Marriage

and

Ministry

A Pride and Prejudice Novel

by

AMANDA KAI

 Regal Swan Publishing

Chapter 1

Charlotte

I did not set out to become a parson's wife. In fact, I had nearly given up hope on becoming anyone's wife. All that changed on the night of Mr. Bingley's ball. I suppose sometimes all it takes is for the providence of God to bring two people into the same room at just the right time.

The grand ballroom at Netherfield was already filling with guests when I arrived. I stepped through the ornate doorway and marveled at the gilded walls, which glimmered in the soft light of the brass sconces and chandeliers. Guests poured in around me like water filling a basin, each lady and gentleman wearing their finest, until the ballroom was a sea of exquisite gowns and jewels and elegant tailcoats with handsome cravats. I wore my best white frock, with a wreath of flowers in my hair. Although I did not own any jewels, I felt dainty and ethereal in the soft chiffon that floated around my legs and billowed as I moved. I milled about, sipping a glass of punch, until the Bennet family arrived. My best friend immediately advanced to my side. I had not seen Elizabeth all week, due to the fact that her family was entertaining company, and thus we were quite eager to speak with each other.

"My dear Lizzy", I effused, embracing her, "how have you been?"

Elizabeth cast a cautious glance backwards. The rest of her party still lingering far behind her, she continued.

"I fear that I now face a most dreadful evening ahead." She sadly intoned.

"Gracious! Do tell. Why must you be so downcast on such a merry occasion?"

"I had my heart set on dancing the night away with a certain handsome gentleman, but now that prospect has withered on the vine," she replied, with a glum and hopeless countenance. I was intrigued. "Could this certain gentleman be our friend Mr. Darcy?" I asked. The matchmaker in me hoped Elizabeth might fall for this handsome and wealthy gentleman in our circle of acquaintances, but she seemed to have taken offense at a comment she'd overheard him make once, and I had yet to persuade her to reconsider him.

"No! His opposite. In fact, one might even say his rival." Elizabeth said. "I have become acquainted this week with a charming lieutenant, a Mr. Wickham, who is stationed here with the militia. He is handsome, genteel, humble, and good-natured."

"And why do you call him Mr. Darcy's rival? Has he done something to offend the gentleman?" I inquired.

"Rather the reverse. Oh, you will not believe what Mr. Darcy has done to poor Mr. Wickham! Once his childhood friend, now forever ruined by his hand!" Elizabeth exclaimed. She continued to relate to me of Mr. Wickham's deferred inheritance at the hands of Mr. Darcy and his denial of the Derbyshire parish rectory that had been left to him.

"I am astonished! But are you certain of your facts? From whom did you learn of all this?"

"From Mr. Wickham himself."

"Quite dreadful. One would not think Mr. Darcy to be capable of such a thing. Perhaps there is a misunderstanding. But of your Wickham— you must introduce me to this man that has captured your special interest so suddenly!" I insisted.

"I wish I could, dear Charlotte, but it seems that on account of Mr. Darcy's presence here tonight Mr. Wickham did not feel welcome in joining our party. I was so hoping to engage him on the dance floor, but I shall not be able to, and now my first two dances have been promised to my cousin Mr. Collins," Elizabeth said, exasperated.

"Ah, yes, the visiting cousin. How is he?"

"Well let's see..." she paused, "obnoxious, overly talkative, dull, homely, always trying to use flattery to win over one's favor."

"A real sycophant," I supplied.

Elizabeth nodded. "Yes, exactly" She sighed. "He's been here a mere few days and I am already sick to death of his company. I am not sure I can stand to be his companion for even one entire evening, let alone have to suffer his presence for any great length of time."

"Where is he now?" I asked.

"There." Elizabeth pointed to the man beside her mother engaged in conversation with Mr. & Mrs. Parks. He was not unattractive, though neither was he particularly handsome. I thought his looks were fairly plain and average, not unlike myself. His hair, though not fashionably cut, was tidy, and his sideburns not overly long. He was dressed in a simple black waistcoat with a white ruffled cravat.

"He does not appear to be as bad as you have painted him, Elizabeth." I mused.

"Oh, but you haven't had to listen to an entire evening of him reading Fordyce's *Sermons* until we all nearly fall asleep by the fireside." She chortled. "Please my friend, I beg you, after the first two dances are up, come rescue me. Keep him entertained for a while, that I might have a respite from his tedium for at least part of the evening."

"It shall be my pleasure." I replied.

∞∞∞∞

William

I had one goal in my mind.

Almost from the moment I arrived at Longbourn, my attentions had been fixed onto my cousin, Miss Elizabeth. I had come to Hertfordshire for the express purpose of selecting a wife, largely at the suggestion of my esteemed patroness, Lady Catherine de Bourgh, and determined that I ought to select such from among my cousins. For, since I am to inherit the estate one day upon their father's death, I might spare their family from inevitable loss, and ensure that Mrs. Bennet and any of her unmarried daughters might always have a home with us if they wish.

Cousin Elizabeth, though not as beautiful as her elder sister Jane, possessed such warmth of spirit, such energy, rapier wit, and pleasant demeanor, that I was immediately attracted to her. When Mrs. Bennet relieved me of my duty to assist her eldest daughter in securing a match— for it would be unseemly to pursue the younger while the elder is still unmarried— by assuring me that Miss Bennet was very soon to be engaged, I could then turn my full attention to Miss Elizabeth. At every opportunity, I positioned myself to be beside her, and made the most of all the little compliments I had arranged in my head to be directed towards her. She received my attention with demure politeness and returned my conversation with the occasional clever remark or bit of humor. Thus, after the past few days' acquaintanceship, I was convinced that I was falling in love. For amongst all her wonderful qualities, my dear cousin was certainly not unpleasant to look at; in fact, one might say her charm and wit made her appear even more comely than her sister— a 'Helen of Troy', though Jane be.

The Bennets had been invited to a ball held by one of the neighbors, a Mr. Netherfield of Bingley Hall, or something to that effect. At any rate, I gathered from what I overheard from my younger cousins that this was the man whom Cousin Jane hoped to wed. This event gave me the perfect opportunity to impress Cousin Elizabeth, and I intended to keep close to her for the entire evening. I congratulated myself on already securing her promise for the first two dances prior to our arrival.

I glanced about for Elizabeth, but she had slipped away to greet her friend on the other side of the ballroom, and though the room was far too filled with celebrants for me to follow her, I was able to observe her animated demeanor as I felt my heart skip. I was forced to look away when Mr. Bennet introduced me to some friend of theirs, and then before I knew it, the orchestra began to tune, and the opening dances were announced. Elizabeth made her way to the middle of the dance floor as I crossed through the crowds to meet her, ready to claim my prize of being the first one to dance with this fine young lady that evening. Other couples lined up beside us. I bowed to Cousin Elizabeth, and she returned with a polite curtsy. The musicians opened with a country dance. Fortunately, it was one I knew well, and Elizabeth also seemed adept. I would have hated to be embarrassed on such an occasion.

"You are quite the skilled dancer, Cousin Elizabeth." I remarked, my face beaming with the affection I felt for her.

She whipped her brunette head back to face me, as per the choreography. "I thank you for your kind words, Mr. Collins. This dance is quite popular in this region. I believe I have performed it at nearly every ball in the last twelve months. Familiarity does breed comfort," Elizabeth remarked. I wondered if that could be an encouragement towards me.

"In that case, I shall hope to become very familiar with you, dear cousin," I smiled, my eyes wide with delight. Elizabeth looked a little flustered and missed one of the steps. I supposed my overtures to be a tad overwhelming in the rapidity of our growing attachment. Not wanting her to feel overly shy, I retreated a little in the conversation.

"Of course, the comfort of familiar things can come from many places. A favorite blanket on one's bed, a childhood stuffed animal, a dish that one's mother prepares every year on holidays, for instance."

"Indeed." Elizabeth gave me a small smile.

"Not to mention, the familiarity of family. It's a pity I never had the opportunity to visit my Longbourn relations until now. I can only hope to better acquaint myself from this point on, including you, Elizabeth."

Elizabeth came up short with an answer to this, seeming a little tongue-tied, but as the song picked up tempo towards the finish, there was no room for a reply anyhow. Once the song ended, she politely responded, "Relationships with family are always a priority to me."

There was a brief pause while the dancers caught their breath. Then the second dance began. It was even faster than the first one, and left us too winded to continue talking, so I simply enjoyed the beauty and skill of my dance partner as I tried to keep up the pace.

ထ၀ဝ၀ထ

Charlotte

Poor Elizabeth looked so uncomfortable all throughout the first two dances as I watched her from the other side of the ballroom. I wondered if her cousin was really as horrible as she had described. She had made him out to be an over-talkative flatterer with a tiresome disposition, but if the man's only crimes were that he rambled on about his favorite topics and tried a bit too hard to please everyone, then I saw it as being merely a trifle. His face was not unpleasant, I thought, and he was quite attentive to Elizabeth. If he meant to make her an offer and secure her family's future, she would do well to accept him. Nevertheless, I kept my word and approached them just as the second dance was winding down.

Tired from the brisk jig, Mr. Collins was a little out of breath, but he greeted me warmly when Elizabeth introduced us.

"Naturally, I am delighted to make the acquaintanceship of any friend of my fair cousin". He smiled and bowed. "Miss Lucas, it would be my great pleasure if you might be my partner for the next dance".

"Thank you", Elizabeth mouthed to me as I stepped onto the dance floor with Mr. Collins, and she made her escape to the waiting arms of one of the officers, who had just asked her to dance.

"Are you enjoying your stay in Hertfordshire, Mr. Collins?" I inquired, as he faced me in the long line of dancers.

"Oh, immensely. I cannot bear to think how sad I shall be to leave. I am quite enjoying the chance to get to know my cousins better and to become acquainted with their neighbors." He beamed.

"Yes, the Bennets are wonderful, especially Lizzy. I think of her as my best friend, and her family is like a second family to me."

"How excellent for you to have such friends," Mr. Collins remarked, his eyes continually glancing down the line of dancers towards Lizzy and her partner.

The dance continued, as did Mr. Collins' conversation with me for the majority of the span of it. When the music concluded, seeing as Elizabeth had disappeared to some other room, Mr. Collins asked me to dance a second time. I obliged him. Following that, I excused myself to locate Lizzy. I found her standing in the card room, watching the groups of whist players.

"How was he to you?" Lizzy asked, a bit worried for my sake.

"Pleasant, and not unduly talkative, as you suggested, though he did go on for a bit about a certain Lady Catherine— ."

"—de Bourgh". Elizabeth finished. "His patroness. He worships her." She rolled her eyes.

"So, I gathered," I nodded. "Evidently, she has done a great deal to elevate his status in society and provide him with a generous living upon his graduation from seminary. I daresay he will make a respectable provider for someone." I suggested.

Lizzy was aghast. "I hope you're not referring to me!"

I simply shrugged and grinned. "Perhaps you have someone wealthier in your sights already!"

"Or at least more romantic!" Lizzy's eyes sparkled as our joint laughter echoed off the high ceilings.

Just then, Mr. Darcy appeared in front of us. To each, he politely bowed, then to Elizabeth, he inquired if she might join him in the next minuet. Elizabeth nodded numbly as she agreed. Lizzy's face was flushed, and she was discomposed.

"Did I just agree to dance with Mr. Darcy?" She asked in disbelief. I, for one, was pleased for her sake.

"I dare say you will find him very agreeable."

"Heaven forbid! That would be the greatest misfortune of all, to find a man agreeable whom one is determined to hate! Do not wish me such an evil." She half-laughed, half-cried at her own irony, and I laughed with her, doing my best to comfort her.

As Elizabeth was engaged for the next dance, but I was not, I distracted Mr. Collins by the punchbowl. While he rambled on about the fine quality of the punch, how it was acceptable for a clergyman to indulge in a little innocent refreshment (I don't think he realized how much alcohol was actually in it; the militia kept sneaking past and altering the ratio by increments!),and how Lady Catherine preferred to serve only wine at her parties, except for her daughter's birthday, since Miss de Bourgh favored punch, and so on, and so on, I took the chance to steal a furtive glance over his shoulder at Lizzy and Darcy. They seemed to be deeply engrossed in each other, almost as if they were the only ones dancing in the ballroom. Although I could tell Elizabeth still bore an icy countenance towards him, I wondered how long Darcy could contain his passion for her. It was clear, at least, that he had eyes for no one else in the room.

I mused in my soul at that juncture that Elizabeth may not need to settle for marrying her cousin, who she so disdained. Perhaps, having caught the attention of this illustrious gentleman, she may find herself in better fortunes even than her elder sister, who at present was clearly enjoying the favor of one Charles Bingley, our evening's host.

With that in mind, it dawned on me that I might assist my

friend in drawing her unwelcome suitor away from her, by encouraging him towards myself. Such an act of service towards my dearest friend could not be unwelcome by her, I was certain. Mr. Collins, in my estimation, was tolerable, plain, but certainly not ugly, and reasonably well-off enough to support a wife and any children they might have.

Additionally, I knew through Elizabeth that he would one day inherit their estate upon her father's death. Naturally, I would not seek to displace my dear friends from their home, but I suspected Mr. Collins could be persuaded on this point. Mrs. Bennet need not move from her home right away after her husband dies; she could possibly even live out the rest of her days there or stay until such time as she might choose to move in with one of her married daughters. Especially if things went well for her two eldest's current courtships, they would have plenty of room for her if she wanted to vacate Longbourn. At any rate, someday Mr. Collins would be living there, a mere walking distance from my family's home. Such a situation sounded blissfully ideal to me.

"…. Do you not think so, Miss Lucas?" Mr. Collin's question broke my reverie. I blushed. "You must forgive me. I was lost in thought watching the dancers. Do repeat your question, sir."

"Are these crab puffs not the most excellent you have ever sampled?" He then bit again into the hors d'oeuvre we had both been handed by the server moments before while I was daydreaming.

"Ah, yes," I also bit one. It had a texture at once light and flaky, with a creamy and savory taste. "They are quite delicious." I pronounced.

"I have only sampled better ones once before, at a party thrown by Lady Catherine. Do you know, she employs a famous chef from Paris…"? He continued to converse, only expecting minimal replies from me.

Well, if this is a sample of my future existence should my hopes be realized, I had better familiarize myself with this sort of conversation, I contemplated.

∞∞∞∞

William

The first set of dances was over soon, and before I knew it, we were being called to the dining room for the meal. The crowds following the candle-lit hallway carried me along with them like a school of trout being swept down the river, but I cut my way through the wriggling masses in search of a certain girl. Confounded by the fact that so many of these brunette girls looked practically identical from behind, I finally recognized the unique pearl hairpins of my target and pressed through the last of the congestion to catch up with her as we reached the dining room.

"Miss Elizabeth, might I have the pleasure of being your dining companion this evening?" I asked as the Bennet family found their seats at the long table.

"Oh, Mr. Collins, I, I..." she stammered, "I'm deeply aggrieved to admit, I've already promised Jane that I should sit by her." Elizabeth managed to finish.

"But of course," I replied, "you must sit by her on one side. But please, do allow me to sit beside you on your other side. For it is my particular desire to be your escort and companion tonight," I boldly declared. Perhaps Elizabeth felt overwhelmed by my pursuit, and the rapidity of our growing affection, for she smiled shyly as she sank into the seat between Jane and myself. As the wine was poured, she looked down into her lap, and I could have sworn I saw a blush creep across her face, though she tried her best to hide it.

After supper, some of the ladies sang or played the piano, including a delightful performance from Cousin Mary. Then the dancing resumed. I tried my hardest to persuade Cousin Elizabeth to dance a third time with me, for that would surely confirm she understood my intentions towards her, but she refused, on the grounds that her feet were too sore, and nothing I said could persuade her otherwise. She did not delight our company with her dancing anymore the rest of the evening. Instead, she settled herself into a plush settee from which she could watch the event. Nevertheless, I succeeded in keeping her entertained with my dialogue on as many topics of interest to young ladies as I could imagine in that moment, only being interrupted by the addition of Miss Lucas, who seemed eager to join our conversations.

Altogether, I congratulated myself on not only being able to spend a considerable portion of the evening with Elizabeth, but also on making a good impression with Miss Lucas. For it is well-known that if one can procure the good favor of a lady's bosom friend, then said friend is likely to give a good recommendation on one's behalf to the lady one is pursuing.

My cousins were all so tired on the return home that Elizabeth and Jane rested their heads gently on Mary's shoulder, eventually drifting off into slumber, and Mary looked as though she might also nod off at any time. Only Kitty and Lydia were still talking animatedly about their adventure, though in more hushed tones than at the party. I, myself, sitting on their side of the carriage, was forced to squeeze as far as I could to the outer edge, but it gave me the perfect vantage to look out the side into the dark open countryside and contemplate my next course of action.

Time was running out during my visit, I realized. I had already been in Hertfordshire over a week and would be returning to Kent on Saturday. With only three full days left, I realized I needed to be bolder if I were to have any hope of securing Cousin Elizabeth's hand before my departure. I mused to myself that perhaps I ought to ask to take Elizabeth on a carriage ride, perhaps with Jane or another of her sisters along to chaperone, so that we might picnic in the countryside tomorrow. Then I recalled her having mentioned that Miss Lucas was invited to come over all day from mid-morning onwards. Perhaps she might chaperone. Then again, if I let the two ladies have their privacy to converse, it may give Miss Lucas a chance to further recommend me. This sort of thinking went on for a bit, as I devised ways in which I might accelerate the process of courting Miss Elizabeth. By the time we reached Longbourn, my resolution was clear. I would request her audience first thing in the morn, even prior to breakfast, and make my declaration and offer of marriage to her.

Chapter 2

Charlotte

I was met by a flurry of confusion upon my arrival at Lizzy's house the next morning.

Lydia answered the door. "I am glad you are come, for there is such fun here! What do you think has happened this morning? Mr. Collins has made an offer to Lizzy, and she will not have him."

I was stunned. An offer of marriage already? What's more, for her to refuse him? After her dance with Mr. Darcy, Elizabeth had assured me that she was still adamant that he was far too proud, conceited, and cold-hearted for her to ever accept him. Could she really be so foolish, then, as to turn down another man's offer, if she had set her heart against Darcy? But this was Elizabeth, after all. Always thinking with her heart and not her head.

Upon entering the breakfast room, I was bombarded by Mrs. Bennet on the same news, who continued even long after Lizzy and Jane's entrance, until Mr. Collins finally arrived on the scene. It was no secret that he was giving Lizzy the cold shoulder after her rejection of him; he hardly said two words to her it seemed. Lizzy, however, was not moved by his display in the least.

"I will be obliged if you could distract Mr. Collins from the matter at hand by your conversation," was her simple request.

This fit nicely with my own plans, for I still deemed that someone or another ought to have Mr. Collins if he were so determined to take a wife, and it might as well be me, if he would have me. I saw myself as having about as good a chance at happiness with Mr. Collins as with any other decent fellow who wasn't a drunk, a gambler, or wife-beater— it seemed highly unlikely that this man of the cloth would turn out to be one of those! The rest of the family had quickly vacated to other parts of the house, eventually leaving me alone with Mr. Collins in the sitting room. No one seemed to care in the least about chaperoning us. So, I seated myself on the cushion next to him and began to speak.

"How pleasant to see you again so soon, Mr. Collins." I greeted, displaying my best demure smile.

"Likewise, Miss Lucas," replied he, but without his usual charm.

"The ball last night was quite an affair, was it not?"

"Humph, a rather lackluster event, from my experience." His sour mood could only be stemming from the morning's turn. The grandfather clock by Mary's piano ticked loudly in the silence that seemed to span for an eternity.

Bracing myself, I dared venture into what I knew was one of his favorite subjects.

"Does Lady Catherine throw a great many parties?"

Suddenly, his face brightened.

"Not overly many, perhaps four or five a year. But those she does give are always the most excellent! She always invites all the landed gentry around Kent, plus a few dear friends from London. Lastly, I have been so fortunate to have her condescend to inviting me on several occasions, though I am but a humble rector."

"How excellent for your social prospects, to have such connections," I remarked.

"Indeed. Her introductions have allowed me to build a good standing in our community and bring many wealthy parishioners into my fold."

"Your Lady Catherine is quite magnanimous then".

"To be certain!" He beamed. His countenance was so altered by my estimation of the lady, that I could tell I had won a major boon by praising his idol.

I spent the rest of the day currying his favor and keeping him occupied. I found it easy to procure his good opinion. I had only to mention Lady Catherine or Fordyce's *Sermons* periodically to make him feel that I valued his interests and feelings, and I could talk about whatever I wished the rest of the time. I could only hope I had enough time during the remaining days for him to develop some feelings towards me if the Lord willed it. For without that, he was unlikely to return to Hertfordshire anytime soon, given the current state of his relationships with his kin.

∞∞∞∞

14

William

I had put my heart on the line for Elizabeth but could not have been more surprised by her response. For a young woman of twenty, with no other serious prospects known, to refuse an offer of marriage from any respectable man, especially one who could enable her family to remain in their ancestral home, was unheard of! What's more, I could not believe I had so greatly misread her. I mistook my cousin for merely being shy and genteel. If she disliked me, she should have rebuked my advances early on, I thought, indignant. How dare she lead me on!

I was still fuming when Miss Lucas arrived. Her presence was a welcome change from the Bennets, who I had grown sick of at present. Elizabeth even had the nerve to ask if I still planned on staying till Saturday; was she so eager to get rid of me? I confess that partially to spite her, I replied that my plans remained unaltered on that account.

Miss Lucas provided the perfect distraction from my problems. Her manner was friendly and engaging, and I enjoyed conversing with her immensely. We played chess, at which she had me sorely beat, we took a walk through the pasture, and she allowed me to read to her for an hour or so from Fordyce's *Sermons*. I scarcely had to even look at Cousin Elizabeth the rest of the day, except at mealtimes. I was a bit sad at the end of the day when Miss Lucas had to return to the lodge. After her departure, I retired to my room to catch up on my reading and to prepare for Sunday's sermon. For though Lady Catherine gave me leave to defer that week's message to a curate as well, on account of my returning only Saturday night, I declined, preferring not to sit in a pew in my own church to listen to another minister's homily.

The following day our whole household was to go to Lucas Lodge. I contemplated remaining behind to enjoy the solitude, but the prospect of spending more time with Miss Lucas proved too tempting. So, I too donned my hat and entered the carriage to pay our neighbors a visit. Sir William Lucas shook my hand and Lady Lucas curtsied. Though I had only met them the day before yesterday, they assured me that any friend or relation of the Bennets was always welcome in their home.

There was still time before dinner, so one of the younger girls suggested we take a walk. The Lucases had a lovely little garden, and a trail leading off behind through the woods. Mary stayed behind with her parents to read a book she'd brought, and Kitty and Lydia clung together with the younger Lucas daughters in a giddy tromp across the footpath. With Elizabeth and me avoiding each other still, that left her to accompany Jane, and me to walk beside Miss Lucas. We gradually fell to the end of the pack, our slower pace allowing some space between us and the others ahead. The late November air was crisp and cool. I thought I saw Miss Lucas shiver in the wind.

"Are you cold, Miss Lucas?" I asked.

"I am comfortable. Merely wondering if we might get our first snow of the season soon."

I glanced up at the clouds overhead. "We may yet see some flurries before I depart."

"Hertfordshire looks so beautiful in the snow. This dull countryside transforms into a winter wonderland once the trees and fields are frosted in white", Miss Lucas said with a dreamy smile.

"If only I were not leaving so soon, I could be assured of seeing such a lovely sight". I remarked.

"Is there any chance of your returning to these parts before the winter is over?" She asked.

"As my business with the Bennets is concluded for the present, I have no reason to return anytime in the near future." I was surprised to see Miss Lucas looked disappointed at my response, and I did not quite know how to respond.

We walked in silence for a few paces. In the sun's rays, Miss Lucas's face appeared rosy and glowing. I thought she seemed rather comely. She sported a burgundy wool cape over her grey dress, and her bonnet bore burgundy silk flowers. I had not given much thought to her appearance before. She cut a womanly figure, more shapely than the rail-thin Bennet sisters, and her face, though not as youthful as theirs, was softly sweet and mellow. Her eyes lit up when she smiled or laughed. Yes, I thought, I could even call her beautiful.

"I do love being outdoors." Her comment broke my brief reverie.

"I do as well". I returned. "In fact, I have a small garden on my rectory which I love to tend in my spare time. My roses are my favorite; their color and sweet scent is only rivaled by those of Lady Catherine's gardener." Realizing I had just bragged a little, I blushed, and sought to make myself humble again. "That said, I have a terrible time with squashes, and my geraniums always wither— they are so temperamental."

"I would not know how to care for any sort of plant, be it a flower or vegetable," Miss Lucas admitted. "I'm afraid I have no experience whatsoever when it comes to gardening. I just enjoy being out of doors amongst flowers and nature." I talked a bit more about gardening, and she seemed interested in all the information I had to offer regarding the best ways to irrigate a vegetable garden, or how to plant a flower bed.

In time, we had circled the loop back to the house. The others had already gone inside for dinner. I offered my hand to her to help her up the back steps. As we ascended, I paused suddenly and turned causing her to step closer to me to keep her balance. Our sudden proximity made my heart pound. "Miss Lucas?"

"Yes?" She looked up into my eyes. Lost in the sparkling blue of her eyes, I faltered a bit. For a moment, I almost decided to kiss her. Then prudence brought me back to my senses.

"I enjoyed our walk immensely," I finally said.

"Likewise," she replied before we entered the house.

The rest of the day passed pleasantly. To my fortune, I was seated beside Miss Lucas, and Cousin Elizabeth was placed at the far end of the table from me. Lady Lucas sat at the foot of the table to my right. Lady Lucas must have sensed the change in the wind that had occurred, for she was doing everything in her power to recommend her eldest daughter's finer qualities. Miss Lucas had indeed captured my special attention. Her manners, amiable nature, family situation and beauty were all exactly as would meet the approval of Lady Catherine de Bourgh, and she appeared quite faultless in my eyes. But I was afraid. I had been fooled once already in the same week into thinking that my feelings were shared by the lady I admired. I had no wish to repeat my error. I had known Miss Lucas only two full days. Was I being rash in thinking she might already bear some manner affection towards me? Regardless, my visit to Hertfordshire had nearly expired; I was due in the pulpit back in Kent on Sunday, and it was already Thursday.

I began to consider my options: I could try to return to Hertfordshire sometime in the near future, though a return visit too soon might be difficult to manage with my parish obligations. I could wait until some business allowed me to return, though the likelihood of that was rare and may be far in the future, and Miss Lucas may by then have found another suitor. Or the most daunting option: I could risk a second humiliating rejection.

Two proposals in a week? Collins, you're a fool, I thought to myself. Yet the thought in my mind remained: I had come to Hertfordshire in search of a wife. It would be wonderful not to go home empty-handed. Such heart-rending contemplation kept me awake long into the night.

∞∞∞∞

Charlotte

Mr. Collin's attention to me was so marked during his visit to my home, it was a wonder Elizabeth did not question me on it. Rather, I think she was so relieved at not having to spend any time with Mr. Collins, she never suspected there might be something more between myself and he. By the time Mr. Collins left that evening, I was almost certain that he had formed an attachment to me. My only concern was his imminent departure. I feared that our connection was not yet strong enough to bear consequence on his actions. With him set to leave before dawn after only one more day, I needed to do something drastic.

My conscience troubled me though. Was it proper for me to be pursuing a man in this fashion? If opportunity presented itself, did that make me opportunistic to grab hold of it? If my plan failed, could I trust that God intended to provide someone else to be my companion and mate, or would I be doomed to life as a spinster?

I awoke Friday morning after a restless night's sleep. It was quite early; no one else in the house was awake, except perhaps the servants downstairs. Not wishing to summon my maid, I dressed myself and donned a shawl before climbing the stairs to my favorite spot in the house— a window-seat nook on the top floor near the entrance to the attic. It was always quiet up there. My siblings never cared for the nook, preferring to read in their bedrooms, the library, or the garden. But for years now, it had been my secret place of solitude, for reading, thinking to myself, or praying. The last is what I needed most in the world at that moment.

"Lord, I'm so confused", I prayed softly. "For so many years I have wanted and prayed for a husband and have been denied. Now an opportunity is at my fingertips— I have only to reach a little further and it will be in my grasp. But is this what You want for me, Dear God?" I sighed. "I want your will for my life. If having Mr. Collins is in your plan for me, then give me a sign, Lord. Show me that this is the path I am meant to take."

The Lord surely heard my prayer and answered me. As I looked out the window, a tiny black speck appeared on the horizon, moving down the lane. It was Mr. Collins! Even beneath the wide brim of his hat, I could tell it was him. His black cape flapped behind him, exposing his awkward, hurried gait, as he headed straight towards my house. In my heart, I knew there could only be one reason he had stolen away from the Bennets' house at so early an hour— to see me!

I hastily thanked the Lord and raced down the stairs. Donning my cloak, I stealthily went through the front door, hoping none of the servants spotted me. My heart pounded. Sneaking out to see a man, even a reputable and somewhat stodgy man like Mr. Collins, was a thrilling thought!

As we approached one another, I tried to invent some excuse to make it appear as though we just stumbled upon one another in the lane.

"Why Mr. Collins, good morning! I am just on my way to—"

"Miss Lucas, I can bear it no longer!" He interrupted and dropped to one knee. Without pausing for breath, as if he might lose his nerve or forget what he wanted to say, he launched his declaration. "I have come with the express design of telling you one thing: I am convinced that you are without a doubt the exact sort of woman I have been searching for. Your kindness and gentility, industriousness, charm, and beauty are as equal to any great lady's. I could not hope for a more suitable wife were I to search the whole country. I never imagined that my feelings could so quickly be changed, but our brief time together has made me realize that one does not need a great length to develop a favorable attachment to another. And now, I only ask that you do me the honor of becoming my wife." He finished, a little out of breath.

I was a little stunned. This was exactly what I had hoped for, but I did not think it possible in so short a time. I had been convinced that at best, he might make me an offer of courtship which we could continue long-distance and whenever visits permitted. But this! Surely God was smiling on me now, to save me from spinsterhood and deliver to me exactly my request. The chilly wind whipped around us as I glanced heavenward, a few tears forming in my eyes as I stood with my mouth gaping. My hesitation must have worried him, for his face dropped.

"Oh dear, have I misjudged again? Oh, I am a fool indeed..." he looked away, his expression riddled with panic.

"You are no fool, Mr. Collins." I let out a deep breath. "I accept your offer."

He looked back, surprised. "You do? I mean, that's wonderful!" He immediately stood up and gave me a quick hug. Holding my hands, he continued. "You have made me so happy, my dear. I cannot think how pleased Lady Catherine will be when I tell her of your many virtues, and what a sensible wife you shall be. How delighted she will be that I have succeeded in my mission in coming to Hertfordshire to select a wife. And you shall be mistress of such a wonderful home. I don't believe I have described my parsonage in Kent to you yet." As we turned back towards warmer quarters, he went on to give me lavish details of his home, Hunsford Parsonage, and its perfect situation in proximity to Lady Catherine's estate Rosings, all the lands he owned as part of the church rectory, and all the benefits that I would receive as the parson's wife. By the time he finished, we were back at Lucas Lodge.

"You have but to ask my father's consent," I reminded him, "but I am sure he will approve of your asking my hand," I assured.

"Miss Lucas, I wondered..."

"Yes?"

"Could we be permitted now to use each other's Christian names?" He asked. I blinked twice. I never realized we had not yet introduced our first names to each other. Funny, to not know such a thing about the person you've just been engaged to.

"Yes, I think so. You may call me Charlotte." I replied. "By what given name do you prefer?"

"William is the name I was bestowed upon my christening." He answered. "I have never cared for any nickname deriving from such."

William. A fine name, I thought. My father's name was also William. It would have been terrible, in my opinion, to be married to a 'Hezekiah', or a 'Jedediah'.

I smiled. "Let us go tell my family our good news, William".

My parents were overjoyed. My mother immediately began talking about wedding plans, and my father congratulated his future son-in-law on his becoming a part of our family. My siblings were also quite thrilled. Emily, for one, began going on and on about how she could now begin planning her coming-out party in time for her sixteenth birthday. Maria, having already been out in society for nearly a year, complained of injustice, since she had been forced to wait until she was seventeen to make her debut. This, in turn, sparked our youngest sister, Louise, to comment that Maria had better hurry up and get married too, then, so that she could also be introduced by the time she was sixteen. Maria said she well thought she could manage that in the next three years. Some comment was made about Maria becoming the next "old maid" in the family, and a fight broke out between my three younger sisters. The fighting ended when our little eight-year-old brother Christopher, who had come downstairs to the breakfast parlour to play since his nurse was ill, chimed in.

"You'd better all find husbands while you can. That way I don't have to take care of you and make you live with me when you get old and gray! Good job, Charlotte, you've made my job easier!" He patted me on the back. Everyone laughed.

"You cheeky rascal!" My mother scolded. "Go back upstairs and play!" She shooed him off. My brother's comment was true though; the responsibility for mine and my sisters' care would have fallen on him and our other brothers should we remain single. Between Maria and me in age, we had two brothers, George and Matthew, who were already living independently in town.

Breakfast was announced. My father emerged from his study, with William behind him. They had disappeared during all the commotion and ladies' fussing in order to have their own man-to-man conversation, presumably about our marriage and engagement. They smelled like cigar smoke, and poor William was coughing, so evidently their discussion had gone well.

My fiancé was invited to join us for breakfast and to stay as long as he wished. He ended up staying the entire morning, only returning to Longbourn just before dinner.

William was emotional when he bid me goodbye by the front door. "Charlotte, my dear, I am afraid I will not see you again tomorrow, for I must leave before first light to catch the early stagecoach. But I bid you well, and please know that I shall return to you again at the very soonest that I am permitted to. I cannot think how I shall bear our separation, but I beg you shall write to me at your leisure."

"I shall." I pledged. He turned to leave, but I caught his hand.

"I have one request," I began.

"Anything, dearest". William crooned.

"I wish to convey the news of our engagement to Elizabeth myself. I fear it may come as rather a shock to her. So please, say nothing of our plans to her when you return. I assure you I will make our news known as speedily as possible."

He chuckled. "It will be hard for me to keep such good news a secret from my relations, but rest assured, beloved, I will honor your request".

He gave me a quick peck on the cheek, then departed.

Chapter 3

Charlotte

Lizzy's reaction to my engagement was much as I expected. Nevertheless, my anger flared at how ridiculous she thought me for entering into such a situation of so little romantic attachment and with such a person as she herself could only find words to mock. Mr. Collins was not a bad man! I censured her for her thoughts and sought to explain myself. "I am not a romantic, you know. I never was. I ask only a comfortable home; and, considering Mr. Collins's character, connections, and situation in life, I am convinced that my chance of happiness with him is as fair as most people can boast on entering the marriage state." This quieted Elizabeth temporarily. I hoped Elizabeth could recognize my situation, and my need to do this to better my own life. At twenty-seven years old, with no money and no prospects, it was plain I was already a burden to my parents. For me, Mr. Collins might be my only chance at a suitable match, and I was not about to throw that away. Life as an unmarried woman was not ideal; I would always be dependent on my parents or brothers unless I could secure work as a governess— the only respectable profession for a single woman of my station.

Things were still tense between us when I left Lizzy's house. I returned home and gave my father permission to pay call to the Bennets to formally announce my engagement. I was certain that the rest of the family's reaction would be even worse than Elizabeth's, and I for one did not want to be there when Mrs. Bennet received the news.

My father's report confirmed my beliefs. He hinted at their bad manners upon receiving the announcement and mentioned that he was surprised to learn Mr. Collins had previously made an offer to Elizabeth. I quickly assured him that while this was true, that it in no way impacted my relationship with Mr. Collins and thanked him for making my engagement known to our neighbors.

I was not surprised that the Bennets were absent from church the following day. Mrs. Bennet probably feared hearing Lady Lucas' bragging about her daughter's marriage and wished to delay having to endure such incessant raptures on the topic for as long as possible. No doubt my mother would pay her a visit soon to do just that, but for now, she was content to mention my engagement to all our family friends in the congregation. It was common practice to tarry in the churchyard following Sunday service, for the purpose of community fellowship, or in my mother's case, gossip. Within a quarter hour, virtually everyone in the parish had heard the news and came up to congratulate me.

I felt a sense of honor and distinction at being an engaged woman. No longer was I looked upon as 'past my prime' by our acquaintances, and my upcoming nuptials gave me a new topic to discourse with my friends, for they all wanted to hear about my fiancé and my plans. I was pleased, for the present.

∞∞∞∞

William

Lady Catherine invited me for breakfast following the Sunday service, and it provided me with the perfect opportunity to announce my good news. She received it with all the approbation that I had anticipated, and heartily congratulated me on my good fortune. She was eager to hear all the particulars about Charlotte and the Lucases, which took me nearly half an hour to exposit. I then took the chance to beg leave to return to Hertfordshire, that I might spend more time with my bride-to-be and her family prior to the wedding, which I hoped would take place as expediently as was reasonable and fitting. She agreed, granting me six days absence from my clerical duties starting in a fortnight. As dismayed as I was at the prospect of waiting for a full two weeks to see my dear Charlotte again, I readily accepted her generous offer. Before bed that evening, I wrote to Charlotte to inform her of all this. My heart was overflowing with excitement as I fashioned some beautiful compliments to include.

Hunsford, near Westerham, Kent, December 1st, 1811

My dearest beloved Charlotte,
You are like a delicate flower blossoming in May. Your face
24

is like my rose petals, soft to the touch. How I cannot wait to press my hand against your fair cheek! You are more beautiful than all the flowers in my garden, and your scent intoxicates me more than their perfume. How I long to be by your side, for my love for you is in full bloom.

My esteemed patroness has granted me leave to return to you two weeks from now. How I shall endure such waiting, I do not know! Were it not for my parish duties to distract me, I should be sick with love from missing you. I expect I shall arrive to Longbourn the evening of Monday, December the sixteenth, but I fear my arrival may be too late to pay call to your family. Alas! That we should have to wait another day to see one another! Nevertheless, I have some business to attend to in London on my way up from Kent which may delay me until such a late hour.

Oh, my darling! I pray that you might soon name the day when you are to make me the happiest of men! Have your parents yet gone to the minister in your local parish, that the marriage announcement may be published? For if the announcement is read by next week, though a Christmas wedding may be too soon, we may yet hope for a wedding on the New Year, it being after the three-week minimum for the requirements of the church. I myself have already published the announcement to my own parish, being so eager to remove any obstacle to our being wed. Do not make me wait overly long to become your husband, for I long to have you established at Hunsford Parsonage as my wife!

Yours truly with all my devotion,
William Collins

Satisfied with the contents of my letter, I folded it carefully and placed my seal upon it. I would send it out first thing in the morning, so to reach my beloved with as little delay as possible.

∞∞∞∞

Charlotte

William's letter arrived with the Tuesday morning post. I opened it while at the breakfast table. As soon as I began reading it, I wished I'd waited until I was in the solitude of my own room. The contents were so unabashedly romantic that my face quickly turned red. Maria saw this and seized the letter from me. She burst out into peals of laughter and, to my embarrassment, began reading aloud to Emily and Louise.

"You are like a delicate flower blossoming in May. Your face is like my rose petals, soft to the touch. How I cannot wait to press my hand against your fair—"

"That's quite enough!" I interrupted, snatching the letter back from her. But she was not dissuaded.

"Your scent intoxicates me? My love for you is in full bloom? Is this man for real? This is the height of absurdity!" Maria exclaimed.

Seeing my crimson face, childish Louise sang, "Charlotte's in looooove!" She proceeded to pucker her lips and make kissing noises.

"Quiet, or I'll send you back to the nursery with Christopher." I scolded teasingly. Louise pouted. At thirteen, she had only recently been promoted to having breakfast at the big table instead of in the nursery with our little brother.

Emily was laughing too. "Are you marrying a man or adopting a lovesick puppy?" she teased.

Fortunately, I was spared from answering by the entrance of my father.

"Good morning, girls," he greeted.

"Good morning," I returned. A chorus of greetings echoed me before I relayed my news.

"Father, Mr. Collins has written that he will be coming back to Hertfordshire in two weeks."

"Excellent. I shall have our housekeeper prepare a room for him." Father nodded.

"He has indicated that he has already accepted an invitation from the Bennets to stay there again."

"Oh? It's a wonder that he should trouble them again so soon. Be sure to invite him to stay here on his next visit. I am certain we have plenty of room to put him up."

"Thank you, Father,' I said. In truth, I was a little grateful he would not be staying with us this visit. I was not used to him quite yet, and I was not sure I was ready to spend so much time in his company. Then again, I would soon be spending every day for the rest of my life with him, so maybe I should not be so grateful and should begin to accustom myself to hearing his constant stream of conversation and long-winded speeches.

The date of our nuptials was still uncertain. My mother had delivered our wedding announcement to our family minister, and it would be read in church for three weeks as the law requires starting that Sunday. However, following Christmas, our minister was meant to travel to visit some relatives, and would be gone until after Twelfth Night, thus William's plan of a New Year wedding would not happen.

I did not visit Lizzy very often, and when I did, it concerned me that our formerly tender friendship still seemed on somewhat tense grounds and we spoke little. It pained me to see that her opinion of me was tarnished, and I resented her idealistic notions of love. It was easy for *her* to turn down proposals and scorn proud men; she was still young and beautiful and had every chance of attracting some other suitable husband. I, on the other hand, did not have that luxury. A decent, God-fearing man like William was probably only going to come around once for me. He was my last hope for ever getting married. For that, I could put up with a lifetime of monologuing and ridiculous love letters.

Truth be told, the love letter was nice to receive, in a way. I had never been praised so amorously before, and it made me wonder how much of the content stemmed from infatuation or a desire to please me, and how much might be genuine admiration.

Since I had promised to write, I did reply to his letter, and the two others that came in his absence, both equally effervescent. My letters, however, were all to the point and matter-of-fact, mainly containing details of what I thought the wedding should entail, or any other news I had to relate. I did not consider myself a romantic, and my letters were absent of any unnecessary flowery language.

The two weeks passed by quickly, and soon it was the day of William's arrival. My outlook surprised me. Instead of feeling dread at his return, I found I was actually anticipating our reunion. It occurred to me that perhaps my emotions had been altered by the outpouring of sentiment in his letters, though I quickly dismissed such notions as foolish nonsense. In his last communication, he had indicated he expected to arrive late, yet I wondered if there was any chance that he might reach Hertfordshire sooner and call on me before the day was over.

Emily, astute as always, sensed my mood. "Your lover's coming today!" She ribbed. She brushed past me while I was arranging my hair at my dressing table.

"He's not my- He's just my—..." I stammered.

"Your *fiancé*". She said with heavy French accent. "I know. You're just marrying him because you're afraid of being 'stuck on the shelf'. By the way," she leaned in and squeezed my shoulders from behind, "your hair looks divine, he's no doubt going to be slain by your beauty, Charlotte!"

I gasped. Before I could even thank her, she skipped off to find something else to do.

Stuck on the shelf. What she said was true, but it still stung a bit. Was it so wrong to not want to endure a life of solitude, to have a companion to go through life's journey with? Is this not the essential key to peace and contentment in life? I was getting exactly what I wished for and I was determined that I was going to be happy about it. Satisfied with my appearance for the time being, I went downstairs to see if my mother needed anything.

∞∞∞∞

William

I hardly paid any attention to my parish duties the whole two weeks, moving through everything mechanically, collecting tithes, visiting sick parishioners, writing my sermons— all about love and marriage, of course! Even visits to Rosings seemed dull, and Lady Catherine's company tiresome for a change. I could not wait to get back to my Charlotte. Only Charlotte's letters provided any solace, so full of her sweetness and simplicity; I could not contain my excitement whenever one arrived, and I read them over and over.

Fifty miles lay between me and my beloved. Such small distance over good roads could be covered in a mere half day's travels if I so desired. As eager as I was to return to Hertfordshire, I had an errand I wished to complete in London, which was of the utmost necessity and could not be further delayed. Therefore, it behooved me to plan a stop near the halfway mark of my journey. I took the earliest mail coach available Monday morning so as to be in town by late morning. After a quick meal at the inn, I set out to do my shopping. I browsed through plenty of stores before I found one that had exactly the thing I was looking for. I just hoped that Charlotte would like it. I glanced at the sky, and then at my pocket watch. If I could catch the next stagecoach out now, I could still reach Hertfordshire before nightfall.

ထထထၜ

Charlotte

I was seated in my favorite nook again when I saw a hired carriage pull up. William exited the carriage and paid the driver before he departed. I closed the Bible I had been reading and ran to my room. I quickly brushed back some stray locks and re-pinned them, pinched my cheeks for color, and checked my teeth for any stray green vegetables, just before the knock at the door came.

William was taking off his hat as I came down the staircase, as gracefully as I could manage. There was a look of utter awe on his face which made me blush. Never having been considered a beauty before, I found his appreciation of my looks to be a trifle excessive. Thankfully, none of my sisters were anywhere nearby, only the maid who let him in. He kissed my hand upon approach.

"My dear, you are as exquisite as a rare jewel, and more lovely to the eye to behold," he gushed.

My father entered the hall. "Ah, Mr. Collins, how excellent to see you again! Will you be joining us for supper?"

"Thank you, sir, I shall," was my fiancé's polite reply. "But before we dine, may your daughter and I take a stroll through your garden?"

"You may." My father winked at me.

"I'll just fetch my cloak," I said, blushing again.

We took a turn around the garden. When we reached the stone bench beside the fountain, William asked if we could sit.

"Charlotte, my love," he began, clasping my hands, "I hope you know that my devotion to you has no bounds. You are unequivocally the brightest star in the heavens. An angel come down from Heaven to meet me. I esteem you in every way to be the fairest creature on the planet; no other woman could compare to your—"

"Thank you, William." I interrupted him, feeling that my

29

shame outweighed the rudeness of doing so. "You don't have to go to such great lengths to profess your love to me. I am aware of how you feel."

"Oh." He was suddenly silent.

I felt bad. Perhaps I should not have stifled his exuberance. Then he took a different direction.

"There's something I want to give you." He began fumbling in his coat pocket. "Something I feel every bride, yes, every *wife,* ought to have." With that, he pulled out a small box and opened it. Inside was a delicate gold wedding band.

"For you to wear on our wedding day. And every day afterwards," he added. I held it up so I could examine it in the fading light. Wrapping the center all the way around was an intricate floral vine pattern carved in gold. It was exquisite, but not ostentatious, just the sort of ring I would have chosen for myself.

"I hope you like it." William said.

"It's beautiful!" I exclaimed. He took it from me and tried to put it on my finger.

"Oh dear!" he gasped. I looked down. The ring was too small for my finger.

"I apologize, Charlotte. Clearly, I overestimated how delicate and tiny your hands are— I mean, they always seem so small and dainty," he stammered as he took the ring back off.

"It is fine," I sought to reassure him. "The ring is lovely." I offered a wistful smile.

William was not satisfied. "Rest assured, my dear, I will get this fixed before our wedding day. I will take this back to London with me on my way home and have it resized for you. I need only to measure your finger with a bit of string and take that length to the jeweler."

I was impressed with his level of determination and his attention to detail. He obviously wanted to ensure that this ring would be perfect for me and had gone to great lengths to select something he thought would suit me. Perhaps his care for me was more sincere than I had realized.

"Thank you for my ring, William." I smiled at him, placing my hand upon his.

"Charlotte?"

"Yes?"

"I wondered if I might," he gulped, "be permitted to kiss you. On the lips." He added.

It was my turn to gulp. "I suppose that might be permissible. We are engaged, after all."

Awkwardly, he leaned in close and puckered his lips, and I did the same. I tilted my head slightly, but he tilted the same way. Attempting to maneuver correctly, I then I tilted the opposite way, but he mimicked me again. So, instead of our lips meeting, our noses and foreheads collided.

"Ouch!" I exclaimed, putting my hand to my head.

William winced as well. "My apologies! I, I, I..." he stammered.

"No need," I mumbled.

"Let's try that again." This time he swiftly leaned in and planted a firm but brief kiss on my lips. The butterflies within me fluttered excitedly at the sensation of his smooth lips and the warmth of his hand caressing my cheek.

It wasn't all that bad, actually, I thought. Maybe I could get used to this.

Realizing the lateness of the hour, I said, "It must be nearly time for supper. We ought to return inside."

The smile on his face as he nodded reflected all the fondness that he bestowed upon me. Taking my hand, he led me from the garden as the last glow of sunset faded.

Chapter 4

William

The memory of Charlotte's lips pressed against mine lingered long after. Her lips were so soft and delicate, and she smelled good, with the aroma of a floral soap or perfume. I kicked myself inwardly, though, at how awkward I had been. I was too ashamed to admit I had never kissed a woman before, only witnessed others briefly or seen kissing in a painting. Charlotte seemed to have taken it all in stride though, and I swore to myself that our next kiss would be smoother.

Despite staying at Longbourn, I hardly spent any time there. I made sure to spend supper there with the Bennets my second night, so as not to be rude, but most days during my stay, I ate with the Lucases, and returned only in time for bed. I felt badly, and apologized profusely for my absence, but I could not seem to tear myself away from Charlotte. My cousins did not seem to mind. After the events that had transpired during my last visit, they seemed reluctant to be in my presence too much. I was grateful that Sir William had extended an invitation through his daughter for me to simply stay at the lodge on my next visit.

On Tuesday night, a new cold front blew in, bringing heavy clouds. I awoke the next morning to see the ground covered in fresh white snow. Having taken public transportation for my journey, I had no carriage at my disposal during my stay. The Bennets were kind enough to lend me their mare, so that I could ride over to Lucas Lodge, rather than be obliged to walk through the heavy drifts covering the lane. Charlotte and her siblings were outside playing in the snow when I arrived. She waved when she saw me.

"Look, William, it snowed!" She was helping Maria roll a huge snowball for their snowman while the littlest Lucas was gathering sticks and stones to decorate it. The other two siblings were building a fort out of snow and amassing an arsenal of snowballs. Then, from behind their snow-wall, Louise threw a snowball, and it hit Charlotte squarely in the shoulders. Charlotte just laughed and returned fire on her sister, pelting her with snowballs. I loved seeing this side of Charlotte, free like a child at play. Soon, all the Lucases were engaged in an all-out battle against one another. I barely dodged a snowball myself.

"I will stable my horse." I called to her.

"Of course, I will be inside in a few minutes", she called back, just before a particularly large snowball came her way, smashing the front of her cloak.

I was already warming myself by the fire in the parlour when Charlotte and her siblings entered through the front door. Charlotte shed her cloak and wet outer garments and joined me on the settee while the rest left to other parts of the house. A maid served us some steaming hot cocoa in dainty teacups.

"You were right, my dear." I remarked, sipping my beverage.

"About what?"

"Hertfordshire is exceedingly beautiful covered in snow."

She nodded in approbation of my assessment.

"And you, beloved," I continued, "are like a snow queen—radiant and lovely playing in the snow, with your fur-trimmed cape like a crown on your head."

She laughed. "I'm more like a silly schoolgirl. I don't know why, but every year something about the first snowfall makes me want to just run and play in it."

"It has been a long time since I played in the snow," I said, "but seeing you frolic with such childlike joy today renewed my desire to enjoy such childhood pastimes as I once loved. My schoolmates used to class me as an expert in the sculpture of snowmen," I chuckled upon reminiscing.

"Well then, perhaps you will join us some time."

"Perhaps." I replied quietly, suddenly wondering what Lady Catherine would think of such immature recreation and what the dignity of my station might allow.

Changing the subject, I asked, "How go the wedding plans? Have your parents yet received a confirmation from your minister, that we might finalize the date upon which I am to become the happiest of men?"

Charlotte shook her head slightly.

"Mr. Pearson has indicated that he will be traveling to visit relatives after Christmas service until Twelfth Night, thus the wedding cannot take place until sometime during the second week of January. A firm date has not yet been decided." She concluded.

"Still, that is only a few weeks away," I said, encouraged. "Ah, Charlotte, you are so good, so amiable! I never expected I would be so happy in all my life, not even with Cousin Elizabeth." My remark must have struck a note with Charlotte because she frowned.

"What's the matter, dear? Have I upset you?" I asked.

"William, did you love Lizzy"? Her question was the last one I might have expected. I chose my words carefully.

"I… believed that I loved her, that I was falling in love with her. I certainly esteemed her and regarded her as the sort of woman who I thought might make me a suitable match. Clearly, I was wrong." I cleared my throat and continued. "Truth be told, I was quite shocked that she rejected me. Even if her affection was less than mine, the economic advantage I was offering should alone have induced her to accept, yet she blatantly refused."

Unaware of fully what conflicting emotions were welling up within me, my eyes began to mist.

"What's more, her treatment of me since then has been so cold. Do you know that she has not spoken to me, except by sheer necessity, since that day? She rather pointedly ignores me and goes out of her way to avoid me, as if we were no longer even friends, let alone family. I had hoped at least that we might just pretend the whole incident never occurred. After all, it was not I who behaved rudely or caused insult. In fact, the whole Bennet family seems less welcoming to me than before, which is partly why I have spent so little time there since I arrived the other night."

"I had no idea, William," Charlotte consoled. "What a pity!" She placed her hand on mine gently.

Returning her gesture, I replied, "No matter, my dear. I only look forward to our future together. I think it is safe to say, I no longer have any feelings for Elizabeth."

That seemed to have put the matter to rest, and we steered the conversation to other things. We spent the rest of the day indoors, reading by the fire and conversing or playing cards with Charlotte's parents and siblings.

At the end of the day, Charlotte informed me that she had plans to call on Elizabeth the following day, and apologized, but that I should expect we would spend the bulk of our day at Longbourn. I told her not to worry on my account, and that I would not find it awkward to be in the company of my fair cousins for such a length.

∞∞∞∞

Charlotte

I arrived at the Bennet home shortly before mid-day. Mrs. Bennet scowled at me as I walked past her into the sitting room. She'd made it no secret that she saw me as her supplanter, the future mistress of Longbourn, and for the moment, she still despised me for it.

William was in the sitting room with the older three of his cousins. Kitty and Lydia had gone to Meryton, presumably to chase officers. He rose and took my hand, pressing it to his lips briefly. "Good morning, my dear," he greeted. I replied similarly. Elizabeth and Jane both rose and gave me hugs; Mary simply nodded and said "hello", before continuing her piano practice.

We talked for a while, exchanging pleasantries, and my fiancé dominated the conversation as usual, until Jane was called away to help her mother, and Mary concluded her practice and left in search of other occupation. Seeing that it was down to just Lizzy, myself, and he in the room, William also excused himself to prepare for his sermon.

"What a relief, now that he's gone!" Lizzy sighed.

Her comment irked me.

"Why do you say that?" I inquired, clenching my skirt as I attempted to keep my composure cool.

"You must get so tired of his company, day in and day out," she said.

"As I expect to soon be in his company daily, I have found I am growing accustomed to it," I said stiffly. Lizzy misinterpreted my demeanor to be discomfort over my future prospects.

"How I pity you, Charlotte," she said, "to be chained to such a man for life. Every day the same monotony, the endless, dull grating of his voice. Isn't there any hope of your breaking free before it is too

35

late? You could always call off the engagement and save yourself from this." That was the last straw for me.

"How dare you, Elizabeth!" I stood, infuriated. "I consider myself extremely fortunate to be engaged to Mr. Collins. He is kind and generous, considerate of my well-being and is eager to please me. While I do not know yet whether I love him, I can at least say with confidence that I have come to regard him as my friend. That is something you do not even consider him, in spite of the fact that he is your distant cousin, and his only offense against you was to offer you a comfortable life and protect your family's inheritance!"

"An inheritance which you were all too quick to snatch up!" Elizabeth accused. "Or do you deny that it was your object to steal my family's home out from under us, behind my back?" The hint of truth behind her words hit me like a slap in the face.

"My object was to secure my happiness and spare my family the burden of supporting me."

"So, you *are* just an opportunist then!"

"Better that than someone who cares so little for other people's feelings!" I shot back. "My feelings aside, how could you treat poor William so? Did you not realize that he cared for you when you cast him aside? And now you treat him as a stranger, not even family to you anymore. I befriended him when he was brokenhearted and bitter and gave him reason to hope that he might still find happiness."

"So, it's 'poor William' now?" Elizabeth raised an eyebrow. "I think it would have been poor for him, and for me as well, it we had gone through with his proposal. We are completely ill-suited for each other. In fact, having known you for so long, I still do not see how you could possibly feel any differently about him than I do. But, as they say, 'one man's meat is another man's poison'. If you want my leftovers, you be my guest."

"I think you are right. You are ill-suited for Mr. Collins. There is no way he could be happy with such a spiteful, selfish person," I spat.

Elizabeth just stared at me. "If you think me so spiteful and selfish, as you say, perhaps you would prefer to spend less time in my presence," she finally said.

"From your lips, not mine." Was my reply. "Tell Mr. Collins and the others that I have an upset stomach and will not be staying for dinner after all. I've suddenly lost my appetite."

I left Longbourn and began walking in the general direction of Lucas Lodge, but instead I began to wander across a snow-covered pasture and into the woods near my house. I truly felt sick to my stomach; that at least was no lie. How could I have said such awful things to Elizabeth, my dearest friend? If our friendship was now at an end, the fault was definitely mine.

Over an hour later, my feet beginning to shuffle long trenches in the snow due to my weariness and sorrow, the path finally led me back to my own garden. I sank onto my favorite bench. It was bitterly cold out, but I did not want to have to explain my sudden return to my family, as they were expecting me to stay at the Bennets' through dinner.

Suddenly, I heard a familiar voice calling out to me.

"Charlotte? Charlotte, where are you?" I looked up. It was William, coming down the path into view. He spotted me and hurried his gait. "Charlotte! I was so worried about you. Whatever are you doing out here in the cold?" He grasped me in a firm embrace as soon as he reached me.

"Just... thinking," I tried to excuse.

"They told me you'd gone home with a stomachache, and I was alarmed you left without even saying goodbye, so I excused myself from dinner to come here and check on you. But when I called, your family had no idea about your condition or your return, so I— what's wrong, dearest?" He noticed how greatly I was trembling and on the verge of tears and it broke his monologue.

I quickly wiped my eyes and lifted my chin.

"It's nothing." I lied.

He was not convinced.

"My dear, I would never wish you to tell me anything you did not want to. However, as your fiancé, I want you to know, I'm happy to listen to anything you want to unburden yourself of," William said tenderly, placing his hand on my back.

I broke down into heavy sobs.

"Oh, I've made such a mess of things! Lizzy and I had an

argument, and our friendship is ruined and it's all my fault!"

"An argument? Good heavens! Over what?"

Between sobs I said, "I got angry with her over her treatment of you, and her disapproval of our relationship. She accused me of only marrying you so I could inherit her house someday. We both said some nasty things to one another."

William pulled back from me in horror. "Oh dear. Oh, this is all my fault!"

I shook my head. "No, William, you cannot blame yourself for any of this. This was all my doing,"

William sighed.

"If I had not told you how I felt about Elizabeth's rejection of me...or if I'd made it clear to my relatives my intentions..." He turned and looked me in the eye. "You know dear, I never intended to steal away the inheritance from my fair cousins. It's only by a silly law written ages ago that the estate passes them by for lack of a male heir. I fully intend to let them use the house for as long as they wish, until all the daughters are safely married, and Mrs. Bennet has passed on or has chosen to move out."

I nodded, dabbing my eyes with my handkerchief. "I believe you."

He continued, "I ought to sit down with them all, or at least Cousin Bennet, and set the record straight."

"That may be very well, but that will not undo all the things I have said to Lizzy. Oh!..."

I began weeping again. William pulled me into another embrace and let me cry upon his shoulder. "There, there." He patted my hair tenderly. "Elizabeth is a Christian woman, and your friend. She will forgive you; I am certain of it. Go to her and apologize, and you can make things right."

"I'm not certain she will even see me, let alone speak to me ever again."

"Go to her later today when you have rested. As the Good Book says, 'do not let the sun go down on your anger'. But now we must get you inside, for it is cold, and if you stay outside much longer you really will become ill." Just as he said this, a large gust of wind blew, and I shivered. William took off his own coat and wrapped it around my shoulders. Then, he scooped me up into his arms and carried me inside. Weary from my wild emotions, I nestled my head against his chest. I felt safe and warm there. It occurred to me that he was much stronger than he appeared to be, to be able to carry me so easily. The thought of his strength made me feel so safe and yet slightly aquiver, all at once. He laid me down on my bed and whispered soothingly that he would inform my parents that I was unwell. Then he left the room and I fell into a dreamless slumber the moment my eyes closed.

∞∞∞∞

William

I was already worried when I left Longbourn to check on Charlotte's condition. I cannot even convey how petrified I was to learn that she had not arrived safely back at home. The thought of her lost somewhere in the woods, out in the snow, and sick, was more than I could bear.

I was relieved, then, when I set out through the garden, and I found her at 'our bench'. It upset me very greatly though, when I discovered that our engagement had come between her and her best friend, that they had quarreled over me and over a matter which I should have easily put to rest long ago. I made up my mind that I ought— no, I *must,* do whatever I could to help set things right.

I remained downstairs at Lucas Lodge while Charlotte rested. The combination of her exposure to the outdoors for so long and her being emotionally overwrought demanded that she take some time to recover. I occupied myself with some reading in preparation for my sermon that week, although I found it difficult to concentrate.

At length, Charlotte awoke, and her parents sent a servant up with some food. When she had finished, she came down to where I had my papers and hermeneutical books spread out in the study. She looked much refreshed from her lie-down; every trace of tears had vanished from her creamy complexion.

"Thank you, William, a thousand times, for coming to look for me, and also for lending your ear to my plight," she said.

I nodded. "Anything for you, my darling. You are the sun and moon to me. For you I would move heaven and earth. I would climb the highest mountain to pick you a star from the sky if you asked it of me." Studying her reaction, I hoped my declarations would please her. She seemed to have too much on her mind still and paid them no consequence. Her expression was worried, and she stared at the floor for a length. When she found her voice, she said, "I would like to take your advice and visit Lizzy today. I don't think I can go to sleep tonight without trying to right the wrongs between us."

"I shall accompany you." I stated. She looked relieved.

"Would you? That would make it so much easier for me."

"Of course," I said. "After all, I have to return sometime tonight anyways, and I wish to speak to Mr. Bennet about the future of his estate following his passing."

Charlotte's parents protested her leaving, on account of the report they'd been given of her taking ill, but I assured them that her ailment was passed, and that we had matters to tend to, so they acquiesced.

The Bennets were quite surprised to see Charlotte accompany me and inquired after her health. Mrs. Bennet invited Charlotte to stay for supper, now that her indigestion was past, but she did not give an answer. Elizabeth was nowhere to be seen. I politely informed them that Charlotte wished a private audience with Elizabeth, and at the same time asked for an audience with Cousin Bennet. As I followed him to his study, I passed Elizabeth on her way down to see Charlotte. She looked like she had been crying. I silently prayed that the two would be able to reconcile. As for me, I was certain my conversation with my cousin would put to rest any fears he or his family may have and might finally induce Mrs. Bennet to view me again with anything but contempt.

∞∞∞∞

Charlotte

I had never been so nervous as when I sat in the Bennets' sitting room to wait for Elizabeth. My heart pounded like the hooves of a wild mustang racing across a plain. The harsh words we'd spoken in that very room just that morning still rang in my mind in an endless refrain, torturing me like a vicious nightmare. I wondered if it was even possible for Lizzy to forgive me after what I'd said. I would not blame her if she severed our acquaintance permanently.

Therefore, I was surprised when, as soon as she entered the room, she ran to me and embraced me, tears rolling down her cheeks.

"Charlotte, I'm overwhelmed with guilt! Can you ever forgive me?" Lizzy sobbed. "I've been a horrible beast! I had no right to call you an 'opportunist', or to criticize your motives for marrying Mr. Collins. I know you well enough to know you would never wish me or any of my family to be homeless or try to maneuver and scheme to take this inheritance."

"My regret devastates me as well, dear Lizzy!" I was crying now too. "I called you such awful things, contrary to what I know of your character. Can you ever forgive me for how I've treated you?"

"I can, and I will. I only hope you will do the same for me."

"Of course, I will!" I grasped her in another tight embrace.

"You were right about me." Lizzy admitted, wiping the tears from her eyes with her handkerchief. "I was cold and unfeeling to Mr. Collins, and I thought little of him. I sought only to save myself from further embarrassment after his unwanted attention to me. What a senseless fool I've been!"

"You are not to blame, Lizzy. I understand how you feel. He can be a bit overzealous in his flattery and affection at times, to the point that I often feel I am blushing constantly for his unabashed professions of love in front of anyone and everybody." My face turned red again just from thinking about some of his latest adorations.

My wonderful friend clearly saw my blush of pleasure, and remarked with a grin,

"But Charlotte, I think you are beginning to enjoy all his attention!"

"Hush!" I scolded, growing redder with bashfulness by the second. "It's bad enough I have to deal with my brother and sisters' teasing at home."

"What was it he said only this morning when we were discussing the weather? 'The snow may be bitter cold, but my amiable Charlotte is like a ray of warm sunshine that warms you inside and out'. Something like that?" She continued to tease.

"I forget." I mumbled, hoping she would drop the subject.

"I think, dear Charlotte, that perhaps you care for Mr. Collins more than you are willing to admit, maybe even more than you yourself realize." Elizabeth had hit upon the swirling mass of emotions within me. I had, in fact, been confused as of late, wondering what my true feelings for William were. I diverted with a joke, "I thought we already agreed, I'm only in this for the money and the house." We both laughed at that. It felt so good to be friends again.

I changed the subject. "Now that I have my best friend back, there is something I've been meaning to ask you."

"Anything!" Lizzy exclaimed.

"Would you do me the honor of attending my wedding as my Maid of Honor?"

"Nothing would give me greater pleasure," she hugged me. "Just remember, when you are leaving and you toss your bouquet, be sure to throw it in my general direction". Elizabeth winked.

"And what groom might you be hoping for? Mr. Wickham? Or Mr. Darcy?" Now it was my turn to tease.

"Darcy, hah! He was not an option even while he was still in Hertfordshire. Wickham is indeed handsome and charming, but I have heard rumors that he may be getting engaged to a Miss King."

"How unfortunate!" I shook my head. "Perhaps Mr. Collins has a cousin." I said.

"You forget, Charlotte. I *am* his cousin!" We both laughed again.

"In truth, though, being his cousin is not so bad in some ways." Elizabeth confessed. "For one thing, since I have no brothers, this match between the two of you is about the closest I can ever get to having you become my sister-in-law!"

"When I am married and settled in Kent, you must come and visit me. I shall miss you so, sweet Lizzy!" I effused, and once again we embraced as we always had in such times. With my friendship finally back at peace, I could now turn my focus fully to my wedding plans. All was well with the world again.

Chapter 5

William

I hated to return to Kent again on Saturday, but my leave of absence had again expired, and it was necessary for me to return to my flock and the various ministrations I was bound to serve them in. My last day in Hertfordshire had passed without any remarkable event. Before my departure, though, I was given a shining ray of hope: a letter from the minister Mr. Pearson arrived at the lodge asking whether January eighth or ninth would be preferred as a wedding date. My future in-laws asked if I had any prior commitments on either of those dates, to which I replied that I had not, and that they should merely let me know which date they have chosen once it had been settled with the minister.

Christmas was the following week. On my return home, I again delayed in London to complete errands. I arranged to have the gift I purchased delivered to Charlotte— a bottle of rose perfume. I hoped she would like her Christmas present. Evidently, she did, for, on Christmas Eve, a thank-you letter arrived for me, along with a precious lock of her own hair. The gift itself, added to the knowledge that she could not have even restrained herself from opening my present until Christmas, brought me such joy, that I felt giddy like a little child again. It had been a long time since I felt that way at Christmastime. My congregation seemed in good spirits too when I greeted them at the Christmas Day service at our parish. I received many "Merry Christmas" wishes along with many "Congratulations" for my upcoming wedding.

The details for my wedding were soon finalized. The date was set for Thursday the ninth of January, and Lady Catherine approved of my plan to return on the third. I spent most of my remaining days preparing my house for my new bride. As much as I hated the separation from Charlotte, the thought that it bought me time to make everything ready gave me consolation. It also painted a beautiful picture of what our Lord Jesus was doing, I thought, preparing a heavenly home for his bride, the Church, before he returns to take her to the Marriage Feast of the Lamb. Everyone in my congregation knew of my impending marriage, so I used this Biblical lesson as the basis for a splendid sermon on my last Sunday to preach as a single man.

When I returned to Hertfordshire, I did not stay at Longbourn again; the Lucases had made up a room for me at Lucas Lodge, which was ideal, because now I could spend many more blessed hours with my beloved Charlotte and also become better acquainted with her family. Everyone in the household dashed about, carrying out countless tasks. All the servants were busy cleaning just about every nook and cranny, and cooking and baking enough food to feed the entire Royal Navy, it would seem. Charlotte and her sisters were wrapping little bundles of moulded pastel mints for wedding favors, and packages of rice to throw at our departure, and the Bennet sisters came over to help with these projects. I was surrounded by women.

On Tuesday before the wedding, Charlotte's two oldest brothers arrived, George and Matthew. According to Charlotte, George, who was twenty-five, practiced law, and Matthew, who was twenty-one, was studying to become a doctor. Both no longer lived at home. I was grateful for some more male company. I myself had no guests coming to the wedding, except the Bennets. I had no brothers, and my parents were no longer living. My one aunt was invited, but she was too old to travel anymore. Furthermore, I had not kept in touch with any of my schoolmates, and I could not invite anyone from my parish without inviting the whole neighborhood, something I could not do.

Being without any groomsmen then, I asked George and Matthew if they might stand up for me, as their new brother-in-law. They said they would be honored. I was a little worried about the wedding party seeming unbalanced; Charlotte had her three sisters as bridesmaids and Elizabeth as Maid of Honor, and I had only two for my side. But Charlotte assured me that it did not need to be equal, and since women know so much more about weddings, I decided to trust in her good judgment.

Finally, it was the day of the wedding. According to tradition, I was not permitted to see my bride before the wedding, for fear of bad luck. Charlotte remained in her room while her sisters and Elizabeth attended to her. I dressed myself in my best black coat with a silver silk cravat. In my pocket, I carried Charlotte's lock of hair, tucked inside the lid of my pocket watch.

I accompanied George and Matthew to wait at the church. The smell of the flowers adorning the sanctuary overwhelmed my senses as I went to take my place at the altar. Lily of the valley, scabiosa, ranunculus, primroses, and other winter blooms I recognized as being taken from the gardens at Lucas Lodge, had been gathered into delicate nosegays with blue satin ribbons and affixed to each pew. More flowers graced the gilded candelabras flanking the altar and in each windowsill. Lady Lucas had clearly outdone herself preparing for this event. The wedding guests began arriving. I observed the Bennets taking their seats in one of the middle pews. Mrs. Bennet was softly crying and wiping her eyes with her handkerchief, which appeared to irritate her husband, for he continually patted her arm with a grimace of apathy on his face. Mary had brought along a book and had already submerged herself in it to pass the time until the wedding began. Kitty and Lydia were, as usual, talking and giggling with one another, not caring in the slightest what commotion they made. Jane was conspicuously absent from the Bennet family. I had heard a report from Charlotte that she had gone with her aunt and uncle after Christmas to stay with them in town for some length. I hoped, in time, she would find a suitable match. It seemed the man she had bet her hopes on, our host at the Netherfield Ball, had left Hertfordshire, presumably for good, leaving her brokenhearted. Ah, how long ago that event seemed, although, in reality, scarcely a month and a half had passed! To think that it was only then that I was first introduced to my Charlotte!

The wedding would begin very soon. I tingled in nervousness and excitement, waiting 'til Charlotte should appear and the ceremony begin.

∞∞∞∞

Charlotte

I could not calm the butterflies in my stomach as I dressed for my wedding. Elizabeth helped me into my white chiffon dress; the same one I had worn to the Netherfield Ball. My hands fingered the delicate embroidery and ruching etched into the bodice while she fastened each tiny white button up the back of the gown. How funny, when my mother first suggested I order a white dress, I told her it would be impractical, and I would never have occasion to wear it. Now, in less than two months' time I had worn it twice! I also found it quite fitting that I should be married in the same dress I had met my husband-to-be in. I dabbed a little of the rose perfume William had bought me on my wrists and neck while Louise finished pinning my hair in place.

My mother entered, bearing a velvet pouch. From it, she drew a string of pearls and fastened them to my neck. "Something old." She pronounced with a kiss to my cheek. "These belonged to your grandmother Charlotte, who you were named after."

"Oh, I love them!" I exclaimed, grasping the white orbs in my fingertips to feel their smooth texture.

Elizabeth presented me with her gift next. "Something new," she smiled as she pressed a flat parcel into my palms.

I unwrapped the brown paper making up the tiny parcel. Inside was a beautiful handkerchief, embroidered with my new initials, C.E.C, for Charlotte Elaine Collins, and a small yellow flower.

"It's beautiful!" I gasped. "Thank you!"

Emily's turn was next. "I saw how worn out your slippers were when you were dressing for the ball," she said, offering me her new white satin slippers.

"But you haven't even worn these yet!" I gasped.

She just shrugged. "I know. That's why they are 'something borrowed'. Maybe your good luck will rub off on me when I wear these at my coming out later this year!" Emily winked.

Lastly, Maria, who had a special talent for making flowers out of silk ribbons, presented me with a bouquet of blue silk roses. "And here is something blue," she said. "Now you are ready to get married. My three sisters, my mother, and Elizabeth crowded around me and hugged me. My emotions overwhelmed me, and tears began to well up. "It's a good thing I have this," I remarked as I dabbed at my tears with the gifted handkerchief, laughing at myself. "It's the perfect present!"

46

I could not fend off a torrent of thoughts about William as we rode to the church. After today I would be spending the rest of my earthly life with this man, and my home would now be with him; never again would I dwell with my parents. I was slightly terrified. How well did I really know him? I thought about our brief time together. I had seen many sides of him already. On the one hand, he could be excessively talkative, with an exuberance and never-ending stream of contrived good manners that could be dull at best and tiresome at worst. But I had seen other sides of him as well. He was vulnerable at times, as when he confessed his hurt at being rejected by Elizabeth. He could also be sweet and tender, a valiant protector, a good listener and strong shoulder to cry on, and a peacemaker. Yes, I could see now that William was a good prospective husband, in many ways. Perhaps Lizzy was right; I was beginning to care for this man I would marry on this day.

I had no more time to dwell on my thoughts, because at that moment the carriage pulled up in front of the small stone church with its gothic windows and tower-like steeple. I had entered this church as a member of the congregation nearly every Sunday for as long as I could remember. But today would be different. Today, I would enter as a bride. My nerves tightened once again, like a violin being tuned sharper and sharper, until I feared the metaphorical strings in my heart might burst. Inside, I could hear the strains of organ begin to bellow, hearkening me to draw near. My mother exited the carriage, gathered her skirts, and entered first, followed by my sisters and Lizzy, then my littlest brother. At eight years of age, Christopher looked adorable as ring-bearer, with his rosy cheeks and too-perfectly combed hair; he took his role so very seriously and walked like a miniature gentleman. Lastly, my father, who had stood waiting by the door, held his arm out ceremoniously, and I placed my hand near his elbow. We walked up the steps to the church and a nearby servant opened the door, which let out a blast of organ music, candlelight, and murmurs from the guests. I looked at my father and gulped. He looked back with a wink and a grin and led me down the aisle.

As I placed one foot in front of the other upon the heavy linen of the aisle runner, I suddenly became aware that all eyes were fixated on me. I gulped again in nervousness and tried to keep my gaze steady as I walked. I was unaccustomed to so much attention. Looking past the smiling faces of our family and friends, my eyes found William's. He was looking at me with an expression of awe, as though I were a beautiful princess. I marveled that he could see me that way— I, who had always considered myself to be plain and lacking in physical beauty.

The music faded as our procession reached the altar.

"Who gives this woman to this man to be wed?" Mr. Pearson asked.

My father cleared his throat. "Her mother and I do," he answered. He kissed my forehead and then took my hand and placed it in William's before sitting down beside my mother. She had her handkerchief out and was already dabbing the tears from her cheeks. My eyes watered too, and for a moment, all I could see was the glow of lights from the candelabras beside the altar.

The minister nodded and then continued. "Dearly beloved, we are gathered here today to witness the union between William Joseph Collins and Charlotte Elaine Lucas..." I listened numbly, hardly paying attention to what he was saying, staring into William's eyes as the ceremony went on. My head buzzed, and I began to sweat. Why did my heart lose its courage at this crucial juncture? I reminded myself to keep my knees from locking and to stay calm.

After the introduction, the minister prayed, and gave a short sermon to us, reading from the holy scriptures many of the words of our Lord regarding matrimony. Then he asked William, "Do you take this woman to be your lawfully wedded wife, to have and to hold, for better or for worse, for richer or for poorer, in sickness and in health, and forsaking all others keep yourself only unto her till death do you part?"

"I do." William squeezed my hands as he replied. The minister then asked me the same question. I felt as though my mind had exited my body and was hovering over the scene in the astral realms, leaving only a wooden marionette standing in my stead. I heard myself also say "I do," scarcely believing the words had come out of my own mouth. Then William took from Christopher's pillow the ring he had purchased for me and put it on my hand. Thank goodness, with the resizing, it fit perfectly.

Mr. Pearson said, "since I have witnessed the exchanging of vows and the sealing of the covenant by the giving of the wedding ring, I now declare by the power vested in me by the Church of England and by the Lord God Almighty that you are now husband and wife. You may kiss the bride."

William leaned in and kissed my lips, short and sweet. It was done. We were married. Still feeling numb, I took William's offered hand and clutched my bouquet in the other as the minister motioned for us to turn towards the congregation.

"Ladies and gentlemen, it is my privilege to introduce to you for the first time, Mr. and Mrs. William Collins."

∞∞∞∞

William

The church and the ceremony were beautiful, but nothing could compare to seeing Charlotte walk down the aisle in her billowing white dress. She looked even more radiant than the day I'd met her, like an angel or a goddess, floating towards me.

The whole wedding passed like a beautiful dream. Soon, I was walking back down the aisle arm-in-arm with my *wife*. How good it felt to pronounce that word in my head in regard to my precious Charlotte! The wedding party and guests adjourned to Lucas Lodge, where a sumptuous wedding breakfast was waiting for us. Lady Lucas's servants had prepared roast quail, apple tart tatin, stuffed breaded pork tenderloin, mincemeat pies, and many other delicious things. For our wedding cake, there was a three-layered fruit cake, chock-full of dates, nuts, currants, and raisins. Following the meal, there was dancing in the drawing room. Charlotte's sister Emily was a skilled pianist, and their brother Matthew was the best fiddle-player in the county. Together, their music made a fine duet for our first dance as husband and wife.

We received many well-wishes of a happy marriage and a glorious future from all our guests. Mr. Bennet said to me, "You and Mrs. Collins are welcome at Longbourn anytime you wish. You needn't wait until the house is yours to stay there," he winked. Behind him, Mrs. Bennet scowled. She only mumbled some half-hearted wish that I might be happy in my marriage, though it was a pity it did not turn out to be with one of her daughters, and at last claimed that there were no hard feelings on her part.

Cousin Elizabeth seemed to have made her peace at last. She warmly embraced me, and said, "I'm happy for you, cousin. I can see that you will take good care of Charlotte."

"You will come and visit us once we are settled, Lizzy?" Charlotte chimed in beside me.

"Of course." Elizabeth replied, giving her an even bigger embrace. "Name the date, and I shall be there."

After greetings from the rest of our friends and tearful partings between Charlotte and her family, we prepared to leave. The guests showered us with rice as we ran to the carriage and climbed in. I turned around and watched with amusement as all the single young ladies gathered to catch Charlotte's bouquet, each waiting in eager anticipation for a chance to be the lucky recipient. She stood and tossed it over her shoulder from the rear of the carriage. A sea of hands reached into the air, grasping for the prize. Kitty and Lydia actually got into a shoving match as they each fought over who was to catch it. As they knocked one another to the ground, Cousin Elizabeth leaped into the air over their heads like an Olympian athlete and snatched the flowers away from all the rest. Triumphant, she cheered as she held up her prize.

"I pass my luck on to you, Elizabeth! Charlotte grinned and waved. Perhaps Cousin Elizabeth might be the next young lady to get married after all, we should see.

∞∞∞∞

Charlotte

My father drove us in the carriage as far as the inn at Meryton, where we had a private coach hired to convey us on our journey to Kent— Lady Catherine's wedding gift to us. Additionally, she had made provision for us to stay the night at her favorite inn in London, about halfway through our journey. I told my husband I was grateful for her generosity, which greatly pleased him, and he said he would be sure to repeat my expression of thanks upon introducing me to her.

William was peculiarly silent on the coach to London. I was expecting to get my ear talked off, but that was not the case. For once, the man who always seemed to have something to say was suddenly as silent as the grave. Feeling tired myself after all the hullabaloo of our wedding celebrations, I had made up my mind to practice gratitude and bask in the peace and quiet respite from William's usual chatter. I read a book for a while and looked out the window at the winter scenery.

Finally, my curiosity got the better of me.

"Dear, is something troubling you?" I asked.

William looked a little skittish, something I found unusual. "Ah, it's nothing," he lied. Sensing I was not convinced, he decided to be forthright with me.

"Actually, I must confess, I am quite nervous."

"Nervous?" I asked, surprised. "About what?"

"Well...about our wedding night. And everything that that entails."

"Oh." I said, a huge blush flooding my face in realization.

"You see, my dear...although you may be surprised to learn it, I have never been, um...intimate with a woman before." William bashfully admitted.

I shrugged. "I am a virgin as well, naturally. In fact, I expected that a man of the cloth would have also kept himself pure before marriage."

"While my conscience is somewhat eased by your saying that, it does not relieve my trepidation on account that I have no experience whatsoever in matters of," he gulped, "lovemaking."

I timidly placed my hand upon his leg. "It may be a case of 'the blind leading the blind'," I said, "but at least it is something we can explore and discover together." I gave him a nervous smile.

He nodded and managed a small smile in return. He was still quiet after that, and at length I fell asleep upon his shoulder.

I awakened to his gently tapping my arm. "Charlotte, we are here."

Looking out the window, I saw the inn and realized the carriage had stopped. A valet took our trunks up to our room. It was dark already. We had stopped once for tea and to change the horses, but that was hours ago, and I was hungry again. I asked if we might have some supper. William agreed that he too was hungry, so we dined on some roast chicken and mashed potatoes that the inn had to offer us. Then we retired to our room.

Once again, William was nervous. "I'm not certain exactly how we, ah...begin." He raked a hand through his hair.

"Nor am I," I replied. "I know a little about what should transpire, from what my mother has told me. There is just one part I'm slightly confused about." Even though we were alone, I was too red and embarrassed to say it out loud, so I whispered it in his ear.

"Oh." William was also the shade of a boiled lobster by now. "Well, as to that, I don't think you need to worry. I think I've got that part covered."

"Then perhaps we might start by just kissing?" I suggested. We had only kissed a few times up until this point, and always very briefly and very chastely. This kiss was a little awkward too, at first, then gradually got more intense as we got more comfortable. William pulled me closer to him and ran his hand down the length of my back. The warm sensation made the hairs on my neck stand up, tingling in anticipation. My emotions bubbled within me, creating a strange new feeling I could not name.

I began working the buttons of his shirt, trying to help him out of it. Suddenly, he backed away, laughing.

"Begging your pardon, it's just that, I'm horribly ticklish!" He explained between fits of giggles. He finished undressing by himself down to the drawers.

"We might as well undo my corset, while we're at it." I said. "It's not the easiest thing to get out of and I don't wish to ring for a maidservant anytime soon."

William obliged, but shaking his head, he commented, "why you women wear these infernal contraptions is beyond me." I had to direct him how to undo the laces, which he fumbled with, almost making me lose my balance and making me regret my choice not to employ a servant to assist, until I was finally left in my chemise and stockings. He tossed my corset aside, happy to be rid of it.

"Now, where were we?" He muttered, eager to return to what we were doing before.

We sat down on the bed. William leaned in and began nibbling on my ear and my neck. Then suddenly, I yelled and pulled away.

"Ouch! You bit me!"

"Forgive me, dearest! I did not mean to hurt you!" William turned away and propped his forehead up with his hand. "Goodness, I really am terrible at all this!" He looked perfectly ashamed.

I felt badly for him. "It is all right. I'm new to this too. I think you are putting too much pressure on yourself." I sought to reassure him. "You know," I said thoughtfully, "nobody ever said we have to accomplish the deed on our first attempt."

William nodded. "Right." However, he looked a little disappointed. A few moments passed, the silence covered only by the flames licking in the fireplace.

I did not want him to be disappointed. Not on our wedding night.

"Unless, of course, you want to." I added.

"I want to!" My husband immediately pulled me into a fierce and passionate kiss, the likes of which quite surprised me.

And so, two became one in the eyes of God that night, as husband and wife joined together in body and spirit for the first time.

Chapter 6

William

The morrow after my wedding, I was the happiest I had ever been in my life. I laid in bed for a while just watching my wife sleep and thinking to myself how beautiful she looked with her long hair trailing down the back of her white nightgown, her deep breathing causing her chest to heave up and down. Our first time together, admittedly, had been awkward, and a bit short. The second time was much better, though. As they say, "practice makes better", so I trusted our relations would only improve from that point on. Nevertheless, by the time we were back in the coach, I was a very happily married man.

I was chatty and excited on this leg of our trip, for in just a few short hours we would be at Hunsford Parsonage. I was eager to show my bride all the improvements I had made to the house in preparation for her arrival, how I had paid attention to every detail that might please her.

"I've acquired a brand-new carved mahogany wardrobe in the master bedroom, for all your beautiful dresses," I told her, "and purchased a vanity for you to sit at while your hair is being arranged."

"Thank you, dear, that's very thoughtful." Charlotte replied with a nod.

"I also repaired the floorboards on the stairs, which were beginning to creak, hunted down a mouse in the attic, and replaced the old rug by the fireplace with a new plush Turkish one." I proudly conveyed.

"Your attention to detail has been most thorough." She praised.

"Thank you. It is all for you, my dear." I beamed. "Lady Catherine herself even paid a visit to see how all the preparations were coming. She was extremely impressed with the new additions I had made, and she seemed pleased I had taken her previous suggestion to install shelving in the upstairs closet in order to better utilize the storage space." I continued to relate details about the house for a while, then moved on to describing the neighborhood and its residents. Of course, my illustration would not be complete without an account of Lady Catherine's personality and her magnificent home, Rosings. On that subject, I spared no detail. I wanted Charlotte to feel at home from the moment we arrived, and to feel as though she were already familiar with everyone and everything.

We stopped at the Bell Inn in Bromley for luncheon. "Lady Catherine always dines here and rests her horses whenever she travels to or from London." I told Charlotte. "She highly recommended that we sojourn here, and that we need only mention her name and we will receive the highest treatment. She could not guarantee the same at any other inn we may happen to pass by on our road." Lady Catherine's advice proved to be true. Upon hearing our connections, the servants immediately leapt to action, tending to our horses, and laying out a feast of ham, poultry, roasted vegetables, fish soup, pie, and other delights for our enjoyment. We indulged until we were fit to bust. When we were back on the road after luncheon, Charlotte asked if she might be permitted to rest a while. I obliged, owing that our journey was quite tiring, and wishing her to be a bit rested when we arrived home.

∞∞∞∞

Charlotte

If William was silent as the grave the day before, he more than made up for it on the second day of our journey. I suppose, in a way, I was glad that I had made him so happy and that he was back to his usual self. But at the same time, it was a bit exhausting listening to his endless stream of talking, and of course, the topic of exposition he never seemed to exhaust was anything related in any conceivable way to Lady Catherine! I was grateful for a respite from it by closing my eyes to sleep the remainder of the journey.

My husband woke me when we arrived. Lady Catherine had insisted that our private coach convey us all the way to Hunsford Parsonage, thus sparing us the hassle of hiring a post chaise in Westerham to complete the last bit of our journey.

I looked out the window as we came up the lane.

"There it is, my dear! Our home!" William pointed out

excitedly.

The parsonage was a sweet two-story stone cottage, covered with ivy. The garden beside it lay dormant for winter, but the trees and shrubs were all well-manicured, and I could foresee that the landscape might be quite pretty come spring when in bloom.

The servants greeted us at the door. I was introduced to Mrs. Perry and Mrs. MacDougall, the housekeeper and cook, respectively. The manservant, Hines, assisted by Jesse the stable hand, took our trunks upstairs. William boasted that we also employed a maid. William's first object was to give me a full tour of the house. We entered through the hall, which was sparsely furnished with a coat rack, an ornate clock mounted on the wall, and a small wood-framed mirror. On the eastern side of the hall was William's study. He opened the door briefly for me to observe the bookcases crammed to overflowing, and his desk with a view of the lane, by which he could observe all of Lady Catherine or her daughter's comings and goings. Turning to pass through the doorway on the western side, we entered the dining room, which was completely taken up by the enormous dining table and chairs. As I squeezed myself between a chair and the wall to get a better view of the room, William remarked, "Lady Catherine selected this dining set especially for our benefit. It seats twelve persons in all! She told me, upon hearing of my engagement, 'Mr. Collins, now that your parsonage is to have a mistress, you must be prepared to entertain a party of guests now and then. I must see to it that you have a suitable table for doing so'. Naturally, I was most grateful for her consideration," he concluded.

Pressing myself into the wall again to extricate myself from corner in which I was lodged, I replied, "I share your thanks, but I do wonder if a smaller table might have been more in keeping with the size of the room." William seemed not to have heard me. He opened the door on the other side of the dining room which led to the kitchen, and I had no choice but to follow him.

"As you can see, we have an excellent kitchen, with a wood-burning stove, and a large window to allow plenty of natural light for Mrs. MacDougall to see to prepare our meals." William continued walking, pointing out the staircase leading to the basement quarters where the servants resided. Another doorway opened into a small breakfast nook with a round table and a sideboard. This dining arena was more in keeping with my tastes, I thought with a smile. William looked to my face to see whether I approved. Finding approbation, he continued his tour by passing through the elegant, yet comfortable, drawing room, with its fine velvet settees facing a broad fireplace. I admired the intricate pattern of the luscious rug beneath my feet.

"Do you like it?" William asked, noticing my close study. "This is the rug I mentioned before. Lady Catherine assisted me in purchasing it from a traveling merchant who brought it all the way from the orient." He continued relating details about the rug and other furnishings. Finally, he stopped beside a closed door.

"This room is my special surprise for you, Charlotte."

A surprise? I thought to myself with a bit of glee. Whatever could it be?

He opened the door to a small parlour, furnished with a floral upholstered settee and matching chair, an end table, and a small desk in the corner.

"I converted this room into a parlour for your own private use. I had some furnishings brought in, but I left the walls bare. You may decorate it however you wish. When you want to entertain a guest or two, or just want a place to escape, you can come here. I won't bother you."

Escape. Funny that he should put it that way. Perhaps he was more aware of his own mannerisms than I thought, if he expected I might need a place to steal away to from time to time. To get a 'respite', is what I would have said in place of 'escape'. For, it was not that I was being imprisoned or held hostage by some brute. Rather, I think every spouse needs a bit of a break from the other now and then, and it seems he knew this too.

"Thank you, William." I gave him a heartfelt embrace.

He then took me upstairs to show me the rest of the house. When we reached our bedroom, he was eager to show me my new wardrobe and vanity. I, however, was more interested in the bed. I heaved myself upon it in a bit of an unladylike fashion and sprawled out across the top. William seemed a little surprised, then, brushing decorum aside, followed suit. Laying on his side and propping up on one elbow, his face so near I could feel his breath, he asked me, "Do you like your new home, Charlotte?"

I thought for a moment, then replied. "Yes, I believe I do."

"You know, there's still time before we need to change for dinner," he said with a smile.

"You're welcome to take a nap if you like, dear." I said. "I'm rested enough from the drive."

"A nap was not what I had in mind." William's eyes twinkled, and I understood his meaning.

It was nice to be desired, I thought, as we shut the world out for a little longer.

∞∞∞∞

William

Having now shown my humble parsonage to Charlotte, my anticipation turned towards being able to introduce her to my patroness. Fortunately, I did not have to wait too long. A message arrived the next day inviting us to dinner at Rosings. I was almost beside myself with delight.

"Lady Catherine will be so pleased to meet the woman who has made me the happiest man alive!" I gushed. "Be sure to wear one of your best dresses, Charlotte. I wish for her to see you in all your glory when I first introduce you. I have already bragged to her of your many fine qualities, your gentility, good taste, common sense, and general agreeableness, among other things." Charlotte looked a little embarrassed, so I said, "Of course, you needn't worry, I know you are too humble to admit all these, but I know they are true."

"Thank you." She murmured.

At half-past four Charlotte descended the staircase, the dark blue fabric of her dress rustling with each step. Once again, I stared in wonder, drinking in her beauty. My eye was drawn to the delicate lace highlighting her bosom. Her hair was also fixed rather becomingly, teasing me with its little curls kissing her cheeks and the nape of her neck.

"I hope my appearance meets with your approval, and with Lady Catherine's." She added.

"Indeed. You look radiant as the moon goddess Diana in all her splendor. No doubt you will be the most beautiful woman at Rosings tonight, even more so than the noble Miss de Bourgh in all her finery." I lavished. Charlotte merely blushed.

Charlotte and I walked across the park to the great manor where my benefactress and her daughter resided. I let my wife soak in the majesty and magnitude of Rosings as we approached. I was confident it would surpass even my detailed descriptions to her. Lady Catherine's butler admitted us to her drawing room and announced our arrival. Lady Catherine reposed upon the settee, with such an air of dignity as befitting a queen. Her graying hair was elaborately curled and fashioned in a style such as could rival the late Marie Antoinette. Since her husband's passing some years ago, she wore nothing but dark colors, but her taste was such that her garments were never out of fashion. Today, she wore a taffeta gown in a wine color so deep, one could not distinguish whether it was dark red or purple. She gestured to acknowledge our presence, giving me permission to speak.

"My dear lady, may I have the privilege to introduce to you my wife, Charlotte Collins, daughter of Sir William Lucas?" I said with immense pride. My wife curtsied before the great lady.

"Come here, Mrs. Collins, that I may have a look at you." Lady Catherine commanded from her seat.

Charlotte timidly stepped forward.

"Your dress and manners certainly befit the daughter of a knight and the wife of a clergyman." Lady Catherine appraised, "but you are older than I expected. By Mr. Collins' descriptions of you, I was expecting a spring chicken. I trust your maturity may be an asset though, for as you know, the wife of a rector is responsible for many things, including maintaining relations with the parishioners and raising well-behaved model children."

"Yes, your ladyship." Charlotte nodded.

Lady Catherine invited us to sit before she continued.

"Have you very much experience with children, Mrs. Collins?"

"A little". Charlotte replied. "I am the oldest of seven children. Some of my younger brothers and sisters are several years my junior. I often helped in the nursery when they were small."

"Heavens, did you not have a nursemaid for that?" Lady Catherine scoffed.

"To be sure, we did. A very fine one. But as my sisters are so close in age, there were many times when she would be tending to one and another might need something, or someone to play with. In this, I was of great assistance to her. Also, my youngest brother is still of nursery age. I often help to feed him and tuck him in bed on his nurse's night off."

"I see." Turning to me, she addressed, "Mr. Collins, you ought to give your wife's fine skills a refresher. Perhaps you might employ her to teach a Sunday School in your parish."

"An excellent idea, your ladyship." I commended. "Perhaps when Mrs. Collins has had a few weeks to settle in, she might be interested in establishing such. Don't you think, darling?" I asked, turning to Charlotte.

"Perhaps." Charlotte said quietly.

I expressed, "I, for one, have been longing to establish a time of learning for the children expressly designed for them for about thirty minutes prior to the Sunday service, but have been lacking a suitable teacher to conduct such. I myself have made a few attempts, but I think the children do not relate to me as I have not the talent for simplifying Bible stories to their level. I can see that they grow bored during the service, too, and that my sermons are too complex for most of them to grasp. I would love for them to have a teacher dedicated to improving their understanding of the Lord God in ways that are more practical for their age."

"I'll do it!" Charlotte suddenly volunteered. I was surprised, but pleased, at her sudden enthusiasm.

"That's excellent, my dear!" I clasped my hands in excitement. "You'll be just wonderful at it, I know."

Lady Catherine chimed in. "You'll have your work cut out for you. It is imperative that you plan a thorough curriculum to cover the entire year, which includes lesson plans for reading, writing, and Bible learning. You must not neglect any of the virtues or the major Bible stories, and you must also emphasize good moral character." She advised.

"You could play a short game each week or have a simple song to help the children remember their scripture memory verses," I suggested.

Lady Catherine jumped in again. "And you must include some children's hymns. Do you play the piano at all, Mrs. Collins?"

Charlotte looked a little overwhelmed. "A little, your ladyship, although not much as of late."

"You must not allow your talent to wither away." Lady Catherine admonished, the lace on her sleeve emphasizing her wrist as she shook her finger. "I know there is no piano at your home, but you may be allowed to use one of mine to practice on, for I have several. Perhaps the one here in the drawing room, when the room is not in use of course, or the one in the housekeeper's room. That one nobody ever touches, and she is seldom in her room during the daytime, naturally."

I smiled at how naturally gracious and generous Lady Catherine was, to think of offering such a thing.

"Thank you so much, your ladyship." I said.

Charlotte, who had been momentarily speechless, found her voice. "Y-yes, thank you."

Charlotte looked a little pale.

I jumped to reassure her. "You needn't be worried about all this, dearest. With your sweet spirit and easy manners, I'm sure the children will all love you, and I will help you to make the lesson plans if you wish." Charlotte nodded.

At that moment, Miss de Bourgh arrived.

"Ah, here is my daughter, Miss Anne de Bourgh". Lady Catherine announced. She spent a few minutes introducing Charlotte and allowing pleasantries to be exchanged. During their discourse, I observed the differences between Miss de Bourgh and Charlotte. The heiress of Rosings was about the same age as my wife, but where Charlotte's complexion was rosy and healthy, Miss de Bourgh's was pale and sickly. She carried her thin frame with all the regal elegance which she was brought up to bear, but I found I preferred Charlotte's curvaceous figure over hers. Miss de Bourgh had once been my ideal standard of beauty, and though I never once considered her as an object, being far too low in stature myself to be worthy, I had originally sought to find a wife in similar appearance and nature. Ironically, though Elizabeth Bennet's waif-like figure reflected Miss de Bourgh's, I had never considered that as a point of attraction.

Were it not for the comeliness of her face and the duty upon me to assist her family, I should have instantly preferred Charlotte over Cousin Elizabeth, I thought.

Before we had further time to converse, the bell rang, and we were ushered into the dining room. The first course we were served was a potato and kale soup, followed by a winter salad topped with butternut squash and Brussels sprouts. The main dish was seared chicken breasts with brown rice pilaf.

"I am very keen to serve only nutritious food at my table these days, on account of Anne's health." Lady Catherine remarked as we nibbled on the chicken. "I recently hired a chef straight from Paris, and I have given him clear instructions to only cook lean cuts of meat, whole grains, and a variety of healthy starches, fruits, and vegetables."

"An excellent plan, your ladyship," I praised.

"Mrs. Collins," she addressed my wife. "You also ought to be careful as to the menu you order in your household. It is your job to ensure the health of your husband and yourself. Too many fatty cuts of meat and too many rich desserts will be a source of many health problems, and it is important to watch your waistline too." She advised sternly. "A portly wife is not an attractive one."

"I am sure consciousness for my family's health is always at the forefront of my mind," Charlotte replied stiffly.

"Your advice is greatly appreciated Lady Catherine," I thanked. "I, for one, have never been too health-conscious, so I am glad now that my wife can care for me and extend my lifetime of happiness with her." I grinned at Charlotte, but she did not smile back. I wondered why.

"I do, however, hope I can continue to indulge in a nice plum pudding from time to time, for that is my favorite," I said.

"Of course!" Lady Catherine said, "one must be allowed *some* indulgences. How one could live without their favorite vice is incomprehensible. I myself have a strong preference for brandy. It is my one weakness I allow," she bragged.

Miss de Bourgh spoke up. "I could not fathom a world without chocolate!" It was rare for her to contribute to the conversation, but it always pleased me when she did. She had a sweet spirit. It was a pity her poor health did not allow her to travel in social circles as much as she might like. "A good chocolate cake, or maybe some hand-dipped truffles, that is what I like!" She said brightly.

"A woman after my own heart." Charlotte smiled at Anne. "I do wonder who the master is— me or the sweets—when it comes to chocolate."

Lady Catherine sniffed and toyed with the ruby necklace around her throat. "Too much chocolate will make one's face break out with acne. A lady must maintain a clear complexion and avoid foods which aggravate the skin. That is why I do not keep chocolate in my house."

Just then, the dessert course was presented. It was a bread pudding, topped with raspberry preserves and brandy sauce. Lady Catherine took the first bite.

"Now here is an exemplary dessert!" She exclaimed. "The brandy sauce truly brings out the taste of the raspberries, don't you think so, Mr. Collins?"

"Indeed, it does!" I replied, tasting my own dish.

"It's a pity there are no fresh raspberries at this time of year."

"Now that I know your ladyship prefers them, I shall be sure to plant some raspberry bushes in my garden early this spring, so that come summer there may be fresh berries abounding," I promised.

Following dessert, Lady Catherine sent us home in her barouche, since it was already dark. Charlotte was quiet during the two-minute ride. When we entered our house and I shut the door behind us, I said to Charlotte, "It would appear that went rather well, don't you think?"

My wife unleashed a fury I did not see coming.

"Went well? You must be joking! I have never been so insulted in my life!"

I was vastly confused. "Insulted? In what way were you insulted, my dear?"

"Lady Catherine is by far the rudest woman I have ever met! In the course of one evening, she called me old, insinuated that I was fat, and implied that I have a poor complexion!" Charlotte complained.

"How on earth did you derive all that from our

conversations?" I asked, still baffled. "She did come right out about your age; I'll give you that. But she credited it as an asset, not a liability. As for the other two items, I think you are seriously overreacting and misinterpreting what Lady Catherine wished to convey."

My words merely added fuel to the fire. "Of course, you would take her side of things!" My wife spat. "You just sat there the whole evening and let her take shots at me, even thanking her for it!"

I was getting angry now too. "I did no such thing! I simply did as I always do in the presence of my betters— to show them proper deference and gratitude. Thank heavens you were at least able to pretend to do that in the home of the woman who has done nothing but provide for us and share her wisdom with us!" I finished.

"Her *unsolicited* advice." Charlotte pointed out. "Or did you not notice that she had something to say about everything, as if she were the ultimate expert on every subject?"

"It is a flaw of hers, I admit, but as she is my superior, I give her leave to say whatever she wishes in my presence. It is still up to us to decide which of her suggestions we might apply to our lives in practice," I tried to explain.

Charlotte merely shook her head. "I am too tired for this. I am going to bed."

"Very well." I resigned. "I have some finishing touches to put on my sermon for tomorrow and will be in my study a while. I'll see you in the morning. I must remind you that we need to be at the church by quarter-past seven to prepare for the service." Charlotte acknowledged and went upstairs. I heard the bedroom door shut firmly as I turned to go to my study. "I'll never understand women," I said aloud to myself.

∞∞∞∞∞

Charlotte

I was so angry when I went to bed that night. After all William had told me about his beloved patroness, I expected her to be a woman of taste and decorum. Instead, she concealed all her condescension behind a thin veil of polite language and masked her need to control and dominate with a pretense of well-meaning. But William had let me down! I was hurt that he couldn't see how badly I

64

had been treated, and that he had defended Lady Catherine's behavior when he should have been offended for my sake, I thought. I was still grumbling inside my head when sleep finally overtook me.

The maid woke me the next morning to dress for church. I looked over at William's side of the bed. He hadn't slept in it. After the maid helped me dress and arrange my hair, I went downstairs, but I couldn't find my husband anywhere. Glancing at the large clock in the hall, I saw that it was already a quarter to seven. With just thirty minutes to spare before we were due for worship I wondered where he could be.

I cautiously opened the door to his study. There was my husband, asleep at his desk. I felt a little bad, especially given our argument the night before. How was it we were married only two days, and we had already quarreled?

I softly placed a hand on his shoulder. He opened his eyes and looked up.

"Oh, it's you." William said. He rubbed his eyes. "I must have fallen asleep while working on my sermon. What time is it?" He asked me.

"Nearly seven." I answered.

"Goodness!" He exclaimed. "Well, I guess this will have to do, for today," he said in reference to the sermon in his hands. "I'd better hurry and call Hines to come upstairs and help me into some fresh clothes if we aren't to be late."

He got up from the desk and walked past me towards the door, but I caught his hand. He looked back at me, puzzled.

"Please forgive me, William," I said, "for getting angry with you yesterday."

William nodded. "Of course, dearest. I regret my behavior also, that I did not take your side when you felt your pride was injured. Please accept my apology too."

I squeezed his hand and smiled to indicate he was absolved. He lightly pecked my cheek. Then he hurried to prepare so we could depart.

The parish church was just next door to the parsonage. Quite convenient, I thought to myself. William busied himself with preparations and supervising the church warden who also came to serve in the church. Soon, the members of the congregation began to arrive, all in their Sunday best. I saw Lady Catherine and Miss de Bourgh sit down in the de Bourgh family pew, but I kept my distance. I knew no others of the parish yet, so I simply took my seat on the front pew. I could hear others talking about me, asking each other if I was the parson's new wife, but I did not assert myself to confirm them.

I later found out that Mr. Collins was known for his long, dry sermons as much as his long, dry speeches. I suppose I should have guessed such, given what I knew about him in our brief time together. Still, I was used to hearing the Word of God move me through eloquent and insightful sermons. Mr. Pearson back in Hertfordshire was an excellent speaker who used witticism and anecdotes to further his poignant messages, and I usually found his passages of scripture to be quite applicable to my life. It was hard to stay awake during my husband's sermon, and I felt his message could have been cut down by at least twenty minutes. I was glad when he gave the benediction and the organ started to play so I could rise from my seat. I joined him at the door to the church as he shook hands with the leaving congregation. Of course, everyone wanted to meet me. I met so many new faces and names, I was sure I would not remember them all, and I depended upon my husband to remind me of them later.

Lady Catherine invited us to breakfast at Rosings on her way out.

"Of course, we would be glad to accept," was William's reply. I was dismayed. Was I to be forced to endure a repeat of last night's episode again so soon? Immediately after the last person left the church and the custodian was shutting up the building, I said to William under my breath, "I really do not wish to return again to Rosings today."

He leaned in and whispered, "Trust me my dear, when I say it is necessary, and please be on your best behaviour, no matter what happens, for my sake," he pleaded. Purely out of respect for my husband, I agreed.

Breakfast followed much the same as the last night's dinner had, with Lady Catherine's mouth opening as a never-ending vat of interfering, busy-bodying, suggestions and offensive remarks. I kept myself calm and collected, turning a thousand cheeks to her brutal sneering. My comfort was in Miss de Bourgh, who it seemed had been longing for a new female companion, and who was happy to keep me occupied in conversation whenever her mother allowed.

As it was daylight, Lady Catherine did not send us home by her carriage, so we set off on foot.

"Remind me again why I must put up with this woman." I said as we walked.

"I would prefer to show you." He replied, heading off in a different direction than our house.

"Where are we going?" I asked as we walked out towards the farmlands that bordered our parsonage on one side.

"You'll see." William took me to a tiny shanty, which hardly seemed a fit dwelling for one person, let alone a family. "This is our tenant farmer's house, built upon the glebe farmlands belonging to us through the church."

I saw several children running around barefoot, and the farmer's wife was in the yard feeding the chickens. The farmer himself was mending a pair of boots that looked well past the point that one should try to continue repairing them.

"Families like his can barely afford to survive," William explained. "Because of the generous gifts Lady Catherine provides to the church, supplementary to her tithes, we are able to let this tenant stay on our property for no charge. They farm the land for us, and we let them keep a generous share of the crops, only keeping for ourselves the food on our table. My hope is that by increasing my favor with Lady Catherine, I may be able to do even more, improving this residence, and building another on the plot of land beside it. What's more," William said, "There are several other church livings which Lady Catherine holds the right of presentation to. Should one of them become available during my lifetime, she may decide to give it to me, thus enabling me to perform similar acts towards the poor in another community." William went on to say, "Without Lady Catherine's support, I would be forced to keep a higher share of the profits just so we ourselves could live, and these people would be living month-to-month with nothing to spare. If any disaster befell, we might not even be able to afford to keep them on at all and would have to farm the land ourselves to survive. Our income from tithes alone is not enough for us to live upon. I shudder to think what would happen to this poor family if we could not afford to subsidize their living," William shook his head.

I had never considered the benefits or ramifications of having or not having a generous supporter before now but seeing how these people lived put it in sharp perspective for me.

The tenant family invited us to stay for dinner, so we spent the afternoon with them. As I became acquainted with them, I saw that they were a kind and hardworking family, who were more than willing to share the little that they had. The dinner we had was not much, just some beef and potatoes, but I knew for them it was a lot. William had mentioned that there were several families whose situation was similar. I realized that, in a way, William considered his ability to subsidize their living as part of his ministry.

I decided then that I needed to do whatever I could to assist my husband in serving his parish and those in need around him. If that included catering to the whims of one Lady Catherine de Bourgh, then so be it. This was the life I had chosen, and I ought to live it.

∞∞∞∞

William

After that first Sunday, I was surprised at the enthusiasm with which my wife threw herself into her new lifestyle. The first week, she accompanied me on my usual rounds to visit the parishioners, so she could grow acquainted with them. Then eventually, she took over most of the social calls, freeing me to focus on visiting the sick and those needing my counsel. The Sunday School was also established within just a few short weeks. Charlotte had selected "heroes of the Old Testament" as her theme for the year, so I assisted her in planning a curriculum that would cover one famous Bible story each week, with a scripture memory verse and a short song to help the children remember the main point of each lesson. Their reading and writing lessons corresponded with that week's Bible story as well. She seemed excited to have a special role in the church, and the children all loved her, just as I knew they would.

As for our relationship, we got along smoothly. Charlotte always treated me with the utmost respect. Even when I opened my mouth like the big fool I was, she never criticized or admonished me in front of others. If she said anything, she would always wait until we were in private, and then say something such as, "It occurred to me dear, it might not be a good idea for you to say…" and proceed to fill me in on whatever social cue I had missed.

She had even seemed to make peace with Lady Catherine. I could tell by watching her facial cues that there were plenty of times she resented our patroness' speeches towards us, but she remained polite as always. I tried to be more sensitive to my wife's feelings and interject as needed on her behalf in front of Lady Catherine- always being careful never to offend the great lady though, of course.

All in all, I couldn't be happier in my new marriage. Little did I know, but trouble was just on the horizon.

Chapter 7

Charlotte

Having begun to be settled in my new home, I then looked forward to Lizzy's promised visit. She was planning to come at the beginning of March, accompanied by my father and sister Maria. Originally, Maria was also to stay for six weeks, along with Lizzy, but plans had changed, and now she would be returning home with my father after only a week. Emily's sixteenth birthday was approaching, and as my mother was hosting a ball for Emily's coming out, she needed every available daughter's assistance to plan it. I was a little sad that I would miss the event, for I missed my sisters and brother at home, and my mother too. Still, I was glad for some company from Hertfordshire, and I knew I would greatly enjoy Lizzy's continued presence, even after my family returned.

The weeks flew by and before I knew it, the day of our company's arrival was upon us. William was beside himself with excitement, making everything ready. He fussed about like a mother hen, rearranging the sofa cushions just minutes after the maid had straightened them, looking out the window every minute to see if they had arrived, and double-triple checking that fresh linens and clean wash basins had been laid out for our guests. Finally, when he had bothered the cook for the third time asking if everything was in order for dinner, she asked me out of exasperation if I might do something about him. I brilliantly suggested that he trim the hedges out front, for that way he could easily see the moment the carriage drove up. He was pleased, and the servants were grateful to have him out of their hair.

The carriage arrived at the expected time. Lizzy leapt out of the seat, shouting, "We are here!" She raced ahead of her traveling companions to be the first to throw her arms around me.

"Oh, sweet friend, I have missed you!" I exclaimed.

"Not as much as I have missed you," Lizzy insisted. "Hertfordshire has been terribly dull since you left. There have been no balls or parties to attend, nothing to divert my attention, save walking to Meryton and corresponding with you and my sister."

"I hope we, here in Kent, can offer you a livelier diversion, to distract you from all your woes," I laughed. Lizzy had intimated in her recent letters that the man she secretly admired, Mr. Wickham, was soon to be engaged to Miss King, whose fortune exceeded her own. I recognized the blow Lizzy must be feeling over the loss of his affections and attention and hoped her stay in Kent might lessen the pangs of heartache— perhaps even introduce a new suitor to replace the colorful Mr. Wickham.

My father and Maria caught up with us and received my warm embraces as well.

"Welcome to our humble abode!" William greeted my father with a handshake and the ladies with a bow. Our guests were shown inside, and their baggage cared for. In similar fashion to my own first tour, William proceeded to showcase all the various rooms of the parsonage, their furnishings as were provided or suggested by Lady Catherine, and to punctuate every advantage of their being so closely situated with such a fine estate as Rosings, and the beneficiaries of such a generous patroness.

Seeing the view of the landscape from the windows, Maria exclaimed, "What a lovely garden you have, Mr. Collins!"

"Why thank you, Miss Maria!" My husband beamed. "It is the spring planting season these days, and some of my flowers are just beginning to bloom again. My wife encourages me to spend time tending to the garden every day, as it is excellent for my constitution."

A full tour of the gardens commenced, as William was so eager to show off his favorite project to our guests. When my husband wanted to go 'round the meadows as well, I interrupted him. "My dear, I think our guests are tired from their journey." He acquiesced, and our party returned to the house. Father and Maria followed the servants up to their rooms so they could change and rest before dinner.

"I'm not tired in the slightest," Lizzy answered when I asked if she needed to rest also. I took her by the hand and led her towards my parlour. Behind me, apparently unaware that we had all left the room, I could hear my husband continue rambling about the garden as he looked out the dining room window. "I have great plans for improvements. I intend to take out the dead birch and plant lime trees along the path in its place. Under the oak tree, I will make a flower bed of hydrangeas and foxglove and place beside it a bench to sit upon. Lady Catherine has also promised to lend me her gardener's assistance to install a fountain, which she says no proper garden can be complete without. I flatter myself that any woman would be happy being the mistress of such a home and garden. Although our gardens do not surpass those of Rosings, I am quite sure there is no better place on Earth than our little paradise..."

Lizzy laughed as I shut the door. "I can see that my cousin is the same as ever."

"Yes. Don't worry, we will not be disturbed here," I assured her. Mrs. MacDougall had already laid out some refreshments for us on the little table beside the settee. "Would you care for a scone? I asked Mrs. MacDougall to bake them this morning especially for your arrival."

Elizabeth happily selected one with plenty of currants from the plate I offered. As I poured some tea for her, I exclaimed, "Oh Lizzy, it's such a joy to have you here!"

"You look very content, my friend." She observed.

"You know, I can honestly say that I am. It gives me great pleasure to run my own household."

"I am glad to hear it. And... how do you manage Mr. Collins?" She asked. "I noticed he mentioned you send him into the garden quite often."

"Mr. Collins and I get along quite fine. It's true we do not spend all day together, but the time we do share, we are always amiable to one another."

"Amiable even in the boudoir?" Lizzy smirked naughtily.

I turned bright red. "Married ladies don't kiss and tell, Elizabeth!" I playfully scolded. I was not about to admit it to her, but there were some aspects of marriage that I rather enjoyed.

Lizzy was full of mirth. "Why, I think you *like* Mr. Collins!" She teased.

"He is my husband, after all." I drily defended. "Besides, he sort of grows on you." I poured some more tea, still blushing.

Elizabeth snorted. "Grows on you? Like a fungus?"

We were interrupted by Maria bursting into the room. "Charlotte, Lizzy, come to the front window and see!"

I stood up and followed my sister to the dining room, Lizzy not far behind me. "What's happened? I expect the pigs have gotten out again." Then I saw out the dining room window. "Oh, it's Miss de Bourgh." She was in her carriage with her companion, Mrs. Jenkinson, talking to William.

"She looks simply splendid, just like Mr. Collins described," Maria gushed. Behind me, Lizzy muttered something under her breath which I could not distinguish. The carriage departed, and my husband came up to the window to talk to us.

"Great news— we've received an invitation to dine at Rosings on Sunday evening." He announced.

"How wonderful." I said with approbation.

William addressed Lizzy and Maria. "Ladies, do not make yourself uneasy about your apparel."

"Just put on whatever dress you've brought that's the best," I completed. Goodness, now I was even finishing his sentences!

"Lady Catherine's never been opposed to the humble in spirit," he added.

Dinner with Lady Catherine! How I hated to hear those words just two short months ago. Now, they were such a part of my daily life, that I did not give it a second thought. At least once per week we dined with Lady Catherine. I had discovered that, despite her tendency to be a busybody and a condescending know-it-all, she also had the capacity to be gracious and generous. More than once, she sent us home with a large roast or bird for our cook to prepare later in the week. She was also accommodating whenever my husband needed to ask a favor of her, and she frequently offered her resources to us whenever a need presented itself.

∞∞∞∞

William

Lady Catherine was pleasant as always, in my estimation. When we arrived at her home on Sunday, she eagerly inquired after the rest of Charlotte's family, and took time to ask Cousin Elizabeth many questions about her upbringing and family life. She also conversed well with Sir William about the political climate, asking my father-in-law his opinion about the current status regarding the trade disputes between Britain, France, and America and what he thought the Prince Regent and Prime Minister Pitt ought to do about them. She even took a slight interest in Maria, asking, now that her eldest sister is married and her other sister would be coming out soon, whether she had any suitors worthy of marrying in her scope.

After a fantastic dinner, we adjourned to the drawing room for cards. The young ladies quickly made up a table for cassino. Miss de Bourgh intended to join them, stating that cassino was her favorite, but her mother called her, "Anne! Do come join our party over here. I need your partnership at quadrille, for Sir William tells me it is his specialty and I intend to best him." Turning to my wife, she said, "Mrs. Collins, you may join your sister and friend at the other table."

"Yes, your ladyship," Charlotte acquiesced.

Anne looked quite disappointed but did not dare disobey her mother. I also sulked inwardly, as I had looked forward to playing against my wife.

As our games progressed, I noticed that our table was rather dull, while the other table seemed to be having great fun.

"Ha, that's twenty-one. I win again!" Charlotte cheered.

"Luck is in your favor at the moment, but the tide is about to change!" Elizabeth grinned as she dealt another hand. Maria chimed in. "Yes, this time *I* will win!" She bragged.

Charlotte shook her head. "Not a chance, little sister. Not a chance!"

"Mr. Collins, it is your bid." Lady Catherine turned my attention back to the game at hand.

"Ah, begging your pardon, ladyship. Ten for me."

The lady scoffed, "Ten! I suppose you think your luck is as good as your wife's over there."

"Perhaps." I replied. Truth be told, Lady Catherine and her daughter were sorely beating Sir William and me. I tried to pay attention, but the laughter from the other side of the room kept distracting me. The women at our table won, and I had a chance to turn again to face the cassino-playing table. Charlotte's smile was magnetizing, and her laughter like an inviting, babbling brook. I wanted to swim in it all night. I noticed that she seemed like a different person when she was around her siblings or Elizabeth, and I recalled the day I'd seen her playing in the snow. I was envious. Would she ever feel so carefree and playful around me?

She was always cool and polite to me, and I always courteous and genteel. What was I doing wrong, that I was unable to bring forth joy from my lovely bride? Was my presence so tedious that I could only see this side of my loved one when in the company of others?

Lady Catherine complained of the late hour, insisting that "Anne must always go to bed on time for the sake of her health." She rang for her carriage to send us home.

I was eager to hear our guests' opinions on Lady Catherine and her incredible house. On the ride home, I turned to my cousin. "Miss Elizabeth, what did you think of Rosings? Is it not the most excellently grand home you have ever seen?"

"It is certainly the largest," Elizabeth admitted.

Sir William contributed to the conversation. "I've been to St. James's, and even their coffered and gilded ceilings do not compare to the ones I saw tonight."

Pleased that my father-in-law was impressed with the house, I felt compelled to tell him, "Lady Catherine had her drawing room ceiling imported from Italy; it was originally installed in a Roman cathedral and cost over three thousand pounds. The one in the dining room originally belonged to a Spanish princess."

"Most impressive!" Sir William exclaimed.

"I, for one, was in awe over Lady Catherine." Maria gushed. "Did you see the peacock plumes in her hair and the size of the jewels 'round her neck? But her presence is most terrifying! When we were introduced, I was so sure that I would faint, the way she looked at me with such intimidating scrutiny."

Elizabeth chuckled.

I raised a quizzical brow. "And what was your impression of her ladyship, cousin?"

"Oh. Um. She was very... inquisitive. And knowledgeable, I suppose," Elizabeth weakly allowed.

"To be sure! Lady Catherine is an excellent source of advice on nearly all subjects," I lavished. "More than once, she has taken great pains to illuminate the best way to raise my chickens, for instance, or given instructions for my cook on how to keep our pantry well-stocked and organized. Additionally, she has—"

"My dear, we are already home now." Charlotte interrupted.

"Ah, so we are." I saw that the carriage had indeed stopped already, and our guests were merely waiting to disembark out of politeness to me. Charlotte was always so helpful in calling my attention back to the present whenever I began to ramble.

Charlotte and I brought up the rear as we entered the house. I stole my arm around her and placed my hand in the small of her back.

"You looked quite delightful tonight, my darling." I whispered in her ear.

In the dark, I couldn't see whether or not her cheeks colored, but she leaned in close. "Thank you, dear," she whispered back, and gave me a peck on the cheek, which did make me blush.

Remembering my thoughts earlier, I decided to be a bit playful. In a bold move, I moved my hand downward and gave a quick squeeze. Charlotte jumped and giggled a little. The light from the house was shining on her face by now, so that time I got a good look at how red she was as she hurried into the house ahead of me.

Must be my lucky night tonight, I thought, trying to hide my ecstatic grin as I entered my home.

∞∞∞∞

Charlotte

Having Lizzy and my family around had put me in a perpetual good mood. Even dining with Lady Catherine did nothing to dampen my spirits. My husband must have noticed it too and decided to capitalize on it. He was certainly *amiable* when we turned in for bed following our guests' first dinner at Rosings...

Miss de Bourgh invited Lizzy, Maria, and my father to take a tour of the countryside with her the following day; my husband and I too were invited, but declined, having already seen plenty of Kent. They were to head out in the morning, and picnic near Hever Castle, then spend the afternoon driving round the rest of the countryside before returning to Rosings in time for tea.

Thus, William and I found ourselves left to our own pursuits for the day. I woke in time to see our visitors off in Miss de Bourgh's phaeton, then I retreated to my own parlour. Since the arrival of our guests, I had not been afforded my usual quiet time in the mornings. I typically devoted a half-hour to an hour reading a passage from my Bible and praying. Then, if time allowed, I would catch up on some other reading or write letters until breakfast. On this particular morning, I was reading from Galatians, and the words reminded me of a hymn I had heard recently. For some reason, I could not recall the tune, try as I might. What was stuck in my head was the song our cook, Mrs. MacDougall, had been singing, "The Water is Wide"-an old Scottish tune. For whatever reason, I decided to try singing the hymn to that tune. Miraculously, the words fit it perfectly.

"When I survey the wondrous cross
On which the Prince of glory died
My richest gain I count but loss
And pour contempt on all my pride
Forbid it, Lord, that I should boast,
Save in the death of Christ my God
All the vain things that charm me most,
I sacrifice them to His blood"

I was about to begin the third stanza, when suddenly, I heard two voices in the passageway on the other side of my door.

"Why, Mr. Collins, whatever are you doing lurking outside your wife's door?" The first voice belonged to my housekeeper, Mrs. Perry.

"I, uh, I was...that is to say." I heard William stammer.

"The missus does sing beautifully, does she not?" Mrs. Perry asked.

While this was going on, I stood and opened the door upon my embarrassed husband and the housekeeper, who bore a smirk on her face for having caught him listening to me.

"Charlotte! I wasn't eavesdropping on you!" William lied, then admitted, "Well, at least, not intentionally. It's just that your voice was so entrancing, like a siren's call. I could not help but want to hear more of it."

Mrs. Perry merely smiled and carried on with her duties, leaving the two of us alone.

"It is all right, William," I reassured him. "When doing my daily perusal of scripture, I felt suddenly inspired by some songs I heard recently and the passage out of the Epistles I was reading." I explained. "I'm currently studying Galatians."

My husband seemed surprised. "You were reading the Bible?"

I nodded.

He shook his head. "Silly me, I should not be astonished. It is perfectly natural for a Christian woman to be reading from the Holy Scriptures, particularly one who is the wife of a clergyman. After all, it is the duty of every minister's wife to set an example for her parish and to raise godly children in the home. One must be properly equipped for such, I would imagine."

There was an awkward pause. "...Yes". I finally agreed.

"But I digress. The reason I happened to be downstairs passing by your door was that I was on my way to the garden." William explained.

I glanced at the little clock atop my desk. "Is it not later than usual for you to be doing that?"

"A bit," he said. "I confess, I did not hear you wake this morning, as I typically do. Thus, I rather overslept. At any rate, a thought occurred to me. If you are finished with your reading and, uh, singing, would you care to assist me in the garden for a change? You may recall the shipment of bulbs that Lady Catherine ordered for me a few weeks ago. Well, they arrived the day before last, and I'm afraid I must get them all into the ground if they are to survive. Truly, I could use the help," he admitted.

I thought for a moment. "You know, some fresh air would be nice. I would be happy to help you, dear." Donning my apron, I followed him outside.

William showed me the flower beds where he wanted the bulbs planted, and we got to work. Though it was March, the sun was warm, and I began to sweat. I used my arm to wipe my brow.

William glanced at me, then chuckled as he turned back to the flower bed.

"What is it?"

"Nothing."

I narrowed my eyes and twisted my lips in a mock scowl.

"Your face. You've got a huge streak of dirt across it," he told me.

"Oh, you think you look so much better?" My impish spirit was coming out again. I grabbed a handful of dirt. "I shall remedy that, posthaste!" I said, before smearing a big clump across his cheek. His expression was priceless. I began laughing so hard my sides felt they might split.

"Oh, you're going to get it now!" he boomed, giving chase immediately. I cannot fathom what wild spirit had gotten into my husband lately; he had a flirtatious side I'd never seen before. With both hands, he scooped an even greater heap of soil. I foresaw what was coming and began running, laughing all the way. William chased me across the lawn. My skirt slowed down my escape and he caught me, knocking the both of us to the ground. We tumbled once before I found myself laying in the grass looking up at him.

Both of us suddenly stopped laughing. William gazed intently into my eyes. Then he pressed his lips against mine. For a moment, I was stunned, then I began kissing him back with a passion I didn't know I had. We paused for breath. "Would you care to move to more comfortable and private quarters, my dear?" William asked. I nodded. Dusting off the dirt and grass, we practically flew into the house and upstairs.

∞∞∞∞

William

My wife did not bother to fully undress as we found ourselves in the throes of passion. Her driving the reins was a new experience for us; one I found incredibly exhilarating. Just being like this was almost enough to push me over the edge already. Trying to make the experience last longer, I distracted myself by daydreaming. I wondered, if I had married Elizabeth as I'd originally intended, would I be this happy, as I was now with Charlotte? Since I'd met her, Elizabeth always seemed so uncomfortable around me. Even now, whenever she spoke to me, I could sense the awkwardness as she struggled to know what to say, and her body language suggested she'd rather be anywhere than there. How could I have once believed her demeanor sprung from shy affection? Thinking about what our lives would be like together, I could not imagine she would be content living under the same roof as me, dining at the same table as me, sharing a bed with me....

Oh, Lord! I sighed. What Charlotte was doing to me at that moment felt unspeakably good! Would Elizabeth have given me *this* kind of treatment? Definitely not! I moaned for her to continue. "Oh...*Elizabeth*..."

Charlotte instantly halted and got off the bed. "What did you call me?" She asked in disbelief. Immediately, I realized what I had said and began cursing myself. "I...." I just stood there with my mouth gaping. No words could come out— I had been rendered completely mute.

Charlotte launched. "We are together, making love, and you're fantasizing about my *best friend?!*" She began pacing the room angrily. "All this time we've been married, you have still been holding onto feelings for her, is that it?"

"No!—"

"And while she is a guest in our house, no less!" Stopping to look at me she scoffed, "Elizabeth's room is just down the hall. Are you going to go over tonight and sleep with her too?"

"I would never do such a thing!" I defended.

Charlotte shook her head. "I'm not certain anymore. How can I trust anything you say at all? You're apparently able to confuse my name out loud with that of your *lover*." She spat venomously.

I desperately tried to reason with her. "There is nothing between me and Elizabeth. No acts of unfaithfulness have been committed against you."

"Except in your head!" She argued.

"That's not what was happening at all!" I threw myself at her feet. "Charlotte, you are my one and only. My beloved. You're the air I breathe...the ground on which I place my feet—"

"Save your breath," Charlotte interrupted. She quickly pulled her drawers back on. "No amount of groveling is going to get you out of this one." Grabbing a rag and the washbasin, she scrubbed her face clean in front of the mirror. Turning back around to me she said, "I can't even stand to look at you right now. I'm going out. Don't expect me back for tea."

"But what shall I tell Lady Catherine? She is expecting us at Rosings."

"Tell her whatever you want. Make up some excuse. You're good at that." With that, she stormed out of the house.

I broke down in tears and collapsed beside the bed in anguish. How could this have happened? I cursed myself again and again. Letting my mind wander like that was foolish. But my mouth! It did nothing but get me in trouble, time and time again. Could I but have it sewn shut forever? I felt in that moment that I could easily endure starving to death if it would keep me from ever speaking again, the way my mouth had betrayed me. Would Charlotte ever forgive me after this? How could I possibly make her see that my heart was true to her? I did not know. I could only pray that somehow, I could fix this awful mess I had made.

Chapter 8

Charlotte

My fury drove me as far away from the parsonage as I could manage on foot. I found myself in the village, wandering aimlessly along the storefronts. I scarcely paid heed to my direction; my mind was so consumed with anger. Just at the very moment when I believed we were starting to mean something more to one another than merely contractual marriage partners— now this! His slip of the tongue had revealed the person who was truly on his mind when we were together. What's worse, of all people, it had to be Elizabeth he preferred! I had played second fiddle to her my whole life, but never had I been so envious before as I was right in that revolting moment of time. I should have known all along that this was coming; after all, I was only his second choice after her, his consolation prize. But he swore to me before we were married that he had no feelings for her! He lied to me!

Still, Lizzy was not to blame. I knew she would never intentionally do anything to hurt me. The comment I made about William sleeping with her was more just to rattle him than anything. She certainly would not be a party to such sin— especially given her well-advertised low estimation of William! No, this was clearly an unrequited love on his part, as it had been from the beginning.

In my swirling reverie of wrath, I failed to discern the young woman entering my pathway as she rounded the corner until I directly collided with her.

"Oh!" I gasped as we crashed. Her parcels tumbled and scattered on the ground.

"I beg your pardon!" I apologized, helping her collect her belongings. "I did not mean to make you drop your things."

"No harm done, madam," she said, brushing her blonde curls behind her ears as she stood up. "I'm afraid I've always been clumsy." She flashed a smile. "Have a good day," she said, then hurried along.

Though I knew most of the villagers, I had never seen her before, and I wondered why.

I noticed that several people were watching us, trying to look as though they weren't. I glanced at my reflection in a store window. Goodness, no wonder people were looking! My hair was a mess; several locks had escaped and flew free in the wind, the bun was dangling by two remaining hairpins, and I discovered a twig leftover from my romp in the garden. My dress was also soiled and wrinkled, leaving much to be desired. Although I had washed my face off before leaving the house, I did not pay much attention to the rest of my appearance, being eager to make my escape. "Tis the consequence of my silly garden-writhing and my wroth departure", I told myself.

Deciding I'd rather not encounter any acquaintance I'd be forced to converse with, I turned and went back home. The parsonage was empty when I returned. William had gone to tea at Rosings, I presumed, and the servants were all elsewhere. Stealthily taking a few books off the shelf from my parlour, I hurried upstairs to my bedroom and did not emerge for the rest of the day.

∞∞∞∞

William

For the next few weeks, Charlotte spoke to me as little as possible in front of our guests, and even less when we were in private. Though married and living with my wife, I felt terribly lonely. When I returned from Rosings after supper that fateful day, I was coldly informed by her that while we should make every effort to keep up appearances in front of our guests, I should not expect to share a bed. Thus, I slept on the sofa in my dressing room adjacent to our bedroom, so no one would know we weren't sleeping together.

The servants all guessed something had happened, for they had heard us shouting, but they hadn't a clue as to what was amiss. I enlisted their help to try to woo my wife back to me. My carnations were now in bloom, and accordingly I picked a bountiful bouquet of them. Mrs. Perry had a gift for arranging flowers, so I asked her to make them up for me and deliver them to Charlotte with my note. Our housekeeper politely notified me later that Charlotte had promptly deposited the flowers in the rubbish heap. A few days later,

I wrote a beautiful poem expressing my sorrows and apologies and asked the maid to deliver it to Charlotte in her parlour. She later told me she had seen Charlotte burning the paper in the fireplace. Still determined to prove my love and devotion to Charlotte, I sent my manservant Hines on an errand to the new confectionery shop that opened up in the village, to bring back the best truffles he could find. A week later, I found the box by Charlotte's vanity table, still untouched. At least she didn't throw them away; they were bloody expensive! I thought.

Charlotte's father and Maria left on Thursday the week of "the incident", as planned. I don't think either of them suspected anything was wrong between Charlotte and me. As for Elizabeth, I don't know how Charlotte could possibly keep a straight face around her, so she must have suspected that something was the matter. I knew not whether Charlotte had confided in her, but I guessed that my wife had kept her own counsel. Surely Elizabeth would have come down hard on me had she known the details of what had transpired!

∞∞∞∞

Charlotte

I was determined to put as much distance between myself and my husband as I could, and also to keep him away from Lizzy. I spent the chief of each day with Elizabeth, hiding out with her in my parlour accompanied by some tea and biscuits, taking long walks with her through the extensive groves of Rosings Park, or asking her to accompany me on errands in the village. In my petty mind, I thought that the more I kept Lizzy apart from my husband, the more it would pain him.

Of course, necessity demanded that I sometimes accompany him to visit Rosings, or to pay a call to one of our parishioners, who I had seen less of on account of our having company, but who still occasionally needed our attention. For these trips, I suggested to my husband that Lizzy need not join us. I was surprised that he readily agreed. Elizabeth also did not seem to mind in the least being left behind, telling us that she enjoyed the solitude and rest.

More than once, Lizzy inquired of me whether something had happened between myself and Mr. Collins, but I consistently denied it, and she pressed no further. I think she could sense the difference in the atmosphere, but at least had the sensibility to maintain a safe distance from the awkward difficulties of another person's married life. I did not under any circumstances want her to know the truth of the matter, for she would certainly try to blame herself, and I couldn't bear to see my beloved Lizzy claim any fault for my husband's adulterous heart.

The second half of Lizzy's visit was punctuated by the arrival at Rosings of Lady Catherine's nephews: the illustrious Mr. Darcy, and his cousin, Colonel Fitzwilliam. My husband went to Rosings to properly greet them, and when he returned, they accompanied him. I was certain it was because Mr. Darcy had heard that Lizzy was staying with us and wished to see her. I could think of no other reason for him to give us the honor of his calling on us, given how little he knew us. I thought that perhaps it might not be too late for Lizzy to capture this attractive gentleman for her own after all, if only she would let go of her pride over the one silly comment he had made the night of their first introduction. Then again, his cousin Colonel Fitzwilliam was nearly equal in appearance, and he was ever so charming and friendly. He wasn't nearly as fabulously wealthy as Mr. Darcy, but he had a solid and respectable position with the military which had him well-set for the remainder of his life. If Lizzy could not see Mr. Darcy as a kind and gentle man, albeit a bit shy, perhaps she might be more tempted by the outgoing colonel.

I spoke to Lizzy about this one day while we were sitting in my parlour. "Lizzy," I said, "have you noticed that both Mr. Darcy and Colonel Fitzwilliam have called on us rather frequently since their arrival?"

Lizzy shrugged. "I presume that they wish to escape from their aunt's pretentious meddling, and that they find the company here to be more pleasant."

"I would agree. But I think the company they find to be most pleasant would be yours." I pointed out. Elizabeth was quick to disagree.

"They can have no particular preference to me. I am certain it is because you are a gracious host, and because even Mr. Collins' nonstop chatter is better than feeling the weight of Lady Catherine's opinions."

Truth aside, I pressed on, "Still, I wonder, if you were to choose one of them to particularly recommend yourself to, which would it be?"

Lizzy laughed. "Naturally, Colonel Fitzwilliam is the more amiable of the two. I cannot help but feel whenever Mr. Darcy is near that he is aloof and somber, and that he somehow considers himself to be above us."

"So, you prefer the colonel?" I asked.

Lizzy nodded. "He is quite handsome and charming, you know."

"Do you suppose that he might have taken a fancy to you?" I suggested.

"Nonsense!" Lizzy laughed again. "I can see no reason to believe that Colonel Fitzwilliam has any partiality towards me, or that he ever shall."

"Still, I see no reason why you could not have him in your power, if you so desired."

"It is up to the gentleman to pursue me if he wishes. I will not go throwing myself at him and making a fool of myself." Lizzy insisted.

"What about Mr. Darcy then? Surely you must have noticed he appears quite keen on you."

"That, Charlotte, is a most ridiculous notion!"

"Not at all."

"Charlotte, why are you so determined to marry me off to someone or other?" Lizzy demanded.

"Because surely you must see the advantage for a woman of your station to be comfortably situated. It's my firm belief that you could have any man you wanted. It certainly seems that no matter where you go, you are every man's first choice." My last comment came out much more bitterly than I wanted it to.

Lizzy seemed confused. "What do you mean by that?"

"First Mr. Collins, then Mr. Darcy and Mr. Wickham, and I'm fairly certain Colonel Fitzwilliam would fancy you too if you only encouraged him a little," I started to choke up.

"Charlotte," Lizzy chose her words carefully, putting two and two together, "are you upset because your husband first made an offer of marriage to me?"

I didn't respond to her.

Lizzy continued, "You know perfectly well that I never cared for him one bit, nor encouraged him in any way."

"I know you didn't." I said softly, wiping my eyes with a handkerchief. "It's just that… I think my husband may still prefer you over me. Much like how I married him because I needed someone to be my husband and provider, he only married me because you turned him down, and he still desired to please Lady Catherine and the others of the parish by installing an acceptable lady as 'wife to the parson'." I strongly urged myself to stick with my resolution and not give any more details than that.

"Now, you know that is not true." Elizabeth insisted. "I have seen the way that Mr. Collins looks at you. He has never once looked at me that way, not even when he was proposing. I don't know what has happened between you two to make things go awry, but I can tell you this: Mr. Collins *very much* loves you and wants to make things right with you."

"You think he...loves me?" William had made many professions of love to me, but I always dismissed them as his attempt to be amiable or as mere infatuation.

Lizzy placed her hand upon my shoulder. "I think you need to open your eyes and see that there is more between the two of you in this marriage than just a business arrangement."

I still was not sure if I was ready to forgive my husband yet, but Lizzy's words had given me much to think about.

∞∞∞∞

William

Easter had passed, and still my Charlotte held me at arm's length, speaking to me only when necessary. We frequently had guests calling in the form of one or both of Lady Catherine's nephews, an honor which pleased me to no end. We also enjoyed the favor of an increase in invitations to Rosings, on account of Lady Catherine's desire to provide her house guests with as much entertainment as possible during their stay.

On one of the evenings when we were at home with no

guests, except Elizabeth, of course, I suggested that perhaps I might read aloud by the fireside. Charlotte nodded her consent. But Elizabeth made excuse that she was tired and wished to retire early and bid us goodnight. I cannot say I was disappointed to have some time alone with my wife.

Charlotte settled into her chair with her embroidery basket, and I picked up my copy of Fordyce's *Sermons* off the shelf.

Charlotte sighed. "Don't you think, just for once, we might read something else?" she asked. I was surprised at her objection, but willing to concede, I closed the book. "Certainly, my dear. Do you have any suggestions?"

Charlotte seemed stunned that I was willing to put aside my favorite book for a change. She blinked a couple of times. "Um...how about you read from...the Bible? Surely there can be no better book on the subject of moral living than that."

"How right you are, Charlotte." I approved. "Do you have any particular passage you wish me to read from?" I asked as I settled into my own chair with my copy of the Good Book in hand.

She shook her head. "Just select something that strikes your fancy. Anything will do."

I allowed the book to fall open where it willed. It landed on the passage of poetry written by King Solomon and his bride to each other.

"How about the Song of Solomon?" I asked Charlotte.

"Truthfully, I'm not sure I've read much of that one. I think the one time I did, I found it all confusing and silly. As I recall, the man compared the woman's hair to a flock of goats, and her eyes to pigeons, did he not?" she laughed aloud.

I grinned. "They were doves, but yes, he did. It's actually an incredibly romantic book if one understands the meaning behind the metaphors and stories," I tried to explain.

"Well, perhaps as a minister of the Word, you can enlighten me on the subject," she suggested.

I picked up reading right where the pages had opened. It was the story in chapter five, when the couple has a fight. How appropriate to our present situation, I thought.

"I sleep, but my heart waketh: it is the voice of my beloved that knocketh, saying, 'Open to me, my sister, my love, my dove, my undefiled: for my head is filled with dew, and my locks with the drops of the night.'

'I have put off my coat; how shall I put it on? I have washed my feet; how shall I defile them?'

My beloved put in his hand by the hole of the door, and my bowels were moved for him.

I rose up to open to my beloved; and my hands dripped with myrrh, and my fingers with sweet smelling myrrh, upon the handles of the lock.

I opened to my beloved; but my beloved had withdrawn himself, and was gone: my soul failed when he spake: I sought him, but I could not find him; I called him, but he gave me no answer."

Charlotte interrupted me. "I see no sense in this. 'My bowels were moved for him?' It sounds like this man has just given her a massive case of diarrhea."

I shook my head. "She's not speaking of intestinal complaints. The Hebrews believed that the seat of a person's emotions was in their abdomen, or bowels. In today's terms, we might say 'my heart was moved'. What is happening here," I explained, "is that there is a conflict going on between them. While we're not told the nature of their previous argument, it is evident that when the husband, Solomon, comes to his wife's bedroom, she is angry and refuses to admit him." Oh, how I identified with Solomon in this story!

I continued. "But he treats her gently; and afterwards, she is repentant and wants to reconcile with him, but he has already left."

Charlotte seemed very curious. "What happens in the rest of the story?" She asked.

"Well, she goes out looking for him, and the daughters of Jerusalem ask her why she loves him, and how to find him, so she goes to great lengths to give them a head-to-toe description of his physical appearance, in which each trait is a symbol for one of his character traits."

"Does the couple reconcile?" Charlotte wanted to know.

"Yes." I said. "She finds him in his garden, and he quotes back to her almost word-for-word the prose from their wedding night."

I flipped the page to the next chapter.

"Here, listen to this:

'Thou art beautiful, O my love, as Tirzah, comely as Jerusalem, terrible as an army with banners. Turn away thine eyes from me, for they have overcome me: thy hair is as a flock of goats that appear from Gilead. Thy teeth are as a flock of sheep which go up from the washing, whereof every one beareth twins, and there is not one barren among them. As a piece of a pomegranate are thy temples within thy locks.'"

Charlotte laughed. "I still think she must have found him to be rather silly and ungainly, for him to be comparing her features to goats, sheep, and pomegranates!"

Not unlike myself, I thought. "Yes, I do admit this metaphor seems foolish to us, but these were terms she would have understood as valuable goods. Furthermore, many people believe each item is symbolic for something else, although no one quite agrees on the exact meaning. But one thing is certain, his speech to her was very provocative and romantic."

Charlotte looked unsure. I decided to take it a step further.

"Here, let me show you, using the passage a few chapters back from their wedding night." I stood and went to Charlotte's side. She looked full of trepidation.

"Behold, thou art fair, my love; behold, thou art fair; thou hast doves' eyes within thy locks". I stroked the front of Charlotte's hair gently with the back of my hand. In the soft glow of the firelight, her eyes glimmered. I pulled her to her feet in front of me. "Thy hair is as a flock of goats, that appear from mount Gilead." Grasping the pins holding her hair, I let it tumble down her back. I ran my fingers through the thick waves spilling over her shoulders. Charlotte stared into my eyes, completely spellbound.

I went on. "Thy teeth are like a flock of sheep that are even-shorn, which came up from the washing; whereof every one bear twins, and none is barren among them." Charlotte smiled, showing me her own beautiful teeth. My heart pounded within me. Could she possibly be ready to forgive me? I kept going with a renewed hope. "Thy lips are like a thread of scarlet, and thy speech is comely" Her mouth parted. I ran my thumb across her lower lip, aching to kiss her so badly, but not daring to. I settled for kissing her forehead once on each side, saying, "Thy temples are like a piece of a pomegranate within thy locks."

Coming behind her and moving downwards, I began to nibble at her neck. Perhaps Charlotte was reminded of our own wedding night, as I was. Letting out a soft groan, she closed her eyes and tilted her head to allow me greater access. I whispered in her ear, "Thy neck is like the Tower of David builded for an armoury, whereon there hang a thousand bucklers, all shields of mighty men." I continued planting kisses down the length of her neck. I was surprised she was so receptive to all this. Tingling with excitement, I moved to the next portion as I embraced her from behind.

"Thy two breasts are like two young roes that are twins, which feed among the lilies. Until the day breaks, and the shadows flee away, I will get me to the mountain of myrrh, and to the hill of frankincense."

Charlotte leaned into my chest, and I stopped speaking momentarily, enjoying our closeness.

"What's next?" She whispered, urging me to continue.

"Thou art all fair, my love; there is no spot in thee. Come with me from Lebanon, my spouse, with me from Lebanon: look from the top of Amana, from the top of Shenir and Hermon, from the lions' dens, from the mountains of the leopards." As I said this, my voice was growing husky. I felt as if my marriage had been thrown into the lion's den. I wanted nothing more than to come out of there and back to the safety we had before. My words caught in my throat, and I couldn't continue.

Charlotte turned to face me again, just as a tear rolled down my cheek.

"Oh, Charlotte," I pleaded, "when will you see, there has never been another for me but you?"

She was getting choked up now too. "I believe you, William. Forgive me for having doubted you."

"The fault is mine, for having given you cause to doubt me." With that, our lips met, our kiss mingled with the salty tears running down our faces.

I hugged Charlotte close and buried my face in her shoulder.

In my ear, she whispered the words I'd been longing to hear for the first time. "I love you, William."

I put my hand to her cheek tenderly. "I love you too. Truly, I do, beloved." Kissing her once more, I scooped her into my arms and carried her up to our bedchamber to continue our reconciliation there.

Some time later, I came out of my dressing room after changing into my nightclothes. I saw Charlotte sitting on the bed still, nibbling on the box of chocolates I had purchased, and I smiled. Yes, I thought, things were once again well in my marriage.

∞∞∞∞

Charlotte

As we climbed into bed to go to sleep later that night, I snuggled close to William. He leaned over and kissed me.

"Are you happy, my dear?' He asked.

"Mm, yes, very." I murmured. "You know," I said playfully with a coy lilt, "you are exceptionally good at explaining the Bible, Reverend Mr. Collins."

"Why yes, Mrs. Collins. After all, I am an ordained minister," he played along.

"I don't believe you finished your exposition of the Song of Solomon." I pointed out with a sly smile.

"Unfortunately, madam, I beg leave to defer the remainder of that study for another night. I do have to give a sermon in the morning." He reminded me with a wry grimace.

"Very well, dear." I conceded, a little reluctantly. Kissing him, I bid him "goodnight."

He nestled down in the bed and fell asleep in minutes.

I lay awake awhile, my head against his chest, listening to his heartbeat and his faint snoring. How I had missed this kind of closeness in the past month! More than anything, the recent distance between us had revealed to me the depth of my feelings. I was not sure exactly when it happened, but I had fallen in love with this man I had married. I knew that by telling him tonight that I loved him, I had brought great joy to William, and our relationship was on a whole new stratum. What a fool I had been, holding onto my anger for so long! Lizzie's advice to me had helped, but it was William's tenderness to me that had shown me what a great misunderstanding

I'd clung to, until I realized there was nothing left to do but forgive him. When we had wed, I'd felt content with my lot in life, never expecting anything more than a comfortable home and an amiable living partner. Never dreaming to find the kind of deep, abounding love we now shared. Now, at last, I felt truly and unequivocally happy.

Blissful thoughts continued to lull me nearer towards the dream castle Hypnos, and William's embrace became for me the waiting arms of Morpheus, as I drifted off and enjoyed the best night's sleep I'd had in weeks.

Chapter 9

Charlotte

Elizabeth was pleased to observe that the relationship between William and myself had been restored. The morning after our reconciliation, I was sitting at the breakfast table with her, when she commented on the subject.

"So, I noticed Mr. Collins whistling when I passed by him on the stairs today. I take it you two are on friendly terms again?"

I nodded. "Very *amiably*," I smiled, referencing our inside joke.

"Oh, even better!" Lizzy laughed. "I am glad you have worked out whatever had come between you."

"Me too." I replied. "I can honestly say things have never been better."

Lizzy grasped my hand. "Oh Charlotte, I know I had some misgivings before when you and Mr. Collins first got engaged, but I was wrong. You are both so suited for one another, like two peas in a pod."

I took the opportunity to tease, "Oh, so now you think me an over-talkative fool too?"

"No!" Lizzy gasped with a laugh. "I only meant you balance each other out. Mr. Collins' manners are much more tempered as of late. He talks less, and when he does speak, fewer ridiculous things come out of his mouth."

"And what of me?" I wanted to know.

"As for you," she continued, "I think your husband has brought out your romantic side."

Thinking about our reading of the Song of Solomon the night before, I could not argue with her assessment. "Perhaps you're right," I admitted. My cheeks colored slightly at the vibrant recollections passing through my mind as I sipped my coffee.

"At any rate, I hope the two of you will cherish each other for many years to come." Elizabeth wished.

"Thank you. Now we just need to find a lover who will be ardently devoted to our finicky Elizabeth! I can see more than ever that you are a hopeless romantic, and nothing less than true love would induce you to accept a man."

Lizzy laughed. "And who would such a man be?"

"I don't know," I said, "but I can picture you, standing under some garden folly in the pouring rain while he madly professes his love for you."

"'Tis to laugh! It is far more likely I'll be sitting by myself on a Thursday and he'll barge in awkwardly and confess to me in a most blathering fashion!" Lizzy postulated.

We had no more time to speculate on either hypothetical situation.

William entered to tell us church would be starting soon, so we left the breakfast table to fetch our bonnets, and that was the end of our conversation.

Another week brought the end of Mr. Darcy and Colonel Fitzwilliam's stay at Rosings. During their final days in Kent, Elizabeth had seemed rather out of spirits. I wondered if it could be caused by feelings for one of these gentlemen, and the sorrow their parting might bring. Lizzy was reluctant to say a word on the subject, even when I pressed her on account of her frequent discomposure and uncharacteristic melancholy. Finally, it seemed she could no longer contain her feelings. She confessed to me that Mr. Darcy had, in fact, proposed to her only the other night! I was about to express my sincere congratulations when she further shocked me by declaring that she had most thoroughly rejected him. To assuage my astonishment, she related the rude manner in which he had prevailed upon her, insulting her family and her low connections. I was ready to concede her rebuttal of him, but she continued on, relating that there was a letter, since then received by her, by which he sought to explain himself. She did not relate any of the particulars, nor show me the letter itself, but she summarized the contents such by saying that she had rather misjudged the man, and that she had been cruelly unjust in her supposition of his motives towards some of their mutual acquaintance.

"Does that mean, dear Lizzy, that you regret your refusal of his proposal?" I asked. "There may still be time to undo what has been done. Perhaps he may yet be induced to enter into an engagement, should a change of heart be made known." I contemplated.

Elizabeth shook her head. "No, sweet friend, I have not changed my resolution on that account. What's done is done, and Mr. Darcy made it clear in the letter that he would not repeat his addresses to me. I have no wish to rekindle the fires that I have so thoroughly extinguished. I merely grieve that I thought so ill over the man. I imagined him proud, conceited, and meddling, but I discovered him to be the opposite: shy, selfless, and well-intentioned. No matter now, though. He is gone, and I very much doubt we shall ever have cause to meet again." Her countenance bore every mark of remorse, and I could not help but feel pained for my friend, believing that there must be more to her feelings towards Mr. Darcy than even she might realize. I wished there were something I might do to help, but although she had done a great service for me in my relationship with William, in this instance, it was out of my power to do the same for her. I did what I could to lessen her sorrow by providing distractions and entertainment for her final week in Kent. Invitations to Rosings were aplenty; Lady Catherine's motive was to ease her own boredom after the departure of her nephews. In doing so, she unknowingly assisted me in keeping Elizabeth occupied and her mind off Mr. Darcy during the remainder of her stay.

On Lizzy's last day, William was to drive her into Westerham in his gig, where she would catch the stage to Bromley and be met by her uncle's manservant to convey her the rest of the way to London. I bid her farewell from our home that morning.

"You must promise to write to me," I begged Lizzy.

She gave me a tight squeeze. "Of course, Charlotte. Thank you so much for hosting me in your home."

"You are welcome back anytime you should wish to escape the scenery in Hertfordshire." I offered.

"Thank you, Charlotte. And you know you and Mr. Collins are welcome to visit us anytime as well. I'll ask my father to formally invite you both soon, and I'll make sure Mamma puts you up in our best guest room— no excuses!"

I laughed. "I'm sure she would put us in the barn if she could."

Lizzy imitated her mother, "Oh, but Mr. and Mrs. Collins can have no need for such a spacious room. Why, any room in the house ought to do, even the servant's quarters. For that matter, they might be just as comfortable sleeping with the horses where there is fresh hay and a clean water-trough!" She mocked.

Still laughing, I said, "I'm sure my own mother will be happy to put me up, so you needn't worry about us, but it would be funny to see your mother's reaction if it were suggested we might stay at Longbourn."

Embracing me again, Lizzy said, "I shall dearly miss you, Charlotte."

"And I you," I echoed her refrain. "The parsonage shall seem terribly dull without your presence to liven it."

"But you shall have the company of one Mr. Collins to keep it from ever being silent!" Elizabeth and I laughed over her remark.

At that moment, my husband emerged from the carriage house, bringing round the gig with his horse.

"Cousin Elizabeth, Charlotte, I'm afraid it is time for you to be parted. Elizabeth, we must get you to your stage." She nodded as William helped her into the small two-seater carriage beside him and they were off.

∞∞∞∞

William

With the last of our guests gone, things were quiet at the parsonage as we resumed our daily routines in a peaceful fashion. I found, though, that I had a renewed desire to spend as much time with my wife as I could.

One morning, when Charlotte was in her parlour, I decided I would rather be with her than alone in my garden. I hesitated outside her door. This was her special sanctuary, and I did not want to go against my promise to her and invade it. Finally, I knocked.

"Come in." I heard her reply. Surprised, I opened the door.

"Good morning, dear." Charlotte greeted.

"Good morning." I returned. Charlotte had her Bible open again on her lap. Oh dear, I had interrupted her personal study time. I stood for a moment, unsure of what to do.

Charlotte broke the silence. "Is there something you wanted to ask me, William?"

"Excuse my intrusion," I said, "I interrupted you. I will return later when you have concluded."

"There is no intrusion. I am reading out of 2 Timothy today. Would you like to join me?" She welcomed, patting the spot next to her on the settee.

"Certainly." I replied, joining her.

We read through the passage together out loud, and then had a lively discussion about the meaning of some of the parts of it. I was astonished that she took such an active interest in studying the scriptures in this way, and that she came at our debate with a fair amount of knowledge of the Bible as a whole. She was easily able to reference other relevant passages and quote then from memory. Here is a woman who is truly a devoted Christian, I thought. When we concluded our discussion, we prayed together. Once more, I was surprised. I had always viewed God as high and mighty, fearsome to behold, and myself as humble servant, a lowly worm below, and thus my prayers reflected this. Charlotte treated the Heavenly Father as if He were her best friend, and spoke to Him in a familiar way, like a loving daughter.

I was a minister of the Gospel, one whom people looked to as their spiritual advisor. I was supposed to be closely connected to God. Yet I found myself desiring the intimacy Charlotte had in her walk with the Lord, something I felt I was missing in my own life.

Then Charlotte put me on the spot.

"How did you know that you were called into ministry as a clergyman?" She wanted to know.

"To be honest, I'm not sure I ever felt 'called', per se". I told her. "The church was just something I chose because I needed a respectable profession. I have no land, except what I will someday inherit from the Bennets, and I didn't want to go into law, or the military. I considered becoming a doctor, but I cannot stand the sight of blood. So, since I'd grown up in the church my whole life, it made sense to pursue a degree in theology and divinity when I applied to Oxford." I finished.

"I see," Charlotte nodded. I was grateful she did not query me further on the subject.

I felt bewildered and confused. Little did I know, my faith would soon be challenged in far greater ways than this.

∞∞∞∞

Charlotte

One morning in May, William and I were planning to go to the village together to complete some errands. But William got called at the last minute to visit one of our parishioners who was ill and had taken a turn for the worse, so I set out for the village alone. The weather was warm and fine for walking. As I neared the town, I came upon Mrs. Barnes and her young son Robbie, who frequently participated in my Sunday School in church. They greeted me warmly, and Robbie ran ahead of his mother, eager to show me something he'd found. "Look Mrs. Collins, I found a shiny penny on the sidewalk!"

I crouched down to his level.

"Very pretty. That's good luck, you know?"

"That's what Mama said too!" Robbie cried eagerly.

"Will I see you on Sunday? We're going to learn about 'Daniel in the Lion's Den'; it will be very exciting!" I promised.

"Will there be real lions?" Robbie's eyes widened.

"I'm afraid not." I chuckled.

"I can roar like a lion. See? Raaawwwr!" He proceeded to bellow out his best imitation of a mighty king of the jungle and bounded on all fours in a circle around us.

His mother and I both laughed at his antics.

"Yes, we expect to be there, Mrs. Collins," Robbie's mother said. "Robbie loves your story times so much; we wouldn't miss it!"

"Wonderful! See you soon." I smiled and parted from them to continue on my way.

I had originally volunteered for the Sunday School to please my husband, since he seemed so keen on the idea, and to prove to Lady Catherine that I was up to snuff in my new role as the minister's wife. I did not expect I would enjoy it so much. Yet, I had grown to love each of the children who participated and looked forward to planning their lessons each week. Truth be told, I had never had a role in the church before. Growing up in my parent's congregation in

Hertfordshire, I had been content to be a regular attender, and I felt like I had graduated, in a way, now having an active part in the ministry.

My first errand that morning was the draper, to order some new dresses. As I approached Emerson's Fine Tailoring, the blonde woman I had encountered a few weeks prior emerged. She was carrying a large bundle of beautiful silks, taffetas, and lace.

I offered her a friendly greeting. "Hello again, good to see you!"

She nodded back politely. "Thank you. It's nice to see you as well. I hope you are doing well."

"I am," I replied. "I don't believe we've been properly introduced. I'm Charlotte Collins. My husband is the local parson."

"You may call me 'Vanessa'," the woman replied, in a regional accent common to Kent. "Pardon me, I would shake your hand, but as you can see, my arms are full at the moment."

"Not to worry," I smiled. "I understand."

"Well, have a good day Mrs. Collins," Vanessa bid me, then continued on her way.

As I entered the store, I saw another of my acquaintances, Mrs. Spencer, who had apparently been watching my exchange through the window as she browsed for fabrics.

"Good morning, Mrs. Spencer," I said to the middle-aged woman.

She scowled at me in return. "I cannot believe you would associate with that woman," she said, referencing Vanessa.

I was slightly offended. "Begging your pardon, I was unaware it was your business whom I choose to associate with."

Mrs. Spencer merely sniffed. "I just expected the 'missus parson' would have better taste, being a woman of God and all. Good day." With that, she left the store. Mr. Emerson, the tailor, chuckled behind me. Apparently, he had witnessed everything.

"Don't pay her any mind, Mrs. Collins. She's been known in these parts as one of the biggest snobs around for many a year."

Perhaps she is related to Lady Catherine, I thought to myself with an inward laugh. I still burned with curiosity about my new acquaintance though.

"Who is that blonde woman, Vanessa, who just came from your store?" I asked Emerson.

"Vanessa? Oh, she's a colorful character all right."

"I noticed she was wearing a very fine dress, although it is daytime, and that she was purchasing so many beautiful fabrics from you."

"Aye, she makes up most of her own gowns, that one does. Absolutely beautiful handiwork! My missus was just remarking the other day how much she admired the embroidery on one of her gowns. We was always sayin' she could give me a run for my money if she ever opened up a shop of her own." Emerson said, his Canterbury accent bleeding through his speech.

A thought occurred to me. "With such elegant clothes as that, could she possibly be an opera singer, or perhaps an actress? Is that why Mrs. Spencer considers her disreputable?"

Emerson shook his head. "She's certainly pretty enough, to be sure. Unfortunately, the only audience she performs for are the ones that pay her a call upstairs at the Drunken Skunk."

A prostitute! So that's why Mrs. Spencer looked down on me for talking to her. This girl was one of the ones living in the brothel above the seedy tavern near the edge of town.

"She may be a 'working girl', but that's no reason to shun her." I said to Mr. Emerson.

"Certainly. She's one of my best customers. As long as she pays me, I've got no complaints about her. But some folks 'round here don't think that way. They don't want to associate with a fallen woman," Emerson said. I understood.

I selected some nice fabrics— a floral print linen for daytime, and a grey-blue taffeta for one of our many evenings at Rosings, and chose the designs with Emerson's help. He promised both dresses would be ready for the first fitting in a few weeks, and I put down a deposit before I left. I finished the rest of my errands for the day, and was on my way home, when I passed by the Drunken Skunk.

Vanessa's dwelling place! I thought, looking up to the windows on the floors above the tavern. I shuddered to think about the sin that went on there on a regular basis. As I stood there, a buxom redhead passed by, dressed in scarlet and purple silks with feathers in her hair.

She could be one of Vanessa's fellow workers, I guessed. The woman did not go through the main door but skirted the side of the building. I casually followed her and watched her climb the stairs behind the building. Their apartments must have a back entrance, I presumed.

I decided in that moment that I wished to call on Vanessa. Cautiously, I climbed the stairs and knocked at the door. A minute later, a gorgeous brunette answered. She was scantily dressed, with her skirt hitched up to the waist, the low neckline of her dress further enlarged by the open buttons exposing her chemise. I tried not to stare, forcing my gaze back to her face.

"Can I help you?" She asked, seeming annoyed by my presence.

"I'm here to see Miss Vanessa. Is she in?"

The brunette blinked a couple of times. "Yes, ma'am. Although I'm not certain of her policy on service to women."

"Oh, I'm not a customer!" I gasped, shocked that she would think that was possible. "Just a friend coming to call."

"Oh. Begging your pardon ma'am… it's just that we don't get many visitors here, except for our patrons." She showed me to Vanessa's room.

"Ness!" She called. "Someone here to see you!" The brunette continued down the hall to her own room. I hoped Vanessa was not entertaining anyone at the moment.

Vanessa opened her door.

"Mrs. Collins...what a surprise!" Vanessa recovered quickly from her shock. "Won't you come in?"

We sat down at a small table and chairs by the window.

"Regretfully, I have little to offer you, only some tea and biscuits." Vanessa explained with a sad look.

"Tea and biscuits will be fine," I assured her. She rang for some hot water. While she prepared the tea, I studied the room.

The large bed was the prominent feature. I tried hard not to look at it, knowing it would make me think of things that went on there. Additionally, there was a wardrobe, a dresser, and a vanity with a gilded mirror. Vanessa kept her tea-things and biscuits in a small cabinet next to the table.

"So, Mrs. Collins, to what do I owe this honor?" Vanessa asked as she poured my tea.

"Please, call me 'Charlotte'," I begged, wanting to put us on equal footing since I did not know her last name.

"Very well. Charlotte, what brings you to my little room this fine afternoon?"

"Ah, well… As the minister's wife, I make an effort to get to know all my neighbors, and to pay a call whenever I make a new acquaintance," was my excuse.

"You can imagine how surprised I was." Vanessa said. "It's not very often that an upstanding Christian woman, let alone the parson's wife, comes to visit one of us." She said in reference to herself and her comrades.

I did not let that dissuade me. "Nevertheless, I felt beholden to come and further our acquaintanceship, and to invite you to join our congregation at the church for Sunday worship."

Vanessa laughed. "I'm not so certain I would be welcome in your little parish. Aren't my lot what your kind call a 'black sheep' or one with a 'scarlet letter'?" She asked.

"Our doors are open to anyone. I know I, for one, would welcome you." I tried to reassure her.

Vanessa did not say whether she meant to accept my invitation, but my welcoming her seemed to open her up to me. A quarter-hour of leisurely conversation helped to foster our relationship, and when it was time for me to depart, she invited me to call again sometime, if I wished. I paid her another visit a few days later, and again the following week. By my third visit, she was beginning to share with me the details of her past, and how she came to be in her current situation.

Vanessa had grown up in a town by the mouth of the River Medway, roughly thirty miles away. Her father, a young carpenter, worked at the shipyard building warships. Daily, he was regaled with tales of danger and excitement by the sailors and soldiers embarking for the wars. One day, desiring to seek adventure and glory for himself, and grown weary of the dull hardship of his trade, he abandoned his wife and small daughter to enlist in the navy. Vanessa was but two years old at the time. Her mother did everything she could to raise her daughter alone, but she had no family on whom she could depend for assistance and life was very hard for them over the next several years. Over time, her mother became severely ill, and they were forced to borrow money to pay her medical expenses. After her mother died, and it became apparent that Vanessa could not pay back the debt, the creditor sold it to his friend, the owner of the Drunken Skunk, a sleazy man named Mr. Bartleby. Mr. Bartleby gave Vanessa a choice, she could work off her debt by coming to live at the tavern as a maid or continue to pay interest on it at an exorbitant rate. Once she was employed as a maid though, he schemed daily to make her life as miserable as possible, promising that her debt could be paid off faster and her life would be much happier if she would simply agree to become one of his working girls instead. Finally, Vanessa relinquished to his coercion. She was but seventeen at the time.

My heart ached for this girl, who still appeared to be no older than perhaps twenty-one. I wondered if there was anything I might do to assist her in her situation. I mused on these thoughts in the drawing room that evening, waiting until William returned home from tea at Rosings, so I could ask his advice on the matter, when he barged through the door angrily.

"Charlotte, I have heard a report about your company and whereabouts of a most alarming nature, which I am greatly hoping you can contradict!"

Chapter 10

William

I remember the day I first heard the report of Charlotte's conduct. I had been invited to tea by Lady Catherine, as I often was. Charlotte was out again. She had been visiting many parishioners as of late. Thus, I went to Rosings alone that day.

Lady Catherine's face bore a scowl that I knew could only mean trouble when I entered her drawing room. She allowed me to be seated before she began.

"Mr. Collins, are you aware of your wife's whereabouts at the moment?" She asked me.

I shook my head. "I know only that she is out paying calls, your ladyship."

"You do not know to whom she is paying these calls?"

I was very puzzled. "If not to our neighbors in the parish, then I am certain I do not know. I can think of no others upon whom she regularly calls." I was beginning to get very worried.

Lady Catherine cleared her throat. "Mr. Collins, my housekeeper's sister has a friend in the village, a Mrs. Thompson, whose shop faces that vile tavern, the Drunken Skunk." Lady Catherine's nose crinkled, as if she smelt an imaginary skunk at that moment.

"She insists that your wife was seen three times in the past week entering or emerging from that establishment."

I was astonished. "Surely there must be some mistake," I insisted. I was fully aware of the kind of debauchery that went on in that place, including the brothel upstairs.

"No, Mr. Collins, my housekeeper herself said she witnessed Mrs. Collins on one of those occasions, when she was at the Thompsons' store. Furthermore," Lady Catherine went on, "another friend of mine, Mrs. Spencer, mentioned to me the other day that she had seen Mrs. Collins talking to a woman of questionable character who works at the tavern. When I referenced Mrs. Thompson's observations, it was her estimation that this must be the person on whom your wife has been calling on at that wretched place."

I was greatly distressed by all this but did not wish to suppose it could be true. I sipped my tea in solemn silence.

Lady Catherine wanted to be certain I knew what I ought to do. "Mr. Collins, you know that you must confront your wife on this matter and put a stop to these meetings. It is unseemly for the wife of a clergyman to be cavorting with wayward women or to be seen frequenting a house of sin."

I did not answer, so she continued. "Or do you not know that the conduct of a minister's wife reflects on the minister, and his ability to shepherd his flock? If a minister cannot control his own wife, then he is not fit to lead his church." Her words had made me angry, but how could I refute them without knowing whether there was any truth to the matter?

"Forgive me, Lady Catherine, but I must go." I stood up and bowed, then hastily fetched my hat.

"Certainly. I do hope you'll come again once your wife has been brought back under your charge." The great lady bade.

I hurried home as quickly as I could. I burst through the door like a madman. Charlotte was in her chair in the drawing room.

"Charlotte, I have heard a report about your company and whereabouts of a most alarming nature, which I am greatly hoping you can contradict!" I bellowed.

My wife's alarm was obvious. "What do you mean?" She arched back from me weakly.

"Have you or have you not, been consorting with a... with a... *harlot* and frequenting a brothel?" I was shaking, I was trying so hard to contain my fury. I desperately prayed that what Lady Catherine had relayed would prove false.

Charlotte took a deep breath, as if she were bracing herself for what would follow.

"It's true. I have befriended a young woman whose...misfortunes have led her to an occupation she would not otherwise choose for herself. The woman in question does indeed work at the Drunken Skunk."

I forced myself to pace the floor and count to four before

responding, to let off some steam. When that time had expired, I inhaled slowly, and made my attempt at speaking calmly, "And pray, what would induce you to visit a woman of such questionable character at her place of work, let alone associate with her at all?" I demanded coolly. "How did you even come to be acquainted with her?"

"I met Vanessa a couple of times in the village, and when I discovered who she was and what she did for a living, I somehow felt compelled to seek her out, in order to minister to her." Charlotte explained.

I frowned. "So, you knew the sinful lifestyle she led before you began visiting her?" I had hoped Charlotte had merely been ignorant of her new friend's line of work before she had called on her a few times.

Charlotte nodded. "Yes. But you must know, she is a slave to her trade. I was actually planning to seek your advice on how we might rescue this girl." Charlotte related the young woman's sad tale to me. As sorry as I was to hear it, I was not moved in the same way Charlotte was.

I shook my head. "It is a tragic story, certainly, and I regret that your friend has suffered such loss. But the fact remains, she is a fallen woman. It is unfortunate that this woman felt she had no other option but to live a life of ongoing sin and depravity, but you must see how inappropriate it is for you, as a Christian woman and the wife of a parson, to be seen visiting her at this bed of immorality."

"Very well. I will not visit her at the Drunken Skunk again." Charlotte said with a gleam of determination in her eye. I felt she was leaving herself a wide loophole and I sought to close it.

"Furthermore," I said, "I must insist that you dissolve this acquaintanceship entirely."

Charlotte stood and looked at me squarely in the eye. "That is something I cannot do," she refused.

"Why not?" I asked.

"Because I cannot simply abandon this woman."

"She is a harlot and a sinner!" I was beginning to grow angry again.

"We are *all* sinners!" Charlotte retorted.

"Yes, but we don't all choose to wallow in our immoral lifestyles the way this woman does!"

Charlotte wasn't dissuaded. "She may yet become a believer and leave her old life behind, if only someone would help her and show her some compassion, instead of pouring out judgment! Were not Rahab and Mary Magdalene prostitutes as well before they became followers of the Lord?"

"It is not up to you to save every lost person in the world." I argued.

"You are absolutely right," Charlotte answered, "but is it not my duty to rescue as many souls as I am able?"

"Your *duty*, wife, is to respect and submit to your husband!" I began pacing the floor again, Lady Catherine's words ringing in my mind and making me fearful. "There are other issues at stake here, madam, besides this woman's predicament. Your refusal to submit to my authority reflects badly upon me. Lady Catherine has intimated that if I am unable to control my own wife, that I could very well be stripped of my position as rector of this parish."

Charlotte's face was livid. "Control me? So that's the issue isn't it? Lady Catherine wants you to be a little copy of herself, able to dominate everyone around you, even your own wife. And because she controls *you*, she can control everyone beneath you too. A master puppeteer!" Charlotte walked to the entrance of her parlour.

"I'm sorry, William," she said sternly, "but you cannot control me or who I choose to be friends with." Then she shut the door to her room firmly. I was severely tempted to barge in after her, but my better judgment retained me. At any rate, I was too angry and hurt to continue speaking to her for the time being. I knew my use of the word "control" in our conversation was a trifle excessive; after all, it was not my intention to domineer over my wife. Still, a wife is supposed to respect and submit to her husband, isn't she? Yet Charlotte had completely disregarded my requests! I had never felt so disrespected in all my life.

∞∞∞∞

Charlotte

Who does my husband think he is? I thought to myself angrily. What gives him the authority to determine who my acquaintances ought to be? At the time, I felt he had no right to force me to submit to him, and I felt justified in disregarding his request that I abandon my new friend.

Supper was cold and silent that night, not a word spoken between us, and bedtime even colder still. While we still slept in the same bed, William immediately turned away from me as soon as we retired for the night. Apparently, he now detested the very sight of me. I felt alone and confused. I had expected that he would have understood my desire to help Vanessa once he heard her story, but he caught me off-guard by coming in with a biased view of the situation before I could even speak! No doubt Lady Catherine's gossip had poisoned his mind. I hoped that come morning, William might see things differently. Unfortunately, that did not happen. My husband was just as frigid as the night before. He emerged from his dressing room prepared to leave the house, a grim look on his face.

"Are you going to visit Lady Catherine?" I asked.

"No," He replied. "Thanks to you, I cannot even show my face there for the time being." He marched out of the room.

What did that mean? I wondered as I made my way downstairs. From the front window, I saw him set out in his gig, presumably to pay call to some parishioners. I turned my attention to writing a letter to Elizabeth. I meant only to communicate the recent developments to her, but I could not help descending into a scathing rant about William's attitude towards the situation. It may have been wrong of me to lambast my husband behind his back, but I did not care. I was too angry and hurt.

The next day, determined to show that I would not back down, I went to the village to seek Vanessa. I had given my word that I would not visit her at the tavern, but that did not mean I was forbidden to run into her elsewhere. I entered Thompson's Mercantile on the pretense of shopping for some goods. As I browsed, I could see the owner's wife, Mrs. Thompson, sneering at me. Of course, I thought, I should have known Lady Catherine's spies would be everywhere. No matter, I would show her too that I could not be cowed into submission. I kept a watchful eye out the store window in the event Vanessa should emerge across the street. I didn't wait long before Vanessa appeared. Leaving behind the one or two items I'd picked up off the shelves, I left the store to meet her. She seemed alarmed to see me.

"Mrs. Collins!" She looked right and left to see if anyone was watching us. "You should not be here."

"It's Charlotte, please," I reminded, "and is there somewhere we can go to talk?"

She shook her head. "No, I'm afraid you need to go. I can't see you anymore."

"Why on earth not?" I wanted to know.

"Your husband, he sent me a letter, asking me to please discontinue our association." Vanessa told me.

The nerve! He just couldn't leave well enough alone, could he?

"I don't want to cause any discord between you and the parson," Vanessa added.

I put my hands on her shoulders. "Vanessa. Do not be concerned in regard to such things. I will manage well enough the situation between the parson and myself. He is not permitted to dictate who I spend my hours of leisure with. Now, why don't you come back with me to my home? We can have a nice visit together."

"Won't the parson be angry?" Vanessa worried.

"He is away for the afternoon visiting a sick man from our parish, and is not expected back until late," I told her. Although Vanessa still had reservations, she agreed to accompany me back to the parsonage.

After we enjoyed some tea, Vanessa had a question for me.

"Charlotte, why is it that you have such a strong desire to maintain a friendship with me, in spite of your husband's objections? Surely you can find better friends who are not so tainted, as I am."

Putting down my cup, I told her, "Vanessa, this may seem odd to you, for I know you have suffered great ill-treatment in your life, but I care about you. I see the way our society has ostracized you and condemned you, and it hurts my heart to see my Christian brothers and sisters treat you with such un-Christlike shunning. For whatever reason, I believe God allowed me to meet you, and led me to be the one to show you what a friend can be."

Vanessa's deep brown eyes began to water. "I've never

110

known anyone like you before, Charlotte. No one has ever truly cared for me, except for perhaps my mother, rest her soul. You have no idea what it means to me, to have someone see me as a valuable friend. To have someone see me as a person, and not just an object or a piece of trash."

I leaned over on the settee and gave her a warm embrace. "I told my husband that I would not visit you at the tavern anymore, but you should know that you are welcome to visit my home anytime."

Before she left, Vanessa asked me something surprising. "I am curious to know more about this God of yours," she said. "Do you think you could teach me about him on a regular basis?"

I was thrilled. "Yes! I would love to." I thought for a moment about our weekly schedules. I knew William had a regular engagement on Tuesdays to visit the orphanage in Maidstone, over twenty miles away, to deliver clothing donations and a portion of the church tithes.

"Would you be able to come on Tuesday afternoons?" I asked.

Vanessa nodded. "I will be there around one o'clock," she said.

Vanessa surprised me yet again when she arrived for our Bible study, not alone, but accompanied by three other girls! "I do hope it is all right," she said sheepishly, "but when I told my companions about you, they were all eager to meet you too."

"Of course, please, come in!" I invited.

Vanessa introduced me to the others, a couple whom I recognized. "This is Lily," she gestured to the redhead I'd seen before, "Isabel," she pointed next to the beautiful brunette who had taken me to Vanessa's room the first time, "and Selina". The last girl was slim-figured and pale, her stark complexion contrasting her jet-black hair.

"It's a pleasure to make your acquaintance." I greeted.

The four ladies squeezed onto the tiny settee in my parlour, as Mrs. MacDougall brought us some tea and refreshments. I made a mental note to move our future meetings to the dining room, where space was more abundant. I read to the women several passages of scripture that spoke of God's love and redemption. Lily, Selina, and Vanessa all had many questions for me, and seemed to be moved by the words I spoke. Only Isabel remained aloof. I did not push her to join in our discussion though, merely allowed her to sit and soak everything in. When our meeting concluded, all the women promised to return the following week.

I was pleased with myself. I now felt that I had discovered the purpose for which God had brought me to Kent— to minister to these lost women. I thought that the conflict over my helping them was limited to between my husband and myself. I was unprepared for the multiple ramifications that were to follow from my actions.

Chapter 11

Charlotte

A few weeks after our initial conflict, William and I were still not on good terms. He began speaking to me again, but only civilly. I knew my disrespectful behavior had offended him, but I was too proud to apologize for it. At the same time though, my heart ached over the rift I had caused between us. I wished William could just see things my way and understand why I felt so compelled to help Vanessa and her friends.

Elizabeth sympathized with my cause. Her reply to my letter showed she was shocked at all that had transpired in so little time since her visit, and how quickly my marriage had fallen into disrepair once again. She agreed wholeheartedly about the importance of my ministry but urged me to do what I could to repair my relationship with my husband as well. The rest of her letter only related to her upcoming tour of the lake country with her Aunt and Uncle Gardiner, all the places they were planning to visit, etc.

Word had spread by now about my being seen with Vanessa and visiting the Drunken Skunk. Gossip travels quickly in a small town, especially with the likes of people such as Mrs. Spencer and Lady Catherine, and I suspected Mrs. Thompson as well.

First, I noticed a drop in attendance in our parish. Several families who were normally present suddenly started missing Sunday services. When my husband or I called upon them to inquire, they skirted the issue. Then, people began openly avoiding us. I was walking down the lane one day and saw little Robbie Barnes again with his mother.

"Robbie, how are you? I missed you in Sunday School the last few weeks."

"Mrs. Collins, I missed you too!" Robbie called to me.

His mother hurried him along. "Come, Robbie, we don't want to be late for our meeting." Mrs. Barnes did not even look at me as she dragged him along the street. Robbie was not the only one absent from Sunday School. Many of the other families with children felt that it was inappropriate for them to be taught by me, now that I had been seen associating with immoral people, so my group of students quickly dwindled down to just a few members.

William fretted constantly over the dropping numbers in our congregation, and even more over Lady Catherine. Her birthday party was fast approaching, and I could see he was conflicted over whether to go.

"Lady Catherine's invitation was made months ago, and it's far too late for her to un-invite us," he told me, "but I wonder if she is hoping we will simply take the polite route and fail to appear."

"Would that not also appear rude to her, though?" I asked him. "If indeed you mean to decline, should you not at least notify her in advance?"

"But whatever shall I do with her birthday gift, if we do not go?" He fussed. A few days prior, a small crate had arrived. When I opened it, I discovered a hideous mantlepiece clock, made of blue and white ceramic, with figurines of a boy and girl attached. It looked ghastly, in my opinion, but apparently my husband had ordered it special from a clockmaker in London and had it shipped to us.

"You could always use it in your study," I suggested, thinking if we kept it, I would want to put it somewhere where I would not have to look at it too often. "Besides, Lady Catherine has so many fine things for her house already, she will probably just put it up on some mantle and forget about it."

William looked miffed that I would think so little of his gift, or of Lady Catherine's appreciation of it.

I continued. "At any rate, I think we ought to go. You should show your patroness that we are not afraid of any gossip, and that we will not be driven out of the community by it." Although I'm not certain he agreed with my reasons, he finally resolved that we would maintain our plan to attend the party.

∞∞∞∞

William

I never thought I would come to dread going to one of Lady Catherine's parties, but I was wrong. Lady Catherine still attended church weekly, so I knew she was fully aware of the community's response to Charlotte's actions. She did not speak to me when she saw me on Sundays though, nor did we call upon one another since that day when she revealed to me what company my wife had keeping.

It was still unbeknownst to me that my wife was meeting with not one, but four prostitute women, and in my own home no less! I did suspect that Charlotte and that woman, Vanessa, were still secretly meeting someplace, but I was glad at least that no further reports of Charlotte being at the tavern came to me, even when I called on the Thompsons and asked them directly about it. Nevertheless, the effect on our position in society was profound. Besides Lady Catherine's disapprobation, I knew there were others of her status who looked down on my wife and I, because of her recent behavior, and that they would be at the birthday party. I debated long over whether we should try to arrive to the party on time or arrive late on purpose. If we arrived late, I hoped we could sneak in through the crowds unnoticed by too many people. There was, however, the chance that everyone would see us the moment we walked in. So, in the end, I decided it was better to arrive punctually, when there would be fewer guests, and we would have the advantage of situating ourselves so as to be seen as little as possible as more people filled in.

Thus, sharply at seven o'clock, we entered the grand hall at Rosings. I hastily deposited the wrapped parcel bearing Lady Catherine's birthday gift onto the designated table and made my way along with Charlotte to where Lady Catherine was standing. I knew it would not do to delay our greeting my patroness on this occasion.

"Lady Catherine," I greeted, kissing her hand, "I wish you a very happy birthday, and hope we shall have many more splendid years to enjoy your radiance and benevolence!"

Charlotte curtsied beside me. "Happy birthday, your ladyship," she said simply.

"Thank you, Mr. Collins, Mrs. Collins". The great lady nodded to each of us without even a smile. "I trust you shall enjoy your evening. I've hired a private bartender for the evening," she said, gesturing to the bar in the corner, "though the offerings may be a bit refined for your taste, Mrs. Collins. We have no ale or beer, as you might find in a *tavern*." Lady Catherine sniffed, and placed an astounding amount of emphasized contempt on that final word. She turned back towards her other guests, effectively dismissing us. I looked to my wife. Charlotte's cheeks were flushed. Good, she ought to be a bit embarrassed, I thought. Charlotte and I made our way to the bar to secure some drinks, after which my aim was to sequester ourselves in a corner and mingle as little as possible until we could safely leave without being rude. Charlotte made no objection to my plan. Plenty of the landed gentry were there that night, from all around the nearby counties, and even from London. Lady Catherine had many friends, all of whom were invited on such an auspicious occasion. Despite my efforts to remain invisible, altogether too many people noticed our presence, and several of them glared at us and whispered to one another. I was sure they had heard about our recent situation, for I knew that her ladyship's tongue loved to wag whenever there was some juicy bit of news, good or bad. This was the first time that I knew of, however, in which my wife and I were the subject of their gossip, and it caused me to be greatly ashamed.

But I was about to discover that someone's approval of a situation could prove even more humiliating than hushed whispers. Supper was announced, and we were seated at the great table far down the line from Lady Catherine, across from Lord and Lady Greenbury. Lord Greenbury was a large, boisterous man. His wife was thin and gaunt and always looked a little as though someone had replaced the sugar in her tea with acid granules.

"Mr. Collins, my good man! How've you been?" Lord Greenbury boomed. "I see you've brought the missus parson along. A pleasure to meet you, ma'am!"

Introductions were quickly made, then Lord Greenbury commented, "So, Mrs. Collins, I've heard you've become friends with sweet Vanessa over at the Drunken Skunk."

Charlotte was shocked. "Are you acquainted with her, your lordship?" she asked.

Lord Greenbury let out a hearty bellow. "Ho, ho, you could say that!" Beside him, Lady Greenbury frowned and stared intently at her soup. Her husband continued, "Vanessa and I know each other *very* well. I'm just glad the little thing is finally getting some good society in knowing you. Lord knows she spends too much time upstairs in that bedroom of hers!" He winked as if to hint he had frequently contributed to that time.

I was too mortified to speak. Lord Greenbury was not exactly a quiet man, and the other guests were aghast that he had no shame in bragging about his exploits before all, including his wife. Worse still, he had revived my wife's recent scandal by including her in his discussion. Lady Catherine was the only one bold enough to speak though.

"Lord Greenbury," she began, "I believe there is no need to 'air one's dirty laundry', so to speak. We are all aware of your philandering ways, and your 'paper marriage', which warrants my sincere sympathy for the heart of your poor, forsaken wife. We are also aware of Mrs. Collins' recent misstep. Thankfully, that debacle, I am told, has safely ended." Lady Catherine took a sip from her wine glass.

I quickly looked to Charlotte's face to see whether what Lady Catherine had said was true. Judging by her expression, I knew Charlotte was indeed still in contact with Vanessa.

I suffered through the remainder of the meal, being shunned by the rest of the guests, and having to bear Lord Greenbury's overwhelming joviality and crude remarks. When the party adjourned to the ballroom for dancing, Charlotte and I seized the opportunity to escape.

"That was certainly the most embarrassing evening I have ever had to endure." I shook my head as we crossed the park separating Rosings from the parsonage. Dusk was upon us, and the moon had risen, providing just enough light to navigate the lawn safely.

"I'm afraid this is my doing," Charlotte apologized. "I never meant for things to develop in such a fashion."

I turned my head to her as we walked. "When will you finally cease meeting with this friend of yours?"

"How do you know I continue to meet her?" Charlotte wondered in surprise.

"Others may not be able to recognize when you are thinking something contradictory to what they have just spoken, but I know each of your expressions, and I have each one categorized and catalogued in my mind, like… a collection of books." This was an overstatement; Charlotte's vicissitudes of mood were frequently a mystery to me, even now. But I wanted to make her think she couldn't hide anything from me, so she might reveal to me the truth of what was going on.

Charlotte answered my question. "I simply must help Vanessa. I don't know how, but somehow, there must be a way to help her break free of this life she's fallen into. Please understand. I don't mean any disrespect to you, but I cannot stand back and watch someone I have become friends with continue to suffer a miserable life. That is why I have been meeting with her. To try to show her a better way."

I bit my lip and walked quietly a few paces. The cricket's chirping and the breaking of twigs beneath our feet helped to cut through the thick tension between us as I weighed what to do. We passed through a clearing, and the moonlight illuminated Charlotte's sweet, compassionate face, further tugging on my heartstrings.

Against my better judgment, I broke the silence by saying, "Help her, if you insist, but do it quickly, and discreetly. Then, I want you to sever all contact with her." A part of me loved my wife for wanting to do something about this woman's predicament. The other part was terrified of what might happen if she did. I prayed that this situation would soon end, and everything would blow over.

∞∞∞∞

Charlotte

I felt guilty for withholding information from William. If he knew I was trying to help not only Vanessa but her friends as well, he would certainly oppose me. His reputation and position were stake, and my continued association with these women put that in jeopardy, or at least so he believed. If anything, Lady Catherine's birthday party proved he was at least partially right, but I still felt that the need I was faced with outweighed the risk to our social status.

My efforts were soon rewarded. The next week at our Bible study meeting, Vanessa arrived bursting with excitement. "Girls, I have some news." She announced. "I'm going to quit working at the Drunken Skunk!"

The others and I were stunned. "What? How?" They asked.

"I'm not certain yet. But I do know this— I've decided to submit my life to the Lord, my redeemer, and I will not turn back. Somehow or another, I will find a different vocation, and I will pay off my debts to Mr. Bartleby. I can't live as a harlot any longer." Vanessa resolved.

I was thrilled. "That's wonderful Vanessa! It fills me with joy to hear you speak of the Lord as you have! I will be glad to assist you in any way that I can."

Some of the others weren't so sure about this plan. "You'll never break free. Cassius Bartleby is not one to give up what's his so easily." Isabel shook her head with arms crossed.

"I don't belong to anyone, least of all Mr. Bartleby," Vanessa insisted.

Selina asked, "But who else will hire you?"

"Maybe someone will take her on as a maid," I commented. "Not everyone is so scrupulous about who they hire."

"If that were true, we'd all be out there working as maids," Lily sighed. "I know I tried many times to get hired, even lied about my previous work experience, but no one wanted to take me on without a reference."

"At least whorin' pays decent." Isabel said, examining her fingernails as she spoke. Like Vanessa and the others, she spoke in a local dialect, and her manners were, at times, crude.

Vanessa shook her head. "Not adequate to pay off my debts quick enough though. Seems like no matter how hard I work, I never end up with anything other than more debt. I need to find a better paying job doing something that I can at least feel proud about, instead of feeling dirty about myself every day."

I put my hand on Vanessa's back. "We'll resolve this together, don't worry." I reassured her.

We hadn't yet begun our Bible discussion for the day. I had spread my Bible on the dining table and was about to begin the lesson when a carriage pulled up out front. I went to the window to see who it was. Miss de Bourgh had come to pay us a call, as she did on rare occasions. I shuddered a bit. I wasn't sure what she would think of my meeting with these women, or what she might say to her mother. Unfortunately, she had seen me through the window, so I could not ask the housekeeper to pretend I was out. I heard Mrs. Perry admit Miss de Bourgh and inform her that I was entertaining guests. Miss de Bourgh replied that she hated to disturb me and only wished to stop in and assure herself of my comfort. Mrs. Perry preceded her into the dining room.

"Miss de Bourgh, here to see you ma'am," she announced.

"Forgive me for interrupting your gathering," Miss de Bourgh apologized. "I was on my way home from a shopping excursion and decided to pay you a call."

"It's quite all right," I excused, not wanting to offend her, "we are just having our weekly Bible study."

Miss de Bourgh's eyes brightened. "A Bible study? Would it be all right if I joined your gathering?"

I glanced around the room at the other women with unease. Should I let Miss de Bourgh into our meeting? I decided I should find a polite way to inform her who they were first.

"Miss de Bourgh, I'd like to introduce you to my friends. These are Vanessa, Selina, Lily, and Isabel." I gestured to each one around the room. I wasn't sure what to say next without being rude.

To my surprise, Miss de Bourgh was keener than I knew. "Please, call me Anne." She insisted. "Vanessa, yours is quite the infamous name around my mother's household these days," she said cheekily. "But don't worry, I'm not one to judge anybody. Regardless of our job or our station, we are all equal in the eyes of God, are we not?"

A true kindred spirit! I thought. I never ceased to be amazed at how different from her mother Miss de Bourgh was, especially when she was away from Lady Catherine's influence and free to express her own preferences and emotions.

Feeling that Anne knew what she was getting into, I proceeded to introduce that day's lesson. Anne joined us again the next week, and the week after. She really took a shine to the women, and her additions to our discussions were lively and thought-provoking.

In my next letter to Elizabeth, I related the good news of Vanessa's conversion and the addition of Miss de Bourgh into our assembly. Elizabeth wrote back of her delight in such news, praising all my efforts, which made me feel additionally rewarded. At least I might find encouragement from her since there was little approval to be found in my own neighborhood. Her tour had been postponed until mid-summer, she relayed, so I was to continue writing to her at Hertfordshire for the time being.

Meanwhile, Vanessa vacated the Drunken Skunk. The draper offered her a place to stay, and a temporary job as his assistant. Mr. and Mrs. Emerson were not the judgmental sort, and they were more than happy to help a young lady like Vanessa to make a fresh start.

Vanessa's former employer was none too thrilled about the situation though. Mr. Bartleby immediately raised the interest rate on Vanessa's debt, charging more than twice what it once was. He justified the difference by saying that the extra income Vanessa had brought to the brothel covered part of the interest, so now that she was gone, he needed to charge her the full amount. If she ever chose to return, she could have her old job and her old room back, and her interest rates would return to what they once were.

I sought to help Vanessa find a solution without yielding to Mr. Bartleby's coercion. I had an appointment for my dress fitting at Emerson's, and Vanessa was assisting. As she marked my hemline, I remarked on the details of the dress.

"My what beautiful lace trim this is, and what delicate embroidery along the neckline!"

"Thank you!" Vanessa replied.

I looked down at her. "Did you do this work?"

"Emerson has been so busy lately; he's tasked me with finishing some of the finer details of his garments. I've even been stitching together some of the lower-cost orders and making up the sample gowns for the displays. I did that one over there." She pointed to a beautiful light-blue calico print with a satin spencer jacket on top.

"Vanessa, it's exquisite! If you can do work like that, you could open your own shop, you know."

Vanessa shook her head. "Mr. Emerson still does all the designs. I just make up his creations."

"But you know how to design as well. Mr. Emerson told me a while back that you sew most of your own clothes. Besides, Emerson's is the only draper's shop in our town. There is plenty of room for another."

"Mr. Emerson said the same to me the other day. He said with the way our town is growing, there would soon easily be enough work to support two tailors." Vanessa said.

"See?" I patted her shoulder. "You could have your own shop and pay Mr. Bartleby back much quicker."

"I haven't any money saved to put towards such an endeavor." Vanessa complained. "How could I possibly venture such a scheme, without any capital laid away?"

The reality of her situation rang true. I sighed. Somehow, we must devise a solution, and quickly, before Vanessa's debts became too insurmountable.

I had little time to dwell on the subject, however. When I arrived home, I groaned at the sight before me. Lady Catherine's barouche was parked beside our gate. The great lady herself was waiting for me in the drawing room the moment I walked through the door.

"Good afternoon, Lady Catherine," I greeted, trying my utmost to be pleasant. "What brings you to condescend to visit my humble dwelling on this fine day?" I mimicked my husband's way of welcoming her.

Lady Catherine's face was stern though. "Mrs. Collins, I must say I am most displeased with you."

I tried to maintain my composure whilst inwardly rolling my eyes. Oh, that? I thought to myself. "Nothing has changed, then?" I smiled dryly.

The Lady went on with discomfort and haste. "Firstly, how could you turn this parsonage I have bestowed on you into a gathering place for sinners? Worse still, how could you allow *my daughter* to become embroiled in your sordid gatherings, mingling her distinguished person with such lewd and disreputable women and tarnishing her reputation?" Lady Catherine's anger burned with every word she spoke in a way I had never witnessed before.

Just at that moment, my husband walked through the door, returning from a visit to someone or other in the parish.

"Why Lady Catherine, what an utmost pleasure it is to see you today!" He beamed.

122

"I wish I could say the same," she uttered. "Sit down, Mr. Collins, for what I have to say concerns you too." Lady Catherine commanded.

As William sank into the seat beside me, I braced myself. All hell was about to break loose, I knew.

Chapter 12

William

I was just returning from making my parish rounds when I saw Lady Catherine's barouche in the yard. Not wanting to waste a moment, I hurried to the door. I hoped her great condescension meant she was over the ordeal of Charlotte's scandal and ready to put the past behind us. I greeted her as warmly as ever. "Why Lady Catherine, what an utmost pleasure it is to see you today!"

Lady Catherine coldly ordered me to sit down. As I obeyed, my body was a basket of nerves. Something must be horribly amiss. I dared hope it might at least be something unconnected to Charlotte's friend. I was wrong.

"Mr. Collins," Lady Catherine began. "Upon your previous assurance that your wife would countenance no further communication with that filthy harlot, I was under the impression this whole dreadful affair concerning them was over."

"Is it not?" I squeaked.

"Perhaps you are unaware then— or at least I fondly hope you are innocent of the knowledge— that your wife continues to meet with not one, but *four women* of this character, in your very own house, no less!" she said with a glare towards Charlotte.

I looked to my wife in shock. The truth was written for all to see. I was speechless. Charlotte, how could you betray me with this deception? Had I known, I could have put a stop to this before her ladyship found out.

I chose my words gingerly. "I assure you, your ladyship, I was unaware that my home was being used in such a manner." I couldn't very well tell her that I knew my wife persisted in helping this Vanessa. But four prostitutes! How on earth had that come about? I wondered.

"But that is not all your wife has done." Lady Catherine continued, "She chose to invite to her meetings none other than *my daughter*, Miss Anne de Bourgh. That she should allow the heiress of

Rosings to mingle with such refuse of humanity is most despicable. Are Anne's chances in society to be ruined forever? It is unspeakable! She is a high-born lady, the granddaughter of an Earl!"

I could not believe my ears. "My lady, surely there must be some mistake—"

"Indeed, there is not!" Lady Catherine interrupted me, "for my daughter confided all to her companion Mrs. Jenkinson, who fortunately saw the danger and came to warn me before the public got wind of this."

Charlotte chose this moment to begin speaking. "Then there is no harm done, I should think."

"You are *wrong*, Mrs. Collins." The great lady shook her head bitterly. "I cannot believe you would allow Anne, not to mention yourself, to be polluted with these women's loose morals and habits. How could you deceive her into thinking this was an acceptable sort of company to keep?"

Charlotte answered, "your ladyship, I did not deceive your daughter in any way. Miss de Bourgh knew full well what she was getting into when *she* asked, not I, to be allowed to join our gatherings. She is a grown woman, capable of making her own decisions, whether or not you are able to see it."

"Charlotte, please don't—" I begged. But Charlotte continued.

"Furthermore, I believe it is Miss de Bourgh and I who are doing the influencing. This is a Bible study, after all, and we have already seen one member come to faith since we began."

Lady Catherine's nostrils flared. "You think you can save these wretched souls? One Bible study does not erase a lifetime of depravity and sin."

"No, but the forgiveness of a loving God can, not to mention a little compassion from those who claim to be Christians!" Charlotte returned.

"How dare you preach to me!" Lady Catherine stormed. "Do you fancy yourself above my station, seated up there on your high and mighty moral horse? I have attended church for well over fifty years, and you see fit to preach to me, your elder?"

The great lady began walking to the door. I immediately rose and followed her, and Charlotte not far behind, still in earshot.

"Your ladyship, my wife is not in her right mind! When I have made her come to her senses, I'm sure she will see—"

Once again, I was interrupted. "I must remind you, Mr. Collins, you are already on very thin ice! I warned you to get a handle on your wife, and you did not. If this should continue, I will write to the bishop about your continued service in the Church of England!" With that, she slammed the door in my face as she exited our house.

I did an about-face and turned on Charlotte. "Now you've done it!" I hissed. "I warned you to be discreet, and you go and involve Miss de Bourgh? Are you mad? You have broken the cardinal rule: to do something which might cause harm to Lady Catherine's daughter. Of all the offences you've committed up to this point, in her eyes, that is the very worst!"

Charlotte's eyes were watery, but she pursed her lips. "As I told her ladyship, Miss de Bourgh makes her own decisions about things. I have committed no sin where she is concerned."

"No sin? You should have refused to admit Miss de Bourgh to your meetings altogether. What's more, since when have you been meeting with *four* women? I had thought there was only one. Are they rabbits, to be multiplying like this?"

"Vanessa's friends saw the effect my friendship was having on her, and it made them also curious to know more about the Lord. I would have thought a minister like you should be thrilled by something like that!" Charlotte argued.

"Ordinarily, I would, but under the circumstances, it only increases my dismay!" I replied. I paced the floor, my hands supporting my forehead.

"Charlotte, do you not see the gravity of the situation now?" I wrung my hands. "We could lose this house. I could lose my job! We have already lost our standing in society. Are we to lose everything over this ideal of yours?"

"I really don't think it will come to all that. Lady Catherine could not be so cold hearted."

"Couldn't she? Perhaps not before you dragged Miss de Bourgh into all this! Now, who knows what she will do to exact her revenge on us?"

Charlotte stood firm. "Even if we did lose the parsonage and your position, would it not be worth it if we could redeem the lives of these women?"

"And then how would we live?" I asked.

"The Lord would provide for us. If He cares for the lilies in the field and the sparrows in the sky, He will also care for us. That's what it says in the Sermon on the Mount in Matthew," Charlotte touted.

"Madam, I wish you would stop acting as though you are the minister here! You do nothing but spout scripture and moralize. You brush off Lady Catherine's threats flippantly, as though we have nothing at all to fear. Do you not even care what happens to our family?"

"Of course, I care!" Charlotte insisted. "I love you. I would never wish anything bad to happen to us. I just wish you could trust God the way that I do."

"This isn't about how much I trust God. If you truly loved me, you wouldn't be putting me through all this right now. When will you give up your stubborn ways?"

I was sick of looking at Charlotte for the moment, so I turned and went out the side door to my garden. Charlotte did not follow me. I puttered around the flower beds a bit, but the angry thoughts rolling around in my head kept me from accomplishing any real work. Why couldn't Charlotte just abandon this cause of hers? It's not as though she were indebted to those women in any way. How could she spare so little regard for our home and livelihood, for my career and status? Did she think I somehow had an ace up my back pocket that I could play, in the event we were turned out in the streets? I had no other trade, no other skills, to find another profession! I had no parents or siblings with whom we could reside. Only an old aunt, who was too poor to sustain us. Our only other option would be to bang on the door at Longbourn and hope that Mrs. Bennett would allow us to stay there prematurely until we could take full possession of the house. Not a fine prospect, in my estimation.

Although I still loved my wife very deeply, the lovely fluttery feelings which I had borne for her at the start of our relationship seemed to have vanished in a puff of smoke. I thought she was being incredibly stubborn and selfish. It severely wounded me that she would put the lives of these prostitutes ahead of our own happiness. Everything was going so smoothly, why did she have to ruin it all? At that time, I was unwilling to forgive my wife for what she had done to us.

∞∞∞∞

Charlotte

I knew I had made an enormous blunder in not coming clean to my husband about my secret Bible study meetings. I could have at least prepared him for the possibility that Lady Catherine might find out about it. William had every right to be angry with me, I realized, but it was too late to rectify according to his wishes. I was too involved in the situation to withdraw, not when Vanessa was on the verge of starting her new life and the other girls chasing the brink on her heels. Surely Lady Catherine wouldn't destroy William's career out of petty vengeance for involving her daughter. Would she? If only William was on my side, he could persuade her that my mission was a worthy cause. She was still a Christian woman, after all, and she had always doted on him, hadn't she?

I did not know how I could persuade William now, though. Not after I had deceived him. I decided about the only thing I could do was pray.

"Lord, I know I've made a mistake by not telling William the truth. Please help him to understand, I love these women, and I want to see them freed from the life of sin they are trapped in. Somehow, with Your guidance, I know there must be a way. Help him to let go of his fears and trust that You will provide for us. Help him to realize that Your work is more important than our social standing and others' opinions of us. Amen." I did not know how the Lord might choose to answer my prayer, but I decided to put it in His hands.

I tried to apologize to William later that night. I went to his study and knocked. "May I come in?" I timidly cracked the door to ask.

"Do what you like." William answered apathetically. "It's obvious you will please yourself, regardless."

"About that," I began, shutting the door behind me. "I regret that I did not tell you about Vanessa's friends, or about the Bible study meetings at our house."

"You knew I would not approve, didn't you?" he asked.

I nodded. "I know it was wrong to keep our meetings a secret from you, but you did say I could help Vanessa."

"Against my better judgment, yes, and look where it has

129

landed us!" William pointed out. "I should have held my ground that you dissolve all acquaintanceship. Had I known you would take things to such a degree, I'm certain I would have walked naked in the streets rather than allow it! Now, will you give up this ridiculous crusade of yours?"

I shook my head. "I've given Vanessa my word that I will help her. Now that she has become a believer in the Lord, she wants to start a business of her own as a seamstress. I am sure the other girls will follow her example if she succeeds."

William took my hands in his and looked up into my eyes from his desk chair. His voice was calm and gentle, as one with which a father speaks to his little child.

"Charlotte, despite what you might think, I do not wish to control or dominate you. I am, however, begging you to listen to me. Despite the good news that your friend is now a Christian, you cannot expect that all these prostitutes will simply abandon their way of life. Even if they wanted to rejoin society, what respectable person would hire them with their past record? You must quit this reform project of yours before things get even more out of hand. You do not understand the forces at work when you try to alter society in such a way," William warned me.

"I think you are more concerned with the way society sees you, especially your 'esteemed patroness'. If she were to approve the plan, I'm sure you would have no objection!" I argued.

"Lady Catherine is but one of the forces to be reckoned with. Have you considered how the community will react to this upset in the balance of things?"

"I'm sure, in time, they will come to welcome the women as I have." I replied.

"What about their patrons and employer? They might not take too kindly to the sudden loss of workers from the tavern."

"They will simply have to accept it. These girls are not their slaves, after all." I had done my best to convince William, but to no avail.

"I am afraid I cannot agree with you, my dear," he said, "I still believe that you are naïve, and have no concept of the trouble you may cause or perhaps fall into."

That was the end of that conversation. I did not know it, but my husband was right about some things. I had set the wheels in motion on a chain of events which would soon spiral out of my control in ways I could not foresee.

I came to Vanessa at Emerson's the next day and told her briefly what had happened with Lady Catherine. I also let her know that, unfortunately, we would need to find a new meeting place for our Bible study. A solution was quick to present itself, however. Mrs. Emerson happened to be in the shop, and having overhead us, quickly offered her drawing room, since Vanessa was residing with them currently. I thanked her profusely.

"Don't worry yourself about it," she said. "It's not easy, doing what you are doing, and I admire you for it. Mr. Emerson and I wish to do all we can to help you and the girls." Then she went on to the back room to deliver Mr. Emerson his dinner.

At the end of my visit with Vanessa, she was walking me towards the door when who should enter but none other than Mr. Bartleby, the tavern owner. Although I had not personally met him before, I recognized him instantly from the times I'd seen him around the tavern. Cassius Bartleby was a slick man, undeserving of the gentleman's attire he wore. He kept his greasy black hair combed back and he bore a mustache. The stench of liquor and cigar smoke that exuded from him was so strong, it was all I could do to prevent myself from gagging.

"Good afternoon, Miss Vanessa, 'Missus Parson'." He greeted coolly, nodding to each of us in turn. Apparently, he had already been made aware of my existence.

"What are you doing here?" Vanessa demanded.

"No need to fret, m'dear, I'm only 'ere to collect me loan payment for this month, seein' as it's already two days' late." Bartleby's sad attempts at playing the gentleman were foiled by his course accent, which betrayed his low-class origins.

"Unfortunately, I don't have the funds yet until I receive my wages," Vanessa apologized, "but I can guarantee you'll have your money by week's end."

"Not ter worry, I'll just tack on the late fee to wha' you owe." He grinned. "You know, 'Ness, some of your regulars are beginnin' to complain that ya an't there. They don't like 'aving their needs met by one of tha others."

"Then maybe they should just stop coming altogether."

"Now you know you daan't wish for tha', otherwise I might 'ave ter raise yer interest again ter compensate." Bartleby suggested slyly. "Ya wouldn't want yer debt to become so steep that ya can't afford ter pay it back."

"Or you could, I don't know, *forgive* the debt altogether. Prove that there is some human decency somewhere in you". Vanessa retorted.

Bartleby wasn't moved in the least. "We all 'ave our debts to pay, Miss Vanessa. I guarantee you'll pay yours off much quicker if you come back to work for me. The Drunken Skunk may not be the fanciest abode, but you 'ad a roof over your head, decent meals to eat. It beats going to debtor's prison, where you'll have to contend with sleeping with the rats."

"Better the rats in prison than living with a rat like you!" Vanessa spat.

"Tsk, tsk, such fire! Nah wonder me customers 're missin' ya!" Bartleby licked his lips, drawing closer to Vanessa.

"The customers tell me yer a real lively bed partner. Maybe if you showed me some of tha' good stuff, I could knock off a few coins from yer debt." Bartleby's cool sneer only fueled Vanessa's anger.

Sensing the confrontation was only going to escalate, I moved to intervene. "Please stop harassing and threatening my friend. She is doing her best to pay you back, as she promised." I pushed myself between them, protecting Vanessa.

"Na, na, Missus Parson, it won't do to get riled up. I was merely suggestin' that Miss Vanessa's presence is sorely missed at the Drunken Skunk."

"She won't be returning." I told him firmly.

"We'll see about tha'." Mr. Bartleby twisted the end of his mustache. "And I do hope you don't get any ideas about stealing away any of me other girls," He warned.

"Your payment will be at the tavern by Friday." Vanessa repeated. "Good day, Mr. Bartleby." With that, she practically shoved him out the door. I hoped that would be the last time I would have to encounter Cassius Bartleby, but I feared it would not.

∞∞∞∞

William

Once again, Lady Catherine's invitations to Rosings had ceased. Additionally, she was also now absent from church. Plenty of stories now circulated the town about Charlotte's little meetings, all with no mention of Miss de Bourgh's attendance, of course. It was my estimation that Lady Catherine hoped to shame me into forcing my wife to quit her mission by completing the ruin of our standing in society. We all knew, with one word, she could turn things back around again for us if she wished.

Charlotte moved her meetings to the draper's home and assured me in a sad voice that Miss de Bourgh no longer attended. I presumed Lady Catherine would have put her daughter under lock and key to prevent that occurring anyhow.

Meanwhile, church attendance had plummeted to an all-time low. The previous Sunday, only five families were in attendance, including the draper's family, the church warden and his wife, and three other families. The majority of the congregation followed Lady Catherine's example to stay away from "the parson's wayward wife". Another portion were men like Lord Greenbury who frequented the Drunken Skunk and had been warned by its proprietor that their favorite companions were being drawn away by the minister's wife. They disliked the threat to the order of society and its vices. Most of these men's wives knew about their exploits and tolerated them, and few dared attend church without their husband's approval.

I knew not what to do to remedy the situation. I had plenty of spare time on my hands, for only a few families allowed or requested that I call upon them during the week. Charlotte was seldom at home, spending most of her days at the draper's shop and residence. I completed all my sermons in record time each week and found myself rereading books for the sake of something to occupy myself. Even my garden was so well-tended there was little for me to do in it each day except pull a few weeds and water the plants. For the first time in a long while, I truly felt quite idle.

Desperate to relieve my boredom, I decided to take a walk by the pond. As I strolled along the banks, I came upon Miss de Bourgh and her companion, Mrs. Jenkinson, coming down the path from

Rosings.

"Good day to you, Miss de Bourgh, Mrs. Jenkinson." I greeted.

Miss de Bourgh smiled. "Good day, Mr. Collins." She returned. Mrs. Jenkinson bobbed a curtsy beside her.

"Miss de Bourgh, I'm pleased to see you out and about. Is your mother aware of your whereabouts?" I asked.

"She has allowed that I am to take a walk daily, for my health, provided Mrs. Jenkinson always accompanies me." She rolled her eyes on that account. I was aware Miss de Bourgh resented having the equivalent of an adult nursemaid looking after her constantly.

Turning to her companion, she said, "Mrs. Jenkinson, would you mind walking a few paces behind us? I wish to speak with Mr. Collins while we walk."

Mrs. Jenkinson frowned, but acquiesced. "As you wish, Miss."

I began walking in the same direction around the pond as Miss de Bourgh. Mrs. Jenkinson made sure not to fall too far behind me and her charge.

Miss de Bourgh whispered, "Do not say anything in the presence of Mrs. Jenkinson that you should not wish to be repeated to my mother." I nodded that I understood. I certainly could not afford to further alienate Lady Catherine in my current predicament.

"What is it you wished to speak to me about?" I inquired.

"How is Charlotte doing? I have not been permitted to speak to her or visit her as of late."

"Charlotte is...doing well." I answered hesitantly. "Though her persistence in her meetings is causing me a great deal of grief, as I'm sure you know."

"Yes, well, my mother can be a bit difficult when one does not comply with her wishes." Miss de Bourgh said wryly.

"I am sorry my wife involved you in this whole affair."

Miss de Bourgh shook her head. "Don't be. I made the choice to become involved, and I do not regret it. Mr. Collins, you may not realize it, but your wife is doing a great deal of good. The women really respond to her and are growing in their understanding of the Lord. Regardless of the social pressures around them, their lives are going to be forever changed for having known Charlotte. I wish you would not try to stop her from seeing her work through to completion." She finished.

I exhaled a long sigh of exasperation. "If only it were that simple. If it were merely my own reservations, I should concede, but the pressure Lady Catherine and the community have put on me make it nearly impossible that she should continue without it spelling disaster for our continued life as it were. Your mother ought to know I am doing everything in my power to adhere to her demands, and I pray she shall be merciful and patient towards us in respect to the living she has bestowed on us and not be hasty in petitioning the bishop for our removal." The last sentence was meant mainly for Mrs. Jenkinson's ears, knowing she would likely repeat all she heard to her mistress.

Miss de Bourgh's countenance fell. "I am dismayed to hear you care more about the comfort of your life than the lives of the women your wife ministers to. I wish I were able to continue assisting her, but that too has been made impossible." I could almost have sworn I saw a tear trickle down her cheek.

We were now at the fork where the path to the parsonage began. "Good day, Mr. Collins." Miss de Bourgh bade as she hurried along ahead of me on the path encircling the pond and back to Rosings. Mrs. Jenkinson picked up her pace to rejoin her charge, nodding sternly at me as she passed by. I remained on the fork to the parsonage, wishing once again that things could simply transform back to normal.

Chapter 13

Charlotte

Vanessa was working so hard every day, but she was still struggling to make ends meet. The weight of the debt hanging over her was crushing, and Bartleby only increased the payments with each passing week. Little did we know, but the whole ceiling was about to cave in.

One day, when Vanessa and I were having tea together at the Emerson's, a letter arrived for Vanessa. When she read it, her face paled.

"What is it?" I asked, worried.

"Bartleby has sent me an official notice. My debt is being recalled in full, effective immediately." Vanessa put the paper down on the table for me to see.

"He cannot do that, can he?" I picked up the letter to study it. The notice was sent from a solicitor's office in London. It stated that Vanessa had until the following Wednesday to pay the debt in full, or she would be arrested and taken to debtor's prison.

"Wednesday is only a week away! That's impossible!" I exclaimed. "Doesn't he have to give you reasonable time to pay back the debts? He cannot recall the debt if you've been faithful to make your payments." I insisted.

"You forget, this is Bartleby we are talking about. He's got his solicitor to find a way to weasel around the laws. "There's no way I can repay all the debt!" Vanessa groaned.

"Don't fret! We shall think of something to do! Let's apply ourselves..." My mind sought hard for an answer 'till an idea sparked.

"My brother in London is a barrister. Perhaps I could write to him for advice."

Vanessa shook her head. "There isn't time to receive a reply and take action."

We both sat in silence for several minutes.

Vanessa put the letter down forcefully. "I'm going to confront him."

"You can't! You mustn't!" I insisted.

"What else can I do, Charlotte? If I cannot repay the debt, I'll be thrown into debtor's prison until I can work it off."

"Talking to him is pointless. If he's bent on destroying you, I cannot imagine what he might attempt if you accost him face to face."

But Vanessa was determined. "I have to try, Charlotte. I'm going."

"Then I'm not letting you go alone."

Vanessa's pace was so quick I had a hard time keeping up with her. She darted past a moving wagon, forcing the driver to pull back sharply on the reins to stall his horses.

"Begging your pardon, sir!" I called to the driver, and he allowed me to pass also, though shaking his head at us. I picked up my skirt and ran after Vanessa. Ahead of me, she pushed past pedestrians, and startled a flock of chickens outside Thompson's Mercantile. I covered my face with my arms to protect it as two of the poults flew right in front of me, halting me until the flurry of feathers dispelled.

"Vanessa, wait for me!" I called. I hastened to cross the street as Vanessa approached the Drunken Skunk. She barged in the front door just as I caught up to her.

I had never been in the tavern portion of the establishment before. In the middle of the afternoon, the place was quite dead. The lamps were not lit. Aside from one candle atop a table, there was only the natural light creeping through the dirty windows to help us see. Assorted wooden tables were scattered across the room, with their chairs upside down atop them so the maid could attempt to mop away the filth and vomit. She was on her hands and knees with a bucket and a rag, trying to rid the cracked floorboards of a foul stain.

Vanessa addressed her.

"Maisie, is Bartleby in? I need to see him."

"Good afternoon, Miss Vanessa. Ma'am," Maisie acknowledged both of us. "He's in his office."

Vanessa began walking, but Maisie caught her arm. "He's with company at the moment, Miss. You mustn't interrupt him."

"I couldn't give a rat's tail about that—" she began, but I

138

stopped her.

"Perhaps, just wait a minute," I advised, not wanting to incur additional wrath.

We heard voices coming from Bartleby's office as he and his guests emerged. Maisie quickly picked up her cleaning supplies and made herself scarce.

"Tell your boss, I'll 'ave 'is money. I just need ter tie up some things first." Bartleby was talking to two rough looking men.

"You'd better. You know he hates to be kept waiting." One of them threatened as he walked into the bar room. The men glanced at us as they passed through and left. Bartleby's fists tightened and his face twisted in a scowl as he watched them exit. Finally, he turned to us, and the most devious smile spread across his visage.

"Well, well, well, if it isn't Miss Vanessa and Missus Parson?" Bartleby's voice rolled like silky-smooth poison. "I expected you'd come back to me someday, 'Ness, and you've brought your friend too."

Vanessa bristled. "I'm not here about that. What's this notice you've given me, recalling my debt in full? I've been prompt in paying you these past months. I've not missed a single payment."

"Of course, of course. But unfortunately, times 're hard, and I simply can't afford ter give ya the leisure of paying it off in installments anymore. I need the money now. But if ya can't pay, I suppose it'll have to be debtor's prison for ya then," Bartleby taunted.

I was confused. "But, what good will that do you? You won't recover your money any faster than if Vanessa continued to work in the draper's store. In fact, she won't be able to work at all, meaning you'll never get your money."

"See, tha's where yer wrong. I've got a friend who's the warden at Marshalsea. He's heard about yer 'talents', Vanessa, and he's mighty keen to see 'em for 'imself. So much so, tha' he's agreed to take on yer debts from me if I send ya to work at 'is prison. I'll get me money, and ya can take as long as ya like to work off yer debts for 'im."

"You're despicable! You know that? Completely despicable!" Vanessa was livid.

"We need to go," I whispered in her ear, trying to take her by the arm.

"Sure you ladies won' stay around? I could find ya some work before ya go!" Bartleby cat-called, his vicious laughter echoing off the walls.

I wouldn't let Vanessa even reply as I dragged her out of the tavern.

Before we were out of earshot, I heard Bartleby call, "Better come up with tha' money by Wednesday, or the constable will come to collect ya for me!"

"That was a complete waste", I said as we left the tavern.

Vanessa was shaking. "What am I going to do?"

"Well, you're not going to go to debtor's prison. Not if I have anything to say about it."

"There is nothing you can do to stop it."

"I'm going to write to my brother George, as I first thought to do. Perhaps he knows something about the laws regarding debts which could help us." I hastily made out a letter to him and took it to the inn to post on the next mail coach. With any luck, a reply could be had before all was too late.

Returning home, I pleaded my case with William.

"Surely there is something we could do to help Vanessa in this situation."

"I'm afraid there isn't, Charlotte. This is a situation of her own making, and we do not have the resources to help her out of it." William coldly replied.

"Bartleby's making. Not hers. He is the one creating this impossible demand. I'm not even certain it's legal."

"It must be," William concluded, "for him to be able to proceed."

"I hope my brother will be able to prove that wrong." I shook my head. "Otherwise poor Vanessa will be dragged off to debtor's prison and forced to go back to doing awful things to survive there."

"It is a situation I should hate to see, yes," William agreed, "but as I said, there is nothing we can do."

"You are turning a blind eye to the corruption before you! How can you be so callous?" I cried. I turned and left the room.

∞∞∞

William

Guilt hung over me like a shadow. Charlotte's accusation had stung like a knife wound, but the lingering feeling that I was not acting as I ought to persisted long after her words had faded. I knew Charlotte was right, that I was being terribly insensitive about her friend's desperate predicament. Yet I was incapable of acting. I feared that any action on my part would only further incense Lady Catherine, and that to offer up our own savings would see us too vulnerable, if in fact Lady Catherine succeeded in ousting me from my position. I could not— I would not— jeopardize my own family's security for the sake of this poor wench, in spite of her dire need. That was my justification at least, acting only out of fear for myself and disregarding any concern I had for Charlotte's friend.

I was saved from acting, for the time being. Charlotte's brother speedily wrote back to her with advice about Miss Vanessa's situation. An exclamation of relief came from her lips as she read the letter.

"Good news, I presume?" I nodded across the breakfast table.

"Very!" She smiled. "George confirmed that what Mr. Bartleby is trying to do is illegal and unfounded. Listen to this: 'A debt cannot be recalled at a moment's notice if the debtor has been faithful to make payments without lapse. The debtor need only to present a letter to the magistrate and proof of their monthly payments— Oh." Charlotte's face fell suddenly as she halted.

"What?"

"Vanessa is not likely to have been given any sort of receipt for her installments. How is she to prove that she has been making payments to Bartleby?"

"Perhaps he has been keeping a ledger?" I suggested.

"It's possible. But he has no motivation to show anyone such records. It would be her word against his that she has not been remiss."

I decided to make a risky suggestion. "If someone were to break into his office perhaps, steal any records he may have..."

"Yes! That could work. Perhaps one of the other girls would be willing to do it. I will ask them at Bible study today." Charlotte threw her arms around my neck and kissed my cheek. I blushed at this nowadays-rare occurrence, feeling like perhaps I had won a boon in my wife's eyes and a temporary pardon from her. Just as swiftly as she had run to me, she disappeared. No doubt she was off to discuss things with Miss Vanessa before their group meeting.

∞∞∞∞

Charlotte

Isabel was against the plan to pilfer Bartleby's ledger book. She insisted that no good could come of it and they would surely be caught. Lily and Selina were on board, though. The plan was that Lily would distract Bartleby while Selina located the book and slipped back out of the office.

"Thank you so much for helping, girls," Vanessa thanked. "I don't know what I would do without you!"

"This will be dangerous," I reminded them. "If Bartleby suspects anything, he may turn on you."

"We understand." Lily asserted. "I'm not going to let that bully get away with something like this."

Vanessa and I waited on edge at Emerson's while Lily and Selina carried out their mission. Isabel claimed she had better things to do and left us. It felt like an eternity before our brave spies returned.

"Did you get it?" I leaped from my seat and ran to them.

Selina proudly held up a brown leather-bound book. "It's all here! And you will not believe what we discovered!"

Lily quickly flipped to the pages containing Vanessa's records of debt. "Take a look at this, 'Ness."

"I don't believe it!"

"What is it?" I needed to know. A quick read of the entries, and suddenly, I realized what they were all gabbing on about. Bartleby was more than just a wicked creditor and brothel master; he was a crook! Vanessa's debts to him had been paid off nearly two years ago, yet he had continued to require monthly payments from her and had lied about the balance owed to him!

"Then, that means, the debt that is being recalled is, in fact, fictitious!" I exclaimed.

Lily grabbed hold of Vanessa and squeezed her against her large bosom. "You're free, Vanessa!" She squealed. "You don't owe

142

that rascal anything!"

Selina, normally a bit quiet and shy, began skipping around like a little girl in celebration.

"I'll go draft the letter to the magistrate. It seems we have some evidence to present to him!"

We met again a few days later.

"How did Bartleby take the news about Vanessa's debt?" I eagerly asked.

"Oh, he was mad as a hornet!" Lily laughed.

"He must have smashed about a fourth of the bottles in the place before the barkeep stopped him!" Selina gleefully added.

"I thought he might end up owing *me* money for all the extra payments I've made," Vanessa quipped, "but his solicitor managed to weasel him out by claiming the additional amount was for room and board. He must have the magistrate in his pocket because his excuse was accepted."

"At least now you can start fresh with a clean slate." Selina remarked.

Lily nodded. "You'll be the first among us, but you won't be the last." She put her plump hands together and smiled. "We've been talking, Selina and I, and we've decided, we are also leaving the Drunken Skunk." She announced.

"Yes," chimed in Selina, her pale blue eyes bright. "I don't want to work for Mr. Bartleby anymore."

"Nor do I," Lily said.

"Wonderful!" I exclaimed.

"That's perfect!" Vanessa jumped up and embraced them both.

Selina sighed. "Unfortunately, we don't have a clue as to what we're going to do to support ourselves."

Lily nodded glumly. "My last job before the Skunk was a barmaid in another town. Sadly, there are no other establishments in our town that I might apply to; folks at the inn have already said I'm not respectable enough to work there."

"I don't have any useful skills," Selina said, "at least, none that will get me hired anyplace decent."

Vanessa gave a wry smile. "I wish I could afford to hire you as my assistants once I open my own shop, but right now I need to save every penny just to get started.

"We don't expect you to hire us," Selina shook her head.

Isabel, who had been quietly reclining with crossed arms through all of this, suddenly spoke up. "If you have no plans for how you will make a living, then what makes you think you can just up and quit on Mr. Bartleby? Where will you live? How will you survive? Or do you think your fortunes will be as good as 'Ness here, who at least knows how to sew a damn dress?" She scoffed.

"There's no need for such language, Isabel," I chided. "I am pleased that Lily and Selina have decided to abandon prostitution in favor of a new profession. I am sure situations can be found for both of them, with a little time and thought put in."

Lily asked, "what about you, Isabel? Will you leave the tavern as well?"

"Me? Ha, when pigs fly!" Isabel mocked, her shrill laughter reverberating off the walls. "With you three all gone, I'll have the run of the upstairs. All the men will come flocking to me, and Mr. Bartleby will reward me with the extra commissions. Why, I'll be working so hard, I bet I won't even sleep!" she bragged.

I merely shook my head. "The life of a lady of pleasure cannot be as glamorous for you as you make it out to be. Someday you may regret your choice. You ought to attempt a different lifestyle now, while you can," I suggested.

Isabel huffed and snickered, pointing her finger at each of the girls. "You all think you can get out, but you'll see. Mr. Bartleby will let you play your game for a while, but then he'll have you back upstairs at the Skunk before you know it." Turning to me, she said, "Charlotte, you ought to stop filling these girls' heads with dreams. We're all soiled women. There is no other life for us but this. If you ask me, we might as well enjoy it to the fullest and make our fortunes while we're still young and beautiful."

My heart cried inside. What had caused Isabel to become so jaded? Could she really see no other option for any of them but to remain embroiled in the life of a whore?

Isabel left our meeting, saying she needed to get back to work.

Vanessa put her hand upon my shoulder. "Don't listen to her,

144

Charlotte. You're doing the right thing by helping us. We are all grateful for your efforts to put us back on the straight and narrow. I know I would never have had the courage to desert my position and venture into the unknown if not for you."

"Yes, that's right." Selina agreed. "Lily and I would not be bold enough to leave either, if you had not encouraged us and shown us it was possible." Lily also nodded.

"Thank you, girls." I smiled. We all agreed to stop dwelling on the negative and get on with our Bible study for the day.

Isabel stopped coming to our meetings after that. I was sad, but I did not know what to do to convince her to return. Selina and Lily both seemed happier to be out of the Drunken Skunk. In spite of their uncertain future, their attitude was lighter, as if a weight had been lifted from their shoulders. I was pleased for them, and Vanessa also, whose business was starting to gain more traction as people liked her work and began telling others about it. It would not be long, I hoped, before she could afford to open her own dressmaker's shop.

But there was still somebody who was more displeased than any other about the absence of the three former workers from the tavern: Cassius Bartleby. I was coming home from Emerson's shop one afternoon, and I happened to take a shortcut through an alley. Mr. Bartleby had been following me. He accosted me, cornering me in the alley.

"What do you want, Mr. Bartleby?" I demanded.

"Nothin' much, missus parson, only that ya stop stealin' me employees away." He replied. His foul breath reeked of liquor as he leaned his arm against the wall to keep me trapped.

"Vanessa, Lily, and Selina all left you of their own accord. I had nothing to do with their decisions," I insisted.

Bartleby twirled his mustache. "See, that's where you're wrong. I'm fairly certain they wouldn't 'ave gotten such an idea if it weren't for your proselytizin' and evangelizin'."

I growled. "If they left, it's because they hate working for a bully like you! They finally had enough of you!"

"Dogs will always return to their master. They'll be back sooner or later. But in the meantime, my business is 'urting. Poor Isabel's got more customers than she can service, and I 'ate to see a poor fella's needs go unmet for lack of a bedfella."

"Why don't you try servicing them yourself?" I said cheekily.

"Ooh, ye've got spunk, tha's fer sure!" Bartleby chuckled. "But I think you'd be better at 'elping me recoup my losses than I would," He leered.

"How dare you! I am a married woman!" I glared back.

Bartleby just shrugged. "So are most of me customers. Marital status doesn't mean dilberries ter them. Why don' I just see how well ya perform right now?" My eyes widened, but before I could stop him, Mr. Bartleby had forced his lips onto mine. I tried to free myself, but his tight grip on my shoulders kept my back pinned to the wall. As I struggled, I felt his tongue invade my mouth. His teeth bit my lip, drawing blood. Grabbing my wits, I kneed him in the groin, hard.

"Ow!" Bartleby gasped, loosening his hold on me. I felt the sleeve of my dress rip as I wrested myself free. I slapped him forcibly across the cheek, then took off running as fast as I could.

Mr. Bartleby called after me. "You tell those girls to 'come home to papa' or there'll be hell to pay!" When I had gotten far enough away, I stole a glance behind as I ran. Mr. Bartleby was just leaning against the wall, legs crossed casually, lighting his pipe and snickering.

∞∞∞∞

William

I was at home enjoying some tea in the dining room by myself when Charlotte returned. She didn't look at me as she made for the stairs, as if she were trying to avoid me. Rising from my chair, I hurried into the hall and called to stop her.

"Charlotte, what are you doing?"

She paused and looked at me. I immediately saw blood running from her lip and was alarmed. "What's happened? You're hurt!"

"It's nothing…" she tried to excuse.

I went to her. "Did you stumble and burst your lip open by falling?" Then I saw her sleeve dangling from her dress. My eyes narrowed. "Who did this to you?" I demanded.

Charlotte was trembling. "Cassius Bartleby... attacked me in an alley," she finally answered.

146

My insides dropped. "The tavern owner?" Charlotte began to cry. Instinctively, I pulled her into my arms. "Did he...he didn't…" I couldn't finish my sentence for fear of what the answer might be.

"No, he didn't succeed in what you're thinking. But he tried. He forced me to kiss him." Charlotte made a face. "It was so vile."

My blood began to boil. I pulled away from Charlotte, fumes pouring from my ears. "How dare he touch you like that!"

"He threatened me on account of the girls' leaving the brothel," Charlotte said. "He told me 'there'll be hell to pay' if I don't convince them to return to him."

"Now will you finally abandon this ridiculous cause of yours? This man is dangerous!" I turned back to Charlotte and clutched her again. "I don't know what I would have done if something worse had happened to you." I kissed her forehead and cheeks again and again, then pressed my forehead to hers.

"Please promise me you will cease your efforts with those prostitutes. Just let them go back as they were before. I don't want you crossing swords with that Bartleby character. He's already hurt you once. I cannot let that happen again."

Charlotte shook her head. "I am unharmed, William. Just rattled. We cannot let this evil man get to us. He needs to be stopped. The girls should not have their lives run by a man like him."

My anger was still burning inside me. "You're right. I cannot let him get away with what he's done to you. I'm going to put a stop to this man right now." I let go of Charlotte once again and headed for the door.

Charlotte tried to stop me. "No, William, you cannot do this, you'll just make things worse!" She grabbed my arm, but I brushed her aside. Charlotte followed me to the stables as I fetched my horse. "Please, you're going to get hurt!" She begged.

"Better me than you!" I shouted as I mounted my steed and took off.

∞∞∞∞∞

Charlotte

I was so worried about William. It was getting late, and he still had not returned from the village. I could not even eat my supper, my insides were so torn up. All I could do was pray he would be all right.

Finally, there was a knock at the door. It was the constable's son, the acting deputy. Behind him, tied to his carriage, he had our horse in tow.

"Good evenin', madam. I'm afraid I must inform you, your husband has been arrested for assault and disruptin' the peace."

I was too stunned to respond.

"We've determined he attacked under provocation and is not an immediate threat to society. The magistrate has seen 'im and issued a fine to be paid to the victim. If you'll bring the money for the fine and come to collect 'im, he can be released tonight." I nodded numbly and went into the house to fetch my reticule. When I returned, I asked the deputy, "Who was it that my husband attacked?" But I already knew the answer before he had even replied.

"Cassius Bartleby."

Chapter 14

William

I drove my horse as fast as he could run until we reached the Drunken Skunk. Hitching him to a post, I left the horse and went inside. Bartleby was sitting at a table, drinking, and playing cards with some of the guests. I stormed towards him. "How dare you threaten and violate my wife!" I roared. As I approached the table, I grabbed him by the edges of his jacket. "You won't get away with this, you fiend!"

Mr. Bartleby merely began chuckling, and the rest of the patrons around him too. He stood up from the table, along with two of his fellow brutes, both being large, burly men, and I suddenly realized I was outnumbered. My knees began quaking, and my courage faltered.

"You think a man like you can do anything to me?" Bartleby mocked. "I'm not sure 'ow a pretty lemon like Mrs. Collins ended up with a gilly gaupus like you, but Parson, I think it'd be best for ya to go home and be thankful all I did was *kiss* yer wife."

That was the final straw. My fortitude swelled along with my anger, making me forget the bleak odds against me. I took a big swing at the proprietor, but he dodged me, and I fell against the table behind him. The crowd roared. I turned and lunged for him again, but the two leatherheads caught me, each brute pinning one of my arms back. I struggled against them, but they heaved and knocked me to the floor. Before I could get up, Bartleby stamped his foot upon my wrist. I screamed in pain.

"Tell yer wife to drop her li'l crusade and send me girls back home where they belong." Bartleby sneered. He raised his foot to smash my face next, but I rolled away and scrambled to my feet. Bartleby moved to tackle me again, but I kicked him in the shin. He shrieked and doubled over, giving me a clear shot at his nose. With a swift punch, I drew blood.

"Why you—" Bartleby gasped and reached for his face,

giving me time to smack him in the eye. Then the two brutes caught up to me again, holding me as Bartleby prepared to wallop me in the abdomen.

"That's enough! Break it up, boys!" a voice interrupted him. It was the village constable. He stood at the door with his firearm in hand.

"Sir, this man came into me tavern and assaulted me. I 'ave this crowd of witnesses ter back me up." Mr. Bartleby told the constable, wiping the blood from his nose. I looked around the room, my eyes pleading for someone to speak on my behalf, but no one dared oppose Bartleby. "Parson, I'm afraid you're going to have ter come with me." The constable told me. Bartleby's men released their grip and I fell to the floor. Meekly, I followed the constable out of the Drunken Skunk.

I had reached an all-time low. I had never been prone to violence before. It was as if some demon had possessed me and drove me to insanity, for me to lose control of my temper to such degree. I was ashamed of how Charlotte's opinion of me must alter when she heard what transpired, of what the whole town would think. This was surely the end of my career now, I thought. The constable brought me to the jail for questioning. He inquired after the whole story of what had happened from my side. Then he put me in the holding cell in his son the deputy's care while he returned to the tavern to question Bartleby and the witnesses.

Left alone in the cell, I had plenty of time to reflect on all that had occurred and why I had ended up there. I realized that it wasn't just my foolish rage and desire to defend my wife's honor that had caused me to lash out at Bartleby. It was anger and disappointment with myself. I hadn't been there to protect Charlotte. In fact, I hadn't been there at all for her when she needed me. She had pleaded with me to help her in her cause, to support her and defend her. But I had thought only of my own pride and standing in other's eyes, had feared only for the security of my job and the comfortable life I had come to enjoy. I had left her to fight alone against the forces of evil. For Mr. Bartleby was evil, and I saw, now, that he would use whatever means necessary to threaten and oppress others. Charlotte was right when she said we must stand against him, against society even, to free others from this wicked oppression.

I found myself desiring to pray. Dropping my knees to the rough stone floor, I raised my gaze heavenward and began confessing my faults.

"Lord, I've been a stubborn fool. I have been selfish and proud, valuing the good opinion of others ahead of what You might have me do to better the lives of those around me. My wife begged me to help her free her friends from the snare of wickedness, but I denied her, for fear of what others might think, for fear of what Lady Catherine might do to me. I failed to be united with Charlotte in the calling You have given her." I was beginning to get choked up. "Please, forgive me, Lord, for leaving her to the wolves instead of standing by her side to support her and protect her. This precious woman you have given me— her heart is so tender towards anyone who is suffering and oppressed, and her integrity is so much greater than mine. Thank you for blessing me with a wife who listens to you and is willing to oppose me when I am not in your will." I wiped the tears that were freely rolling down my face now. "Lord God, help me to right the wrongs I have made. I want to take a stand on matters of right and wrong, not according to what the world says, but according to Your word. I pray that it is not too late for You to use me mightily in this parish You have placed me in. Amen."

I opened my eyes. My heart felt lighter again, and my spirit felt much closer to the Lord than I had in a long time. What would happen next remained to be seen, but I trusted that God would carry out His plans in due course. I felt at peace, now that I was working with Him and not against Him.

The constable returned, along with the county magistrate. "Well, you're in luck, Mr. Collins. It seems most of the witnesses believed ya were provoked and are not a danger to society."

The magistrate addressed me also. "You are still being sued for assault by Mr. Bartleby. Do you plead the 'benefit of the clergy'?" he asked, referring to my option to be exempted from a public trial and receive partial clemency for a minor transgression such as this.

"I do, your honor." I prepared to give my vow. "I, William Collins, do solemnly swear that I am devoted to God Most High, and promise to uphold the laws of moral conduct given in the Holy

Scriptures and by the laws of this land, which I have broken. May God judge me if I do not uphold my vow," I concluded.

"Excellent," The magistrate said. "By your vow, your sentence shall be reduced. In lieu of a prison sentence, I am ordering a fine of six crowns to be paid to Mr. Bartleby for compensation."

"Yes, your honor," I agreed.

The constable spoke again in his light accent. "I'm sending my deputy to fetch your wife. Once she arrives, ya can be released tonight to go home with 'er."

I breathed a sigh of relief. "Oh, thank you, sir."

∞∞∞∞

Charlotte

As we rode to the jail, the deputy gave me a colorful description of what had happened.

"Mr. Collins came into the tavern and picked a fight with the tavern owner. Apparently, your husband took a couple pretty good shots at 'is face. Gave 'im a black eye and near broke 'is nose!"

If it hadn't been so serious, I would have laughed.

"It weren't looking so good for him at first though. Bartleby may not be the best fighter, but 'e had 'is friends there to help. Poor Mr. Collins was taking quite a beating until 'e managed to turn it around."

"Oh dear, is he all right?" I asked, worried.

"A couple bruises maybe, but 'e could have fared worse."

We arrived at the jail. I did not wait for the deputy's assistance, simply leapt from the carriage, and hurried ahead of him inside. The constable opened the cell.

"William!" I cried as my husband ran to my arms.

"Charlotte, forgive me! I was such a fool!"

"Hush! I'm only glad you're all right."

"It's not only about tonight. I have not supported you when you needed me through everything that's been going on. But I'm here for you now. Whatever you need to do to get those women free of Mr. Bartleby's clutches and back in respectable society, I'm willing to help you do it."

"William, do you mean it?" I asked.

"I do," he said. Then he captured me in a kiss of pure, blissful

152

relief and boundless love.

The constable cleared his throat. "I don't mean to be interruptin', Mr. and Mrs. Collins, but perhaps ya'd like to pick back up where ya left off when ya get back home," he politely said. I blushed profusely at being caught in such passion.

"Yes, constable. Good evening." I bade, releasing my hold on William and still grinning. Then I took my husband home to do exactly as he suggested.

∞∞∞∞

William

If church attendance had been sparse as of late, it was anything but that now! By Sunday, the whole town knew about my misadventure with Bartleby. Curiosity brought out even some of those that had never darkened our doors before. Like spectators at a dog fight, they piled into the church. Even the choir loft was opened for seating, and still it was standing room only. Lady Catherine, of course, did not deign to attend, but my spirits were momentarily lifted by the sudden burst of visitors. There had been no time to write a new sermon since my arrest, so I planned to simply deliver the one I had already prepared. The topic was fairly straightforward— the dangers of gluttony— but I found I could not get my heart into it.

"When it comes to comestibles, beware the peril of indulging oneself in a manner unbefitting to a believer of the Lord. One must not consume in great excess those foods which are not nutritious to the body and which can only lead to a multitude of impediments to one's health. Also, do not develop a propensity for overeating, which is altogether another form of gluttony. For we learn in First Corinthians, 'For he that eateth and drinketh unworthily, eateth and drinketh damnation to himself, not discerning the Lord's body'. And also, we are given this commandment, 'Whether therefore ye eat, or drink, or whatsoever ye do, do all to the glory of God'." I paused for breath. The congregation around me seemed bored again. Mechanically, I attempted to continue.

"Therefore, I implore you, whenever you are dining, be on guard, then, that you do not eat greedily, nor ask for more helpings when your belly is already satisfied, nor overindulge in those delicacies which may, upon first glance, appear innocent and harmless, but which can render your heart guilty of the very same iniquity which caused so many others before you to stumble."

Looking around at the many faces in my congregation, I found that this simply was not the subject I wanted to address, nor was it what any of them had come hoping to be taught. What was on my heart, what they were all dying to hear about and needed to hear, was the topic of my recent encounter with Bartleby and my new perspective on the women he was subjugating.

Stepping down from the pulpit, I walked out onto the steps of the altar to be closer to my audience. Members of the congregation took notice and sat up or woke up a fellow near them who had been nodding off.

"Friends," I began, "I know you all did not come to hear me talk about gluttony and its many perils. Well, perhaps Mr. Pickett here did." The audience laughed as I gestured to a heavy-set gentleman near the front who had no shame in munching on some chicken legs in the middle of my service. Mr. Pickett grinned, taking it all in stride as he raised one chicken leg in the air and said "hear, hear!" before continuing his snack. I smiled. It was the first time I had used humor in my address, and it felt good.

Continuing on, I said, "Most of you came today because you heard about my recent visit to the parish jail, and how I came to be there. You wondered whether I would have anything to say on the subject of violence, or if I would try to justify my actions." I had the attention of everyone in the room now.

"Well, I will begin by saying, violence is not the answer. I was wrong to attack Mr. Bartleby, no matter how much he may have deserved it. 'Vengeance is mine', saith the Lord.

A murmur crested like a wave across the room, but I put it to silence.

"That said, we also know that we ought to take a stand against the evil in this world. We are to put on the full armour of God, in order that we might stand against the Devil's schemes. I stand before you today to tell you that he has a scheme in place to ruin lives— the lives of young women, desperate to make ends meet. Cassius Bartleby is his pawn, a man so corrupt that he would coerce these women into working for him and use threats and extortion to keep them on his leash. These prostitutes did not choose a life of sin for themselves, but their situations left them with no other option, and now they are trapped. No one will hire them with the stain of immorality cleaving to them, and the debts they owe to their employer keep them chained to him for as long as they remain useful to him."

My audience hung on my every word. I continued on, "We must ask ourselves, 'How can we help these women?'. The answer is this: we must clothe ourselves with compassion and do everything we can to help them break free from their wicked master. We must welcome them— not by condoning their sin, but by encouraging them to repent of it and leave behind their old life, providing for them a way to do so. As for Bartleby, we must put a stop to his tyranny, shut down his house of sin altogether, so he is cut off from his lifeblood."

Some of the congregation began shaking their heads. I knew my message would be hard for some to accept. They enjoyed the many pleasures the tavern had to offer, including for some, regular visits to the brothel portion. They did not want to see these changes happen. Others feared going up against Bartleby. He was a powerful man with many friends in the area, including the mayor and the county magistrate, and he could make things miserable for them if they began threatening his business. A general murmur began, and about a third of the church rose and left the building, one after the other. I expected this might happen, due to the unpopularity of my message, and it did not faze me. I was pleased so many chose to remain.

To the rest, I said, "I commend you, those of you who have stayed to bear with me. Please, if you can find it in your heart to overlook these harlots' colored past, help us to free them from the clutches of this evil man and start anew. Thank you," I concluded. Confident that I had conveyed all I wished, I stepped down from the altar.

∞∞∞∞

Charlotte

I could not have been prouder of my husband. Whatever had occurred the other night, it was apparent he was a changed man. The Lord had answered my prayer and spoken to William to soften his heart. I knew that with him by my side, along with many others now, we had a much greater chance of succeeding in our cause where my friends were concerned. Families immediately came forward following the service, asking how they could help. I told them that Lily and Selina still needed a better living situation. They were currently sleeping on cots in the backroom of Mr. Emerson's shop, since the Emersons had no more room in their home. Two families offered temporary housing until the girls could find employment and get back on their own two feet.

Meanwhile, I heard rumors that customer influx at the tavern had taken a dive. Many people were not so willing to patronize the establishment, now that they knew what kind of man the owner was, and how he was operating his side-business upstairs. I felt that things were looking up for my cause. If only I could help Vanessa open her store and find positions for the other girls, I would feel I had accomplished what I had originally set out to do.

William noticed my glum mood one morning as we sat down to breakfast.

"What's wrong, dearest?" he asked me.

"I am feeling sad for Vanessa's sake. She has worked tirelessly to establish a business, thanks to the generosity of the Emerson's allowing her temporary use of their store for her customers, yet she cannot afford to open a storefront of her own. The barber, who owns the vacant building neighboring his that she wishes to occupy, must be a friend of Bartleby's. He has refused to budge on the price of the rent. In fact, last I heard he's even increased it. It's not fair," I pouted.

William sipped his coffee. "I agree. Bartleby has too many friends in this town." Putting down his cup, he said to me, "I've been thinking though, I may have an idea how we can help."

I perked up. "Really? How?"

"Well, as you know, my income may not be lavish, but we are well-off, thanks in-part to Lady Catherine's benefice."

I nodded reluctantly. "Do go on," I encouraged.

"It occurred to me that we might use some of our savings to generate a small loan, which might enable Vanessa to purchase supplies and begin renting a space," William suggested.

My face brightened. "Would you do that, dear? Oh, that would be wonderful!" I exclaimed. It pleased me to no end that my husband was so willing to help out of our personal funds. Such a thing would never have occurred prior to his change of heart. Then my countenance fell again. "But that would put us at risk, would it not, if what you fear Lady Catherine might do should actually come to pass?"

William shifted in his chair. I saw the inward struggle he must be feeling written across his face. Sighing, he said, "Well, that's a risk we are going to have to take, I think. As you have taught me, I need to be more trusting that the Lord will provide for us no matter what, so long as we are doing the right thing."

I put my hand atop his. "Thank you, dear. I know Vanessa will be so grateful."

William leaned across the table to plant a kiss on my cheek. "Ask her what the sum she requires is, and I shall endeavor to meet the need."

∞∞∞

William

The amount of Vanessa's need was considerable, but fortunately not beyond what I could afford. The majority of my funds were safeguarded at the local bank. Not wanting to trust anyone but myself, not even Charlotte, to carry around that much money, I went to the bank personally to make the withdrawal.

As I emerged from the bank, who should I run into but none other than Mr. Bartleby, who was on his way in. We frowned at one another.

"Mr. Bartleby," I grunted.

"Mr. Collins," He hissed back. Glancing down at the leather valise I carried, he commented, "I see ya 'ave withdrawn a considerable sum."

I merely raised one eyebrow. "You know not what the contents nor quantity of my bag may be."

Bartleby chuckled. "Well, given that this is a bank, me educated guess would be that ya 're carrying money, an' judging by the way yer shoulder is saggin', there must be enough of it ter prove quite heavy. What on earth could ya be doing with all that coin? Not 'elping certain ladies avoid returning ter their employer, I 'ope!"

"My business is none of your concern. You've already been compensated for my actions towards you, so we can have no further business," I scowled.

Bartleby shook his head, with a "Tsk, tsk, that fee was merely a slap on tha wrist. The magistrate clearly could have fined ya more for me troubles." He patted his eye, which was turning yellow now that the bruise was healing. I couldn't help feeling slightly satisfied

158

for what I had done.

"Nevertheless, I have paid what was demanded. Now step aside, Bartleby." I pushed my way past him and continued down the street towards Emerson's Fine Tailoring. Bartleby called after me. "If you're plannin' on givin' any of that money ter 'Ness, you'll find it's all a waste. You're just throwin' it away! Nah good'll come of it!"

I chose to ignore him and press on.

"You will regret this!" Bartleby threatened as I left him in my dust.

Miss Vanessa was at the worktable in the back when I entered the store. Hearing the bell announcing my arrival, she emerged from the back room. Despite three months having passed since my wife's acquaintanceship began, this was the first time I had personally met Vanessa. I recognized her though, having seen her around town.

Vanessa gave a friendly smile. "How can I help you, sir?"

"Miss, allow me to introduce myself. I am Mr. Collins, Charlotte Collins' husband."

Vanessa seemed a little startled. "Oh, of course! My apologies, I should have recognized you."

"No need to worry. We have not formally met prior to now."

"How d'you do?" Vanessa curtsied. "Mrs. Collins told me of your generous offer. I cannot express my gratitude to you enough."

"You're welcome. Actually, that is the reason for my visit today. Given the recent threats made by your former employer, I felt it was safer to deliver your loan to you personally," I told her.

Vanessa nodded. She led me to the back room.

The worktable dominated the room, with a pair of stools near it. A basket of fabric samples was on the floor, and one of Vanessa's projects was spread out on the table.

"Mr. Emerson was kind enough to give me some of his remnant fabrics. I'm making cushions and handbags to sell to supplement the garment orders I've received," Vanessa explained.

"Oh, excellent. Perhaps I shall have to order something as a little present for Mrs. Collins. She's often complained about the color and age of my sofa cushions. They were selected by my patroness for one of the previous rectors, but I believe that it was quite some time ago, as their stains betray the length of time since they bore their original lustre." Realizing I was rambling again, as was my tendency when I was nervous, I apologized.

"Pardon me, I don't mean to go on in such a fashion."

"It's quite all right, Mr. Collins." Vanessa excused.

Seating myself on one of the stools, I deposited the valise onto the worktable.

"Here is the sum you required." I said.

"Thank you ever so much, Mr. Collins." Vanessa smiled. "I shall repay you as soon as I am able, with interest."

"Take your time, miss." I offered. "What you undertake is no small feat. Do what you must to establish your store first, and don't even think of paying us any interest."

Vanessa was moved to speechlessness, and I wondered if she might cry.

I shifted on my stool uncomfortably. Taking a deep breath, I began, "I must apologize for my previous behavior, for writing that letter to you, and all the other obstacles I erected. I should not have tried to prevent Mrs. Collins from being your friend and assisting you."

Vanessa nodded silently. "I cannot say I blame you," she acknowledged, "for wanting to distance your wife and yourself from me. I'm well aware of how my association with Mrs. Collins has stained your reputation in these parts."

"Be that as it may," I continued, "I acted judgmentally and with consideration only for my own interests. Please consider this loan as my way of attempting to make up for the wrongs I have committed."

Vanessa smiled again. "Thank you, sir, I shall."

As a side note, I added, "I hope you might decide to join us some Sunday morning, and bring your friends along. I think you might find there has been a change of heart in our congregation; people will be far more welcoming of you now than perhaps previously."

"I shall consider it," Vanessa told me. Thoughtfully, she said, "You know, I have not darkened the doors of a church since I was a small child. My mother used to take me, but that was before Father left, and before she became ill. The Lord has been very merciful to me in bringing me back to Him, and that was largely due to Charlotte's efforts. You truly have a gem on your hands, Mr. Collins."

I smiled to hear this. "Yes, she is a far more priceless woman than I could ever have imagined when I married her."

"Take care of her, Mr. Collins," Vanessa urged.

I nodded in response. "I shall."

The conversation with Vanessa was still in my head when I returned home.

"'Who can find a virtuous woman? For her price is far above rubies'" I recited as I entered the room where Charlotte was.

She looked up from her needlepoint. "Quoting King Solomon again, are we?" Charlotte teased. "That's from Proverbs thirty-one, am I right?" she asked.

"Right you are!" I praised. Continuing my recitation, I said, "'The heart of her husband doth safely trust in her, so that he shall have no need of spoil. She will do him good and not evil all the days of her life'."

Charlotte put down her sewing and came to me. Wrapping our arms around one another in an embrace, we shared a tender kiss.

"Is everything settled with Vanessa in regard to her loan?" She asked.

"It is," I replied. "I hope no further misfortunes will befall her." Biting my lip, I sighed. "I saw Bartleby when I was entering the bank."

"That man!" Charlotte fumed. "You did not fight again, did you?" she worried.

"No, we behaved ourselves and kept our exchange civil, but seeing him does make me want to throw another punch," I admitted. "Bartleby did, however, make veiled threats when he surmised that I might be withdrawing funds to help Vanessa."

"Do you think he might do something?" Charlotte asked.

"With that man, anything is possible. We ought to be on guard, lest he should do something more despicable."

"Well, hopefully if Vanessa's business is a success, it will show him that no amount of crime or manipulation can deter her from making a fresh start."

"Let us hope that you are right, dear. Now, where were we?" I grinned, pulling Charlotte into my arms again.

"I think," Charlotte smiled slyly, "that you were in the middle of praising my virtues."

"Yes. But I think I can find a better place for me to appraise all your talents." Then I took her by the hand and led her upstairs.

I awoke before dawn the next morning to the sound of my servants shouting, "Fire! Fire!" I leapt from bed and ran downstairs, still in my nightclothes. Charlotte, having awoken also, was on my heels. Mrs. Perry was headed towards us, coughing from the clouds of smoke behind her. "Sir," she said, "the kitchen is on fire!"

Chapter 15

Charlotte

Smoke poured out from the western side of the house, making me cough as I raced down the stairs after William.

"Sir, the kitchen is on fire!" I heard Mrs. Perry tell my husband, her face panic-stricken.

"Try to remain calm, Mrs. Perry," William told her. "Get everyone outside and form a bucket brigade starting at the well."

I was impressed with his level-headedness in the face of such an emergency. I followed him through the front door, where we joined the servants who were lining up with buckets and any large containers they could find.

The smoke from the kitchen side of the house was rising high and the flames lit up the dark sky. Mr. Collins' manservant hurried next door and began ringing the church bells to sound the alert. Soon neighbors arrived from the nearby farms, and some of the servants from Rosings. Jesse, our stable hand, ran to the village to summon more help. Our firefighters quickly increased in number as members of our parish arrived. I noticed Mr. Emerson and his wife join the brigade, followed by Vanessa, Lily, and Selina. Soon, half the town was working to douse the flames. By the time the sun was fully up, the fire was put out. Fortunately, it hadn't spread too far in the house. The kitchen was completely gone, sadly, as well as the servant's hall, but the rest of the house was spared.

The morning air was cool, making me shiver in my thin cotton nightgown. Wrapping my shawl around me tighter, I was grateful that it was summertime. William trudged to me, exhausted from his firefighting efforts. His face was covered in soot and ash, and yet, he had never appeared more handsome in my eyes.

"The last of the embers is dying out now," he told me. I allowed him to pull me into his open arms. I rested my head upon his chest and wrapped my arms around his waist, wishing I could remain there forever.

"I'm just thankful that no one was hurt," I said, not caring in the least if the smoky smell transferred from his garments to mine. Finally, we broke our embrace. "Do we have any idea how the fire began?" I wondered.

William shook his head. "Mrs. Perry told me one of the maids woke up and smelled smoke. When she emerged from the basement quarters the kitchen was already on fire. Mrs. Perry thinks perhaps someone left something burning, such as a candle or tobacco pipe, and forgot about it."

I bit my lip. "I'm not certain that alone could cause a fire to break out."

"Neither am I," William frowned. "But at the moment, we have no clues to recommend an alternative scenario." He sighed heavily.

Turning my head sideways a little, I commented, "You were very cool and collected this morning. Thanks to your quick thinking, we were able to form the brigade before the fire could spread too far. You are quite the hero!" I praised.

William smiled bashfully. "Truthfully, I was completely terrified. Everything in me wanted to panic and run under my chair like a little mouse. But I knew everyone in our household was counting on me to take charge, so I just did the first thing I could think of to solve the problem."

Before we could continue any further, a carriage rolled up. Lady Catherine stepped out, and Miss de Bourgh after her. Before Lady Catherine could stop her daughter, she ran to me.

"Charlotte! I'm so glad you are safe!" Anne embraced me. "I was terribly worried when I heard about the fire."

"Yes, we are fine, praise the Lord, though the kitchen is lost," I told her.

Lady Catherine decided to overlook her daughter's behavior and addressed William instead. "Mr. Collins," she said stiffly, "I offer my condolences for this unfortunate loss. I trust you and your servants are all unharmed? No injuries to speak of?" She asked.

"Yes, your ladyship," William answered. "We have all been spared, according to the Lord's mercy. We thank you very much for your care and concern over our well-being."

"Judging by the condition of your house, I suspect that it will be some time before your servants have a place in which to prepare your meals," the lady estimated.

William nodded glumly. "It would appear that way, Lady Catherine."

The great lady raised her chin slightly. "Far be it from me to deny my rector the ability to eat his meals. You and your wife are to come to Rosings to dine until your kitchen is rebuilt. Your servants may also eat with mine. I shall contract laborers to complete the renovation as expediently as possible."

"You are too magnanimous, your ladyship." William bowed slightly.

"I hope that this gesture will prove to you that I am not without compassion, even against those who have offended me." Lady Catherine sneered proudly.

"We are ever so grateful for your wondrous generosity," he praised again.

"Certainly," the lady said. "After all, I must make the parsonage fit to live in again, in the event I should need to fill it with another tenant."

"I pray that shall not be necessary, your ladyship," William pleaded.

"Indeed," was Lady Catherine's blunt response. Changing the subject, she said, "I shall have my cook send over coffee and rolls for all your volunteer firefighters, and I shall expect you for dinner this evening at five." She turned to head towards her carriage. Glancing back, she called, "Come along, Anne! The carriage is leaving." Miss de Bourgh reluctantly followed her.

Turning back to William, I complained. "Every meal at Rosings! How can I stand such a thing? After all she has put us through?"

"From her perspective, the same could be said about us. Charlotte, Lady Catherine has extended us an olive branch. We would be wise to accept. It may be our only chance to repair relations with her and help her to accept our course of action. Besides, where else would we partake our meals?"

"With our friends, perhaps? Surely others in our parish will invite us over to dine. Or we could always go to the inn," I suggested.

"We may receive a few invitations in the beginning, it's true," William admitted. "But that will not last until the repairs are complete, nor would it provide a solution for our servants, who need to eat just as much as we do."

I was forced to agree with his logic. "Just promise me that I can still be excused to eat elsewhere from time to time."

"If you wish," he nodded. "Just, not tonight, please." William begged.

"Very well, dear," I agreed reluctantly. I hoped it would not try my patience to be dining with Lady Catherine again.

∞∞∞∞

William

Soon after breakfast had been served and our parishioners dispersed, the constable arrived. He and his deputy began investigating the wreckage. A while later, they reported to me their findings.

"Mr. Collins, we 'ave some bad news." The constable said. "This fire was no accident."

I frowned. "What do you mean?"

"We found the burnt remnants of a pile o' rags soaked in what smells to be lantern oil, placed near the stove. There was no lantern or any candles nearby."

"Were there any other clues as to who might have done all this?" I asked.

"We did inquire to all the servants. We 'ave no conclusive leads, but the maid who discovered the fire declared she saw someone running into the woods, though it was too dark to tell if it was a man or woman. Unfortunately, without further clues, we 'ave nothing to go on and no arrests can be made."

I was deeply troubled by all that the constable had related to me. I shared the details with Charlotte.

"Arson!" She exclaimed. "Is the constable certain about all this?"

"He said it isn't definitive, but based on his inspection, that's his belief, yes."

"Goodness! How can we have any peace? How can we feel safe in our own beds even, if there is a pyromaniac on the loose?"

"I am just as alarmed as you are, dear."

Charlotte mused. "Do you think the constable might find anything that could tie the crime to Bartleby?"

"You think he's behind this?" I asked.

"Dear," Charlotte tilted her chin down, "you said yourself he made veiled threats to you only yesterday."

"Yes, but I hate to think he might have done this. It would mean he is even more dangerous than we originally thought. Isn't there anyone else who could be displeased about our recent affairs?" I wondered.

"Well, there's Lady Catherine," Charlotte suggested. "I mean, not that she would have done it personally, but she could have hired someone."

I shook my head. "I can imagine no situation in which she would stoop to destroy church property to get revenge or to frighten us, nor employ a person to do any sort of dirty work for her."

Charlotte nodded. "I suppose I must concede that to you. Despite her many faults, such a scenario would seem out of character, even for her."

I thought for a moment. "Could it be a disgruntled servant, or perhaps a neighbor? We have not exactly been the most popular in town, even after a large portion of the parish came over to our side."

"Possibly." Charlotte mused. "Though I can name no one off the top of my head who has enough motive, besides Mr. Bartleby."

At that moment, there was a knock on the door, and Mrs. Perry admitted Vanessa to us. The latter seemed distraught.

"Charlotte, I have bad news." She ran to my wife. "The money you and Mr. Collins have lent me— it's gone!"

"What did you say?" I exclaimed. Vanessa turned to me.

"Sir, when I returned home with the Emersons after your fire had been put out, someone had broken into their home and gone through the bedroom where I am staying. All my things were strewn about, and the valise of money which you had given me was taken."

"How horrible! Were there any other items missing from the home, of either yours or the Emersons?"

Vanessa shook her head. "Not one thing. Whoever they were, it seemed they were only after the money."

Charlotte interjected. "And all this occurred during the time of the fire this morning?"

"Indeed. No one was home at the time. We all came to help with the fire."

My wife was furious. "This can only have been a planned attack in connection with the fire. The thief had to have known about the money and used the fire as a distraction to lure everyone away from the Emersons'."

"I agree, with Charlotte's assessment," I said, "have you reported this to the constable yet?"

168

Vanessa nodded. "It was the first thing I did. Naturally, I tried to make the connection that since Bartleby is one of the few people who knew I had the money, he must be involved somehow. The constable agreed it was suspicious. But Bartleby seems to have a solid excuse. He went to London yesterday afternoon and was seen having breakfast with his solicitor at the inn in Bromley early this morning. The mail courier who runs the route from town confirmed this when he arrived with the post," she explained.

My frustration welled up in me. "That slimy snake!" I exclaimed. "Of course, he would have covered his tracks. He must have ordered some of his men do the dirty work."

"Did anyone in the village see anything?" Charlotte interjected. "Were there any witnesses who saw the break-in?"

Vanessa bit her lip. "Well, there was one thing." She looked away, troubled.

"Go on," I urged.

"It's quite strange. Emerson's next-door neighbor claims she saw a woman with blonde hair that resembled *me* entering the Emerson's house. The woman had on a wide bonnet, so her face could not be seen well, but she used a key to enter. A short while later, this neighbor saw the woman emerge and walk down the street carrying a valise. All this happened during the morning hours when we were all here at the parsonage putting out the fire. Emerson's neighbor herself has a limp, so that is why she did not come to assist when the alarm was raised. But her son did go, and that is why she was watching out the window, awaiting his return." Vanessa finished.

"How curious," Charlotte mused. "Did the neighbor mention anything else about this woman's appearance that might direct us to the real identity of the thief?"

"Only that she wore a black lace shawl over her dress.'

"Do you own such a shawl?" I asked Vanessa.

She shook her head. "Nothing like it. It most definitely was not me that she witnessed."

"This is turning out to be quite the mystery!" Charlotte exclaimed.

"At any rate, we can do nothing until the constable's investigation is complete." I reminded her.

Vanessa agreed to keep us updated on the constable's progress before leaving.

"Let us make our way upstairs to dress for dinner," I told Charlotte. "Lady Catherine will expect us to be punctual."

We arrived at Rosings precisely on time. After brief greetings in the drawing room with Lady Catherine, we were summoned to the dining room.

"I apologize that Miss de Bourgh cannot join us this evening," Lady Catherine said. "She is unwell and will be dining in her room."

"How unfortunate. Please pass our regards for her swift recovery," I wished.

"Yes, please. I was looking forward to seeing her," Charlotte echoed. She appeared a bit peeved. Perhaps she believed that Lady Catherine was keeping Miss de Bourgh from us on purpose.

"Well, this has certainly been an interesting day," Lady Catherine commented dryly as the soup course was served.

"Indeed, your ladyship," I agreed.

"Such an unfortunate accident," she added, shaking her head.

Charlotte joined the conversation. "The constable thinks perhaps it was not an accident."

Lady Catherine's soup spoon clattered. "Not an accident!" she exclaimed. "You mean to tell me that someone set fire to your home on purpose?"

"Yes, Lady Catherine," I told her. "There is evidence suggesting arson."

"Well, I never! I know you've been rather unpopular as of late," she rolled her eyes, "but who ever heard of someone going after their minister in such a despicable manner? I hope when they catch the rascal, I can make him pay me back for the damages to the parsonage. It will not be cheap to rebuild a whole wing!" Lady Catherine complained.

Charlotte glanced at me, and I smiled and shrugged as if to say, 'see, I told you she would not have done it'.

"Our suspicions are that Mr. Bartleby may be the culprit," I said. "After all, he has the most motive."

"You mean that filthy tavern owner you assaulted?" Lady Catherine asked.

"Indeed, your ladyship. After all, besides his still being sore about that, he is displeased that we offered financial assistance to one of young women who were formerly in his employ. There was also a robbery that occurred at the same time as the fire. The money which we gave this woman was stolen. We believe the arson and the robbery must be connected."

"If that is the case, then surely there can be no better time for you to abandon your cause. If there is such a dangerous criminal threatening you, then you ought to leave well enough alone and let things return to normal. No cause, no matter how noble it may seem or how dear to your heart, can be worth the cost of one's life and property!" Lady Catherine insisted.

"Tell that to the first century Christians who gave up their lives for their faith!" Charlotte interjected. "They were willing to face torture and imprisonment, even death in the Colosseum, for the sake of their cause."

Lady Catherine looked uncomfortably silent for a change. "Well, things were different then. It was a barbaric time, after all," she finally said. "Still, it wasn't long before even Rome accepted the faith and Christianity became the religion of the civilized world. Nowadays, one should not have to die for their beliefs in a Christian nation such as this." Lady Catherine casually took a sip from her wine glass.

I thought perhaps this could be the moment to sway Lady Catherine towards our cause.

"Could I then respectfully ask that you please stop your own persecution of us, your ladyship?" I begged.

Lady Catherine was offended. She slammed her goblet on the table, sloshing wine onto the pure white linen. "Me, persecute you? I have done nothing but attempt to show you the error of your ways! I have told you from the very start that we must separate ourselves from the sins of the world, lest they pollute us, and that it is important not to disrupt the natural barrier between the upright and moral who walk the straight and narrow, and the depraved and wicked who wander the wide path to hell, lest we be tempted ourselves! Now that you have entangled yourself with those sinners, you have angered their kind and brought calamity upon your household!" Lady

Catherine stood from the dinner table. "My discipline towards you was out of an effort to spare you from pain and hardship. To instruct you how best to comport yourselves as ministers of the faith, without becoming involved in the deeds of evil… exactly the class of events that have occurred today. Now, as your benefactress, I must insist that you relinquish your connection to all these worthless riffraff once and for all, before they burn the church down next!"

Charlotte argued, "The church is not a building, your ladyship. It's the people who worship together. The building may burn, but the church will live on, in spite of any acts of terror."

"The 'church building', then, if you insist on my using theologically correct terminology, was built with my late husband's grandfather's fortune," Lady Catherine refuted. "It has sat on this estate for over seventy-five years, and I will not see it, nor any of the other church property, destroyed because of your stubbornness. None of this would have ever occurred, Mrs. Collins, had you not come to this parish and began ruffling the order of things. Your husband never once disobeyed my authority until you came along and bewitched him, you 'Delilah'!"

Lady Catherine had incensed my fury. "You've gone too far, Lady Catherine!" I rose from the table and threw down my napkin. "Mrs. Collins is no 'Delilah', she is my wife! I love her, and I support her with my eyes wide open, and I *will not* see you treat her thusly!"

Walking around the table swiftly, I placed my hands on Charlotte's shoulders. Charlotte was so shocked by all that was happening, she could do nothing other than sit there with her eyes wide and her mouth gaping.

I did not stop. "My wife and I are united; we will not stop our mission to see our former prostitute friends become independent from their previous employer, and to see him restrained from oppressing others. You have bullied us long enough, and we will not back down. Your manipulation and callous treatment of us over this subject must stop."

Lady Catherine glared at us. Stone cold silence filled the room. Had a pin been dropped, we could have all heard it.

The servants entered to present the main course, but Lady Catherine stayed them with her hand. "Mr. and Mrs. Collins have had an unexpected need to return home. Send a tray to my room, and do not serve the rest of the meal in the dining room." The servers nodded and took the food back to the kitchen with them.

"Please leave immediately." Lady Catherine commanded us, in as few words as I ever heard from her lips.

"Gladly." I replied, even more tersely.

Lady Catherine began to exit the room. At the last moment, she turned back to us. With a sneer, she said, "Oh, and to show that I am still not without a heart, you may take your meals in my kitchen along with your servants during this interim."

I had not the heart to thank her.

∞∞∞∞

Charlotte

Never in my wildest dreams could I have imagined such a confrontation taking place as the one I had just witnessed. The gall William displayed in standing up to his benefactress was unparalleled! I really did not know what had come over him. Apparently, neither did he. As soon as we were walking home, I could see the regret written on his face, his complexion pale, and his voice shaky.

"Lord help me, what have I done?" He quivered. "I have just insulted our patroness, calling her manipulating, callous, and a bully! Lady Catherine will finish us for certain!"

I tried to reassure him. "You did the right thing, dear. I have been waiting for you to put Lady Catherine in her place since the day you first introduced me to her! Now it is time for us to let the chips fall where they may, where she is concerned."

"I must have been out of my mind back there, to say such things!" William put his hands on his head in disbelief over his own behavior.

"You were rightfully offended. Everything you said to her needed to be said a long time ago, dear." I placed my hand on his back.

"But what shall we do? It's well-known that Lady Catherine is friends with the bishop. She has only to write to him, and I will be removed from the church, and then where will we go? Perhaps I ought to go back and apologize to her before she does something." He turned to head back to Rosings, but I caught his arm.

"Don't disappoint me after that amazing display of backbone!" I could not keep back a small laugh. "You have, by magic, transformed from a spineless sea creature into a heroic champion, nay, even Poseidon!" I joked.

William merely let out a whimper and rerouted his footsteps towards the parsonage once again.

I reminded him, "Even if things don't turn out the way we desire, we will still have one other."

My husband nodded. "True. I certainly need you now, Charlotte. Pray, do not let go of my arm, or I am certain I shall turn back into a spineless jellyfish and run to undo what I've just done. Everything in my instinct is telling me I've just made a horrible mistake."

"Then let me be your conscience," I said, "and reassure you that you have made the right choice, and that the Lord will look out for us as He always has." I stopped walking long enough to cut in front of William and plant a nice kiss on his lips. Apparently, the gesture was just the remedy he needed to gain some courage. Puffing up his chest, he grabbed my arm and marched straight the rest of the way home.

Chapter 16

Charlotte

I loved seeing this new William, the one who would stand up for himself and his beliefs and make the right choices even in the face of difficult consequences. He was maturing, and his actions reflected it. Still, I knew it was not easy for him. In many ways, he still felt completely out of his element. I realized that there were some things about him that would never change. His tendency to fret and fuss when he was worried or upset about something, for instance. Poor William could not get the quarrel with Lady Catherine out of his head, and try as I might, I could not dispel his constant anxiety over what might happen next. The next morning, William's eyes were bloodshot from lack of sleep, and he spent a great deal of time discoursing with me about the "what if's". I tried to occupy him with small meaningless tasks; reorganizing the bookshelves in his study, pulling weeds in the garden, sorting old sermon notes, but none of them kept him busy for too long. All I could do was pray that somehow things would turn out right after this incident.

Nevertheless, I was eager to discover who was behind the fire and the robbery. My bets remained on Bartleby, if only we could find any proof that he was somehow responsible. I was preparing to pay the constable a visit to see how the investigation was proceeding (and find some respite from William's fretting). As I put on my bonnet to leave, Mrs. Perry interrupted me.

"Begging your pardon, ma'am, but Jesse, the stable-hand, wishes to speak to you and the master. May I show him in?"

Perplexed, I agreed, and William was summoned from his study.

When we were both comfortably seated, Jesse was shown in. He looked deeply troubled, and his knuckles were white as he gripped his cap in both hands.

"What is the matter, Jesse?" William asked him. "You look positively grim!"

"Sir, I have a question for Mrs. Collins, if I may." Jesse replied.

William nodded. "Go on."

"Ma'am, you are friends with Miss Isabel, are you not? Have you heard from her or seen her yesterday or today?"

I was startled. "You are acquainted with Miss Isabel?" I returned.

Jesse looked even more uncomfortable. "Well, I, um, have paid her visits a number of times…" he coughed slightly.

I let out a breath and glanced at William. We were both disappointed at this kind of behavior from one of our servants.

Jesse continued. "The truth is, tha' over the course of our time together, we've fallen in love, you see. We were meant to run away together last night on the evening mail coach. Only, she never showed."

"We will deal with the impropriety of your frequenting a brothel as customer later, Jesse," my husband reprimanded. "When you say you were going to 'run away together', tell me, what was your plan?"

Jesse then went on to relate how he had professed his love to Isabel and asked her to make a new life with him at his uncle's farm in Lancashire. She told him they could do it, if only she could get her hands on some money to afford it. He had promised to do anything to help her and was instructed that they just needed a diversion and then she could get the money.

"Wait a minute," I interrupted. "This 'diversion'," I began putting the pieces together, "It was you who set the fire, wasn't it?"

Jesse hung his head in shame, then looked up at me with pleading eyes. "I didn't think you would lose the whole kitchen," he admitted. "I just did what Isabel told me to. She gave me the lantern oil and some matches. Said if I would just set fire to sommit, then everyone would be busy putting out the fire, and she could get us the money. She would lie low somewhere, and then meet me at the inn at midnight so we could leave. Are you going to press charges against me? I wouldn't blame you if you did, only... I fear they may have me hang for this." Jesse was trembling.

William was merciful. "You came clean to us, Jesse, so no,

we will not be pressing charges. But what about Isabel?" He brought the subject back to Jesse's original concern. "You said she failed to appear at the appointed time."

Jesse nodded. "I tried going to the Drunken Skunk this morning, but there was no answer when I knocked at her door. I inquired to Mr. Bartleby as he passed by, and he simply told me that Isabel was unwell and shooed me away. When I asked one of the maids, she said that Isabel departed her room late last night and did not return. Her room was completely empty when she checked it. Someone had removed all of Isabel's things and left nothing but a bare room. I fear that something may be terribly wrong here."

"I'm afraid you may have been taken advantage of," was William's pessimistic response. "Miss Isabel must have taken an earlier coach without you and left you to take the fall for her."

I was skeptical though. "If that were the case, wouldn't Mr. Bartleby have simply said she was gone? I believe you, Jesse. Something is amiss, and I think Bartleby must know the truth."

I was fully ready to break down Bartleby's door and demand to know where she was. It was clear to me that she had used Jesse to create a diversion while she broke into the Emmerson's house and stole the money from Vanessa. But there was still one piece of the mystery that hadn't been explained.

"Miss Vanessa mentioned one thing to us, though. She said Emerson's neighbor witnessed a blonde woman entering the Emersons' residence at the time of the fire. Isabel is a brunette. Can you explain that for us?" I asked.

Jesse looked extremely uncomfortable. Finally, after a pause, he said, "Isabel has a blonde wig that she uses to, er, entertain customers with. Even I, um, fancy seeing her in it sometimes."

I put my head to my hand to hide my embarrassment at hearing such details from him.

Thankfully, William spoke. "Well, that would make it even more likely that she is indeed the culprit. I think it's time we went to the constable with all this."

"But dear! If the news of this is made public, would not Lady Catherine want to charge poor Jesse for the arson? It is her property, after all," I reminded. Turning to Jesse again, I asked,

"Is there anywhere that Isabel may have gone to lie low? A secret meeting place you two have?"

"There is a place in the woods surrounding here where we met a few times," he said. "I checked there this morning, but we can search again, if you like." We agreed and set out at once.

∞∞∞∞

William

Jesse led us through the woods that stretched beyond the parsonage and Rosings. We came to a clearing with just one large tree, hollow at the base and with a massive branch that had twisted low to make almost a seat of sorts. I could imagine two lovers sharing that branch, making their hopeful plans for the future. Jesse looked wistful. Perhaps he was reminiscing about their last tryst here, much like I was imagining. Isabel was nowhere in sight, though.

"Isabel? Are you here, my love? Isabel? Isabel?" Jesse called out repeatedly, his voice gradually faltering along with his hopes. We listened, but there was no sound other than the wind whipping through the trees. Jesse sighed. "It's just as I expected. She is not to be found in this place."

"Still, if she has been here, there may still be some clues," I said. We began to search around. Suddenly, Charlotte cried out. I turned to look. She had put her hand inside the large hollow of the tree.

"Charlotte! Are you hurt? Has some animal bitten you?" I ran to her as quickly as I could and took her hands in mine.

"I am fine, really!" She brushed me aside. "Look and see! There is something jammed inside the hollow here. I think it may be your valise!"

I peered into the dark crevice above the hollow. Sure enough, there was something brown and leathery, much like the valise I had given to Miss Vanessa. With Jesse's help, I pulled the bag out from the tree and we opened it. Coins glittered in the sunlight filtering through the trees.

"Vanessa will surely be glad of this!" Charlotte exclaimed.

"Indeed," I replied.

On the return path, Jesse suddenly spotted something we had overlooked previously.

178

Caught on a bush was a piece of black lace.

"Do you recognize it?" Charlotte asked as Jesse examined the fabric.

"It's from Isabel's shawl," he replied. I recalled at that moment that Vanessa had mentioned such a shawl from the description of the burglar woman. But what alarmed me was the sight before my eyes on the ground beneath the shrub.

"Blood." I pointed.

"Not Isabel's!" Charlotte exclaimed.

"No way to know for certain, but it appears that a struggle took place here." I pointed out other signs of the altercation— broken branches, footprints in the dirt, and what looked like a set of heel marks being dragged along through the woods away from the main path.

Jesse looked miserable. "If only I had known sommit would happen to her, I never would have agreed to this plan of hers."

"Is there any way to tell who her attackers were?" Charlotte asked me.

"I couldn't say for sure. I'm certainly no expert. But the size of these footprints here makes me think there must have been at least one man. Or a woman wearing a man's shoes," I pointed out.

We followed the prints as far as they led, but the trail disappeared as the grass grew thicker. Finally convinced we had reached a dead-end on our search, I suggested we head to town to return the money to Vanessa. Jesse chose to return to the parsonage rather than accompany us.

Vanessa was alarmed as we related everything to her.

"I never once would have suspected Isabel to be involved with this, or your stable-hand," she confessed, "but I am certain Bartleby must be behind her disappearance."

"Agreed. But without proof of that, we have no recourse," I frowned. "Regardless, time is running out if it hasn't already. There was blood near where the piece of Isabel's shawl was found, which means that if foul play is at hand, it may already be too late." My heart was heavy as the words came out of my mouth.

Charlotte looked overwhelmed.

Vanessa was more perceptive, though. "If the money was still hidden when you found it, then Isabel will still be alive. Bartleby did not find it, so he will need her help to find where she had hidden it. It's imperative that he not discover that we have recovered it, though, or we will lose the only leverage Isabel has to her defense."

I looked at Vanessa intently. "Please think, Miss Vanessa. Is there any place that Bartleby may have taken Isabel? Any place he could be keeping her besides the tavern?"

Vanessa thought for a moment. "There is an old shed near the outskirts of town, off the road that splits towards Hosey Hill. Bartleby used to keep supplies there, before he acquired the storage building adjacent to the Drunken Skunk. It hasn't been used in some time, but I believe it is still owned by him. You could try there."

"I'll go with you!" Charlotte exclaimed.

"No, Charlotte, it's too dangerous for you. I won't see you come to any harm by this man. If he really did kidnap Isabel, then we have no idea what he is capable of," I insisted. "I think it is time we go to the constable over this. I'll make sure to avoid any mention of Jesse's involvement and impress upon him the need to keep the money's recovery in confidence. Miss Vanessa," I turned to her, "do you think you could describe for the constable how to find this shed? I don't want you coming along either."

The constable was against my being a part of the search party, fearing trouble between myself and Bartleby after our recent altercation. I finally persuaded him that I ought to do what I could to assist in the recovery of the young woman, given that her disappearance involved a sum of money which I had originally lent to her companion, thus making me involved in the situation. The constable and his deputy rallied a group of men from the village, including Mr. Emerson. Armed, we set out towards the shed.

"Careful, men!" the constable warned. "We don't know how many we may be up against, or whether or not they are armed. We venture into dangerous territory; be on your guard!"

His warning stirred up the cowardice lying at the bottom of my soul, radiating fear outwards to my hands and feet, until I froze in place, my arms quaking so much I thought I might drop my firearm. I had never been a particularly brave man. Why on earth did I think I could muster the courage to mount such an expedition as this? Danger was almost a certainty; we already knew what type of man Bartleby was. How much more so might a whole band of his thugs be? Realizing I had fallen behind the search party, I knew I had to make a choice. Surely, no one would fault me if I turned and went home to Charlotte. But was this the sort of man I wanted to be? One who abandoned others in their time of need for the sake of my own safety and comfort? Suddenly, the Word of the Lord spoke to me, bringing to my recollection a passage I had come across that morning when I was sorting my old sermon notes: "Be strong and of good courage, do not fear nor be afraid of them; for the Lord your God, He is the One who goes with you. He will not leave you nor forsake you."

"Yes, Lord, I believe you!" I answered, my eyes raised to the clouds above. My soul was fortified once again as I trusted in God's protection, and my liberated feet raced to rejoin the search party.

The shed was so ramshackle, it was a wonder it was still standing. The rotting wood was falling off in places, and the sheets of metal slapped onto the roof were rusting through. Only two men were guarding the building. One sat on an old metal pail and the other on a broken crate and they were playing cards upon a tree stump. The smaller fellow bolted as soon as the search party approached. The other one, a big ugly brute that I recognized as one of those who had helped Bartleby gang up on me in the tavern, could not get away so easily. The constable and the other men surrounded him before he could escape. Mr. Emerson and I ran to the shed. Together, we broke open the door. Inside the tiny room, poor Isabel lay in a heap on the rough-hewn floor, battered and wounded.

"Miss Isabel?" I asked, checking her pulse to ensure she was still alive. Thank the Lord, she was, though unconscious. "Emerson, help me carry her. We must take her to the parsonage and send for the doctor!" I pleaded.

"Mr. Collins?" I heard a weak voice and looked down to see that Isabel had woken.

"Do not worry, Miss Isabel, you are safe now," I reassured her.

Isabel did not respond, but merely fainted once again.

∞∞∞∞

Charlotte

William insisted we wait at the parsonage while the search party went out. He felt it would be safer there. Vanessa fetched Lily and Selina and told them about Isabel's disappearance, and the four of us stayed in the drawing room to await news of the constable's search. As we took turns praying aloud and reading scripture to calm our fears and pass the time, Selina suddenly had a question.

"Why are we trying to help Isabel? Didn't she rob you, Vanessa? If she were kidnapped, wouldn't you say she received the justice coming to her?"

Vanessa placed her hand on Selina's. "You forget, Selina, that Isabel is our friend. Whatever she may have done, she doesn't deserve whatever fate Bartleby may have in store for her."

"Vanessa is right." I praised my pupil. "As Christ has forgiven us, so we are to forgive others who have wronged us."

Selina digested that thought for a while.

It was late when the search party returned. I brought the lantern outside as the girls followed me. William and Mr. Emerson were leading the pack, supporting Isabel side by side. She appeared to be injured and her face was bruised. I heard the constable thank the rest of the search party and dismiss them. He helped Mr. Emerson and William carry Isabel upstairs to one of the guest bedrooms.

Shortly after, the doctor arrived to tend to Isabel. I went downstairs where the constable was waiting.

"Did you catch Bartleby?" I wanted to know.

"Unfortunately, ma'am, I cannot make an arrest until I've received a statement from Miss Isabel, when she 'as recovered enough to do so," the constable explained. "She was too battered and driftin' in and out of consciousness when we recovered her. We did manage to apprehend the ruffian who was guardin' her. We are hopin' to convince him to turn on his employer in favor of a reduced sentence, and that, along with Miss Isabel's testimony, would be enough evidence to prosecute Mr. Bartleby."

I nodded. I could not imagine Bartleby escaping after such ruthless behavior, and with the threat of the noose dangling over his head, I was sure the ruffian would not be willing to protect even a man as formidable as Cassius Bartleby.

The doctor concluded his business and pronounced that the

constable could come interrogate the patient. Once he had taken Isabel's statement, the constable departed to procure what testimony he could out of the prisoner being held at the jail. Vanessa and I were permitted to see Isabel, finally.

She was awake, but weary, when we entered the room. Isabel tried to sit up but found that she did not have the wherewithal to sustain. Laying down again, she started to shake, then she began to cry. Gone was the cold, aloof woman of the world. In her place was the scared girl who had been hiding within her all along.

"I'm sorry, Vanessa! I didn't want to do it!" she insisted. "He made me do it!"

"Who did? Do what?" Vanessa asked.

"Bartleby. He forced me to break into your bedroom and steal the money. Believe me, Vanessa, I never wished you nor anybody else harm!"

I was still puzzled. "But why would you listen to him? What power does he have over you?"

"Besides, we were under the impression it was your plan to run away with Jesse," Vanessa mentioned.

"Jesse?" Isabel choked out a laugh. "That poor fool thought I loved him. But no, he was just a pawn in this whole thing, like I was. The truth is, Bartleby threatened to throw me out in the streets if I didn't help him. What's more, he was going to hurt my father."

"Your father?" I asked.

"My father is very ill," Isabel explained. "He has to go to a particular doctor in London for his treatments and to get his medication. There aren't many doctors who can treat his illness; it's very rare. Mr. Bartleby assisted me in finding my father's doctor, a man he is friends with. Bartleby said if I didn't help him, he would tell his doctor-friend to stop treating my father. If that happens, we will not be able to find another doctor able to treat him, and he'll die!" Isabel continued to sob. "Bartleby also said he'd write a letter to my father and tell him what I've been up to the last several years. My father thinks I have a respectable position as a governess. If he knew that the money I've been sending him came from working as a prostitute, the news of that alone might kill him."

I patted Isabel's back. "Oh, Isabel, I had no idea."

183

Isabel went on. "I might have been fine if I had followed through with the plan. But I did something rather foolish. I thought to myself, 'why should Bartleby have this money? I could just keep it for myself, make my plan to run away be for real. Once I'm safely out of his grasp, I can go to my father in London, find some other line of work, and use the money to pay for my father's treatments'."

"Bartleby found out you were planning to double-cross him, is that right?" I asked.

"Yes." Isabel's tears were flowing even more freely now. "When I failed to show with the money, he deduced that something was going on. I went to the woods and hid the money, intending to wait until the afternoon coach to make my escape. But Bartleby sent one of his ruffians, Grimkoff, to follow me. He didn't see where I hid the valise, but he caught up with me in the woods. Then, he dragged me all the way to the shed where Bartleby and others of his men met him. They beat me and tried to get me to give up the location of the money. When that didn't work, Bartleby left Grimkoff there to guard me. He and his men were out all night searching the woods for the money, but they never found it."

"What about Jesse?" I asked. "You were never going to take him with you, were you?" I knew the answer already as soon as I spoke. Isabel just shook her head.

"Poor man! I think he really loves you, Isabel. He was terrified for your sake when we saw the signs of foul play in the woods."

"I cannot convey the depth of my regret for what I did to him, to you, Vanessa, and to you also, Charlotte." Isabel's contrition was enough to move even the hardest of hearts.

"Why didn't you come to us for help?" Vanessa asked.

"Because I was afraid," Isabel answered. "I didn't want Bartleby to go through with his threats, and I didn't think there was anything you could do to help me stop him."

"Well, thanks to his kidnapping, perhaps we can finally get that scoundrel. I won't press charges against you for the money since we have recovered it." Vanessa insisted.

"Just be certain you do not mention Jesse's involvement to anyone." I instructed. "We have been careful to keep his name out of all our conversations with the constable, so that Lady Catherine cannot charge him for the arson. Perhaps, with your testimony, we may even be able to pin that on Bartleby as well since it was mandated by him as part of the plan he concocted."

"True. He is unaware, to my knowledge, how I managed to accomplish the arson and the robbery at the same time. He only maintained that I ought to 'get someone' to do that for me as a fitting diversion while I robbed the Emersons."

"At any rate, you are to remain here, in safety, until all is completed," I reassured her. "I've already spoken to William and he will not hear of you leaving until Bartleby is safely behind bars."

Isabel tried to stop the flow of tears running down her cheeks, but they just kept coming. "You are too nice to me, both of you. After everything I did to you."

I patted her hand. "That is what friends are for." I smiled. "Speaking of which, before we entered, I heard from Mrs. Perry that a certain young man has been waiting to see you. May I tell her to show him in?"

Isabel nodded. "I suppose I owe Jesse an apology too."

Chapter 17

William

With Isabel and the money safely returned, I was sure it was only a matter of time before Bartleby would be put where he belonged: a deep dark cell with no hope for escape.

Grimkoff, Bartleby's man who had been apprehended, was expected to turn easily when faced with the threat of the gallows.

I went to the constable first thing in the morning to see how things fared with getting a confession out of Grimkoff and whether Bartleby had yet been apprehended.

"The chap sang like a bird when we began questioning 'im," The constable informed me. "We have more than enough to put that Bartleby fellow away now."

"So, you've arrested him already, then?" I asked.

"Unfortunately, no."

"Why ever not?"

"He's fled. Folks at the inn said he made for London during the night. I've sent my deputy to Bow Street for help in finding 'im. The Runners will hunt 'im down, wherever the rascal is hiding. I'll make a point to inform you as soon as he's found. Don't worry, we won't let 'im get away with this."

The constable assured us that he had already been in contact with Bartleby's solicitor, who claimed to have no knowledge of Bartleby's whereabouts. The solicitor had last seen Bartleby the morning of the fire, when he was given instructions from Bartleby regarding his estate. One of those was a written mandate that all of Bartleby's assets were to be sold as expediently as possible. When asked why, the solicitor was compelled to reveal that Bartleby himself was in a state of heavy debt. In fact, if he did not get out of debt quickly, he stood to lose everything he owned, including the tavern.

"No wonder, he's been acting out in such a fashion!" Charlotte exclaimed as we walked back to the parsonage.

"That is still no excuse for his bad behavior," I reminded.

"I'm not excusing him," Charlotte argued, "but this at least gives us a clue to his motives."

∞∞∞∞

Charlotte

A few days after Isabel's kidnapping, I found myself with some spare time before our Bible study meeting, so I decided to take a stroll around the rectory grounds. I was surprised to see the door to the church was ajar. I went inside. Isabel was sitting in one of the pews, gazing at the beautiful stained-glass depiction of Christ hanging on the cross.

"Isabel, what are you doing here?" I asked her.

"Forgive my intrusion in being here, Charlotte, I only came here to think by myself for a while," she apologized.

"No, it is quite all right. You are always welcome here," I told her.

I seated myself beside her on the pew, and for a time, we merely relished the silence together.

Finally, Isabel spoke. "Charlotte, do you think God will ever forgive me for everything that I've done?" A single tear traced down her cheek. "I've behaved so horribly. I hurt all my friends. I stole from Vanessa. I lied to Jesse and used him abominably. I wasn't even kind to you, who has been so caring and generous towards me. Towards all of us. I know you are always speaking about 'God's forgiveness', but maybe there's some, like me, who are too far gone to ever be forgiven."

I put my hand atop hers tenderly. "Isabel, He already has forgiven you. You need only to accept His forgiveness. That picture you were looking at when I came in?" I pointed to the stained glass. "That was the moment when He forgave you, when His son Jesus willingly took the punishment for your sins upon himself. In that very hour, Jesus' last words were 'it is finished', and the debt for every sin ever committed in the history of mankind, past, present, and future, was paid for and forgiven by God."

Isabel's watery eyes looked up at the portrait of the Saviour. "But why would He do it?" She asked. "Why would God let His own son die for my sins?"

"Because, Isabel, He loves you. He knew you before you were even born and planned good things for you all the days of your life. You have only to accept the gifts He is offering in order to receive all the fullness of His love, forgiveness, mercy, and many other blessings."

Isabel was still skeptical. "It all sounds too good to be true. How can I know that this is all real, and not just something people believe to make themselves feel better?"

"Jesus' followers did not believe at first either. Before the crucifixion, Jesus told them that he was going to die for their sins, but they did not understand what he meant. He also told them that he would be coming back. Three days after he died, he rose to life again, and his followers saw the empty tomb and later met him alive in the flesh. After that, they knew and believed that everything he had told them, everything he promised them, was true," I told her.

"You mean to say, because Jesus came back to life like he promised, we can believe that he really is the Saviour?" Isabel asked me.

"That is right!"

Isabel was silent for a few minutes, and I watched as the internal struggle played out across her face.

Finally, she said, "I am ready. How do I do this? How do I receive God's forgiveness?"

"All you have to do is talk to God through prayer. Tell God you are sorry for your sins, and that you believe in what Jesus did to pay for them. Then, ask for His forgiveness and invite Him to be the Lord of your life." Isabel nodded. As she prayed, I felt a calm presence all around us, and I knew that the spirit of God was with us, filling the church. When she finished, Isabel told me, "For the first time in my life, Charlotte, I feel peace." I smiled and embraced her.

∞∞∞∞

William

If someone had told me a few months prior that I would not only be welcoming harlots into my home, but I would actually be participating in Bible study with them, I would surely have laughed in their face! With Isabel still convalescing at the parsonage, her friends resumed having their meetings in our dining room. They welcomed me into their meetings almost as if I had always been there, rather than having been the one to toss them out unceremoniously.

The last to arrive were Charlotte and Isabel, coming from a visit to the church. The latter was beaming from ear to ear.

"Isabel, you look quite changed, what's happened?" Vanessa asked her.

"I'm a different person now." Isabel replied. The others gave her puzzled looks, so she went on, "Charlotte tells me we are all now sisters in the Lord."

Charlotte grinned, and Lily exclaimed, "That's wonderful!" The five women all gathered together in a cluster embrace. I stood witness to the whole thing, feeling incredibly proud of my wife. She was reaping the harvest of her labour, right before my eyes. Because of her faithfulness, four of her friends had turned to the Lord, and I knew she would see many more souls redeemed so long as she continued loving others the way she had with these women.

In that moment, I knew that I too had a calling, to help the lost, the needy, the outcast, the poor in spirit— any who were in need of a Saviour. I may have joined the clergy for selfish reasons, to better my standing in the community, and enjoy a comfortable life, but God knew what He was doing all along. He put me right where He wanted me and called me from the very beginning; it was I who was only just now realizing that purpose I had been given. I knew then that even if God should allow me to lose my title and my home, no matter where I went or what profession I led, my purpose would remain the same.

Charlotte began reading that day's lesson, but it was not long before we were interrupted by the sound of hoofbeats. It was the constable, come to call.

"Good afternoon," he greeted. "I've come to provide news which I am sure you are all eager to hear. I've had word from London. Mr. Bartleby was killed last night. I'm sure you'll be reading about it in the papers 'afore long."

The women were all too stunned to speak.

I filled the silence by inquiring, "May I ask how this happened, sir?"

The constable told us, "Cassius Bartleby apparently owed a

great deal of money to another man. He went to London hoping to win the money by gambling, but he lost everything he had. The man who he was indebted to had become angry and impatient, knowing Bartleby had not the funds to repay 'im, and told 'im he had run out of chances. He murdered 'im in cold blood in a back alley behind the gambling hall. A servant boy witnessed the whole thing in hiding and went to the authorities after."

Everyone else was still too shocked, so I continued, "Well, it is not the justice we imagined him getting, but at last this whole thing will finally be put to rest."

"Indeed." The constable replied.

As he left, Charlotte finally spoke. "Naturally, I'm relieved that Bartleby is no longer a threat. But what a terrible way to die!"

"It seems Bartleby finally found the end of his rope," Vanessa added. Her words underscored the grim atmosphere in the room.

∞∞∞∞

Charlotte

We soon learned that the tavern and all its contents were to be auctioned off by the bank, in their effort to recover some of the enormous debts Bartleby owed. Half the town turned up to witness the public auction, held inside the tavern itself. Of course, William and I were eager to know who should become the new owner, so we went, as did the four women. Even Lady Catherine was curious enough to attend, though she remained at the rear apart from the rest of the crowd.

The first bid was made by the innkeeper, followed by several other business owners, and a few wealthy landowners, including Lord Greenbury (who probably hoped to save his favorite late-night retreat). Then a mysterious gentleman in a grey suit began his input. Lord Greenbury raised his bid, but the mystery bidder upped theirs as well. The bidding war continued for several minutes, each unwilling to concede the sale to the other. Finally, Lord Greenbury threw up his hands in defeat.

"Going once, going twice," the auctioneer called, "sold! To the gentleman in the grey suit for twenty-five-hundred pounds."

But when the gentleman was called forward to complete the transaction, he declared himself to be only a proxy bidder, revealing

190

the real winner of the auction to be none other than.... Anne de Bourgh! The crowd gasped. I was also rendered speechless. Miss de Bourgh had been lurking in the corner under the disguise of a black cloak. Throwing back her hood so that all could witness her identity, she came forward to the auctioneer, prepared to make good on her transaction.

Lady Catherine marched to her daughter, livid. "Anne, I forbid you from buying this property! Have you no understanding of what this place is?"

"I understand perfectly, Mother," Anne replied. "Hence, I want to ensure that it is no longer used for the purposes that it has been."

"Well, I am not going to give you the money to go through with this. Lord Greenbury can have his den of wickedness for all I care!" Lady Catherine flipped her hand. Lord Greenbury huffed but said nothing.

"You don't have to give me the money," Anne told her mother. "I have been to visit father's old solicitor, Mr. Dawson. He was helpful in informing me that as of my twenty-fifth birthday, I became legally entitled to my inheritance, a fortune which allows me to more than easily afford this purchase." She then thanked the man in the grey suit for his assistance, introducing him to them all as this same Mr. Dawson, who confirmed everything to Lady Catherine.

The lady persisted. "I will not permit you to squander your inheritance on this!"

"Mother, you have no say in the matter. According to this," Anne presented a document that Mr. Dawson had provided, "I have sole discretion over the funds in my account. And I do not plan to squander them. It is my plan to turn the Drunken Skunk into a home for needy women, particularly those who are former prostitutes, or who find themselves in desperate circumstances and need an alternative to resorting to prostitution to save themselves."

I spoke up. "That is an excellent plan! I, for one, will be happy to assist you in the founding of such a home."

"We both will." William added, placing his hand on the small of my back. I looked to him and smiled.

Lady Catherine turned on us both. "You two! If it weren't for you, my daughter would have never concocted such a plan, to waste the de Bourgh fortune and bring our family to ruin!" Rounding about towards the door, she whipped back to look at us one more time. "I'm not finished with you yet! I've had a letter from Bishop Kingston. He'll be here to conduct the investigation of your conduct by the end of the week!" With that, Lady Catherine swiftly climbed into her carriage waiting outside the door and ordered her driver to speed off.

I looked at William's face. He seemed pale.

"Well, now it's come," he whispered, watching Lady Catherine's barouche disappear into the distance.

Chapter 18

William

Everything I had feared was coming to pass. Lady Catherine had been friends with Bishop Kingston for many years. Now that she was lodging a formal complaint against me with him, I was certain he would take her side in the matter. Where will we go? What will we do? I fretted. My consternation persisted as I moved about from room to room in the house, never feeling able to settle down in any place.

"Find something useful to do, or you'll drive yourself mad," Charlotte insisted.

Desperate to escape my anxiety over the bishop's inquiry, I decided to pay my dear old aunt a visit. Aunt Violet lived about a three-hour ride away, so I planned to head out mid-morning, spend the afternoon with her, and likely return sometime that evening. Charlotte assured me she would not be alone all day, as the girls were planning to call on her for their Bible study. With that knowledge, I kissed her goodbye and set out for my aunt's house.

The day was pleasant, and the roads easy, so I reached Aunt Violet's little cottage in no time. The sweet lady was enjoying the nice weather under the shade of her oak tree, sitting in her rocking chair with her quilting when I arrived.

"William! What a pleasant surprise this is!" Aunt Violet exclaimed. She put her quilt down and planted a large, wet kiss on my cheek. "How is my favorite nephew?"

"Your *only* nephew." I corrected her with a smile.

My aunt waved me off. "Minor detail! But where is your lovely wife? I was so hoping to meet her. In your letters, you speak of nothing else but her beauty and grace!"

"I promise, Aunt, that we shall both visit you soon. But today, I merely required an escape from my troubles and cares and could think of no better time to come and see you."

"Dear me!" Aunt Violet gasped. "Is everything all right?"

"Not exactly. In fact, I am very much in need of your advice right about now."

My aunt brought me inside and made me sit down while she prepared some food. As we ate, I told her about my recent troubles.

"That's quite the pickle you're in!" Aunt Violet commented. "It sounds like you've had rather a rocky start to your marriage— in fact, you've been stuck between a rock and a hard place from the get-go!"

"I could not have said it better myself, dear aunt," I smiled wryly. "But I need to know, what should I do when Bishop Kingston arrives? He is expected by the end of this week."

"Dear boy, you needn't worry about that. From what I can see, you are doing a generous work in your community, and many people respect you for it."

"But what of my patroness, Lady Catherine de Bourgh? She has set herself against me, and she is a dear friend of the bishop," I worried.

"Ha! I remember her from my days as a young woman, when your mother and I had our 'London season'— your grandmama's attempt to elevate us into higher society." My aunt rolled her eyes. "Lady Catherine entered society the same year I did. I could certainly give you some dirt on her if you like. She wasn't always so squeaky-clean as she'd like you to believe; she was a bit of a rebel, back in her youth," Aunt Violet said with a twinkle.

"As tempting as that sounds, I'm not certain that mudslinging is going to win me any favor with the bishop. I think the main object is for me to prove my conduct irreproachable," I reminded her.

"Very well, very well," Aunt Violet conceded with a laugh. "But just so you know, if she ever gives you any trouble again, you can always remind her about 'that time Miss Violet lent her a petticoat the night of the Masquerade Ball'. I guarantee that would set her mind about differently."

Amused, but not certain I wanted to know the particulars of that incident, I changed the subject.

"Suppose the bishop declares me unfit to lead my parish. What am I to do? If I were still single, I could perhaps try for the law or the military or go into trade. But now I must think of how I shall provide for Charlotte. I cannot support both of us and pursue a new profession at the same time," I explained. "Plus, there is the issue of where we would live. Without the parsonage, I am essentially homeless."

Aunt Violet shook her head. "Not homeless, dear boy. You will always have a home here with me, for as long as you wish."

"Oh, Aunt Violet, we couldn't possibly impose on you like that."

"Nonsense. You are family. I would never wish you to be anywhere but here, if you had no place to call your own."

"But your house is so small, and we are hoping… at least, I am hoping, that our family will grow in time."

"And what a blessing that would be!" Aunt Violet imagined. "To hear the sound of little voices and tiny feet pattering in my house. It would be almost as good as having grandchildren! You know, sometimes I wish your uncle and I had raised children. Sadly, I was not able to have any while he was alive." My aunt looked so very wistful, I was reminded how painful it must have been for her, becoming a childless widow about ten years ago. I vowed to myself that I would make efforts to come visit her more often and bring my family.

"At any rate," my aunt continued, "we will certainly make do, one way or another. That is, if what you fear should come to pass," she finished.

I thanked her and realized that I was not without the love of family in this world.

Aunt Violet's generosity gave me encouragement that at least I had a fallback plan should things not go in my favor with the bishop. My anxiety was, at least temporarily, calmed.

∞∞∞∞

Charlotte

The events of the day prior having played out as they did, we saw the return of a much-missed member of our group. Anne, having officially rebelled against her mother, was determined that nothing should stop her from spending time with whomever she wished. We welcomed her with many tears and sweet long embraces.

"It's so good to have you back!" Vanessa spoke for all of us as she squeezed Anne tightly.

"Mother is so furious right now," Anne gleefully told us, "that she would be on the verge of disowning me. Except, in fact, I am now in possession of my own fortune, and am an independent woman."

"Does that mean that you are now the mistress of Rosings?" I asked.

"Not yet. Mother retains control over the estate until her death, at which point the entirety of Rosings Estate will belong to me. But at least for now, I have enough money to live as I please, and I am to begin managing some aspects of the estate."

"Will she try to throw you out; make you fare on your own then?" Lily asked.

"Not likely. In time, I expect she will get over this and things will return to some semblance of normalcy. I am still her daughter, and she does still love me, after all."

Changing the subject, she asked, "How is Mr. Collins faring? I expect he's nearly driven mad over the bishop's impending arrival."

"Yes, in fact, I sent him off to visit his aunt this morning, to get some respite from his worry."

"Poor man," Selina commented. "I know you will both suffer if the bishop decides to remove him, but he seems to be taking the possibility incredibly hard."

"It's his nature." Charlotte shrugged. "I am worried too, but I am trusting hard that the Lord will take care of us no matter what."

Isabel spoke up. "It doesn't seem right that this bishop fellow should get to say what happens to you. After all, you've done nothing wrong. Merely tried to help all of us to get a better life. I don't know where I would be right now if you hadn't come along and shown me there was a different way. Probably, I'd still be a working girl, serving customers night and day until I was too old and got thrown out to live as a beggar."

The other three girls all nodded, thinking much the same.

Anne clasped her hands together. "That is why I came up with the idea to turn the Drunken Skunk into a home for women just like you four. I want to provide schooling, education in useful trades such as weaving and sewing, and so on."

"A place for fallen women to get a fresh start," Vanessa mused.

"What would you call this place?" Charlotte asked.

"How about 'Magdalena House?'" Selina suggested. "After Mary Magdalene, the prostitute in the Bible who decided to follow Jesus."

"I love it!" Anne exclaimed.

"I can help teach reading, writing, and arithmetic. Those are my best subjects," I volunteered. "And, perhaps William could come in one day a week to teach history and Latin to anyone wishing to pursue a profession as a governess," I added.

"That would be excellent! Please, ask him."

I agreed that I would.

"I could be a 'dormitory mother'. Be someone to look after all the girls staying there." Lily volunteered.

"I will also need someone to run the operation." Anne stated.

"I assumed you would do that," I said, surprised.

"I would, and I will certainly be heading up the major decisions. But now that I also have Rosings Estate to manage, I need someone to be handling the day-to-day business." Turning to Isabel she asked, "Would you do it? Would you help me run Magdalena house?"

Isabel was stunned. "I'm not sure I'm the best person to do it. Maybe Vanessa should do it, not me."

"I would, except I am already planning to open my store. Actually, I just came this morning from meeting with the barber. He's agreed to lease me the little shop next door to his that I've had my eye on!" She showed us the lease agreement.

"Congratulations, Vanessa!" I gave her hand a squeeze.

"Of course, I will still be a part of Magdalena House. I'd love to teach sewing classes when I'm not at the shop."

Isabel was still reluctant about Anne's offer. "Selina, you could run Magdalena House, couldn't you? You even named it."

"True... but actually, I've had news recently too. With all that's been going on I have not had a chance to tell you, I had an offer from a wealthy family in Manchester. They want me to be their nursemaid. My position starts right after Christmas."

"That's wonderful!" I exclaimed.

"So, that means you'll be leaving us?" Lily asked. I knew she would miss Selina the most, given how close the two were.

"I suppose it does, yes."

There was silence for a few moments. Finally, Isabel spoke. "I guess that only leaves me to run Magdalena House for you, Anne."

"I know you'll be wonderful at it!" Anne cheered.

"Yes, you'll be amazing!" Vanessa added.

"Then it's all settled what our roles will be!" I joined in the glee.

"Assuming you're still here, and Bishop Kingston doesn't force you to move far away from us." Isabel's cold reminder of the truth brought our celebration to a stillness.

I gulped. "Let us hope for the best."

∞∞∞∞

William

In spite of my belief that the Lord would take care of us no matter what, I was still scarcely able to tolerate the effects of these events upon my nerves. Bishop Kingston had written us a line which arrived that Friday morning, informing us that he expected to arrive about one o'clock. I anxiously paced about the drawing room, stopping every few minutes to sigh and put my hands on my head.

"Sit down, dear, before you wear a hole through the rug!" Charlotte ordered. I obeyed, stealing a glance at the clock as I did. Still only quarter-past twelve. I wished the bishop might arrive early; better to get things over with sooner.

"I cannot help it Charlotte, it's in my nature to worry about such things."

"I know, but there's no use fretting at this point. The Lord has commanded us not to worry! 'Che sarà sarà', 'whatever will be will be'," Charlotte reminded me.

I smiled weakly.

"Now, why don't you drink some tea?" Charlotte suggested, pouring me a cup. "It will help calm your nerves."

Bishop Kingston arrived right on schedule. Pleasant greetings and introductions were made, which the bishop was happy to receive.

"I must say, that is an excellent black cassock which you are

198

wearing," I remarked. "The stitching is fine, and the fabric hangs so as to make the wearer appear taller. You must tell me who is your supplier of clerical robes and vestments."

Before the bishop could answer, Charlotte interjected, "My dear, perhaps our guest might like to sit down after his journey."

The bishop, seemingly thankful for the interruption, made his way to the sofa.

Charlotte offered him some tea, which he accepted. Setting down his cup after a few sips, he began, "I have already called on Lady Catherine de Bourgh, to hear further testimony regarding the matter which she summoned me regarding. She has provided me with a list of witnesses who she claims will support her allegations."

I nodded timidly. "I see, my lord."

Bishop Kingston went on, "I would like to request that you provide me with a similar list of references, people who can testify as to your character and the work you are accomplishing here in this parish."

Charlotte was already prepared. "I have a collection of names here for you, my lord," she said, handing him a sheet of paper. "Please feel free to inquire amongst all our friends in this community. Noticing my surprised look at how prepared she was, Charlotte returned it with one that suggested I should have been the one prepared. I mentally kicked myself for not putting in more research into clerical investigative procedures.

Noting that the paper was covered with names on both sides, the bishop said, "Thank you for your extensive references. It shall take me some time to query all the people on my lists. While I am here though, I would be pleased if you could offer me your own testimonies."

"Certainly," I told the bishop, feeling my throat tighten and my hands growing more and more clammy.

Bishop Kingston began by clarifying the accusations against us. "Lady Catherine claims that you have been disrupting the order of society, by encouraging your parish to mingle with known sinners, and by inciting anger from the locals. She also insists that you have set a poor example of moral conduct and are responsible for the moral decline of others, including her daughter. I have heard her side of the argument, along with all its particulars. Now I would like to hear yours."

"Bishop Kingston," I began, "what Lady Catherine alleges couldn't be further from the truth. This all began a few months ago, when my wife befriended a young woman who was working as a prostitute." I reached out to grasp Charlotte's hand, and she smiled back at me. "Before long, she was leading four such women in a Bible study and has seen them all come to faith in turn. Subsequently, they have all left their former profession and are now aiming to lead respectable, sin-free lives."

"What you should know, my lord," Charlotte supplied, "is that we do not condone sin, but we encourage repentance through acceptance of the person, without condoning their sinful actions. The example we strive to set for our parish is one of love and compassion, free from condemnation and hypocrisy. For, as you know, all men are sinners, and God judges the Gossip and the Murderer alike. No sin is worse than another, in His eyes, and all are in need of a Saviour."

"Quite so," The bishop replied. "But what of the claim that you have disrupted society? I presume that not everyone was so eager to follow your example. Certainly, Lady Catherine has had her qualms about it."

"Sadly, not everyone is willing to repent. The tavern owner, Mr. Bartleby, for one, and many of his patrons, enjoyed living in sin or making a profit by engaging in illegal acts. For some, their sins eventually catch up to them," I said, thinking of the recent demise of Mr. Bartleby.

"Yes, I heard Lady Catherine mention something about her daughter being persuaded to buy the property of the late tavern owner. Apparently, there's some story that he was murdered?" The bishop asked.

"That is right, my lord. His gambling debts caught up to him in the worst way, and he paid for it with his life," I answered.

"Terrible." Bishop Kingston shook his head.

Charlotte spoke again. "Miss de Bourgh hopes to turn his former house of sin into a house of redemption, a safe haven for former prostitutes and other destitute women. 'Magdalena House', as she plans to rename it, will provide housing and education, in an effort to keep women off the streets and out of the brothels."

"I see." The bishop nodded. Rising from his seat, he said, "Well, I think I have all the testimony I need from you for the moment. If you'll give me a few days to interview the other witnesses, I shall be in contact with you." With that, we thanked him, and bid him farewell.

Over the course of the next few days, it was all I could do to keep myself together. Poor Charlotte tried everything to keep me distracted, but my mind was already preoccupied. Even sleep brought me no respite, as my nightmares tormented me with visions of dire consequences. In my most bizarre one, I sat in a courtroom with the bishop as a towering judge holding a gavel large enough to smash me like an insect, and Lady Catherine as the prosecuting attorney, complete with barrister's robes and wig. The Lady Catherine-barrister kept making all sorts of accusations, until finally the bishop-judge pronounced me "guilty", and stripped me of my title, home, and everything I owned. I stared in horror as his gigantic gavel came crashing down upon me. Then I woke up.

At last, after three days' time, the bishop sent notices to both me and Lady Catherine, requesting we meet him on neutral territory— outside the church— for him to present the results of his investigation. Charlotte went with me, naturally. Lady Catherine was already there when we arrived, but the bishop was not. "Mr. Collins," Lady Catherine nodded to me with a sniff.

"Lady Catherine," I nodded back stiffly.

Bishop Kingston was not far behind us. He wasted no time, addressing Lady Catherine first.

"My lady, I have researched your claims, and interviewed the witnesses you provided me. Meeting with Lord Greenbury was especially interesting." The bishop raised his eyebrows slightly." Then he turned to us. "Mr. and Mrs. Collins, I have also questioned the people on your list of names. The Emersons and Miss de Bourgh, in particular, were most helpful to me."

Lady Catherine scowled at the mention of yet another betrayal on her daughter's part. "And have you come to a conclusion, my lord? Do you agree with my claims that this man is unfit to lead the church in this parish?" she asked.

Mine and Charlotte's ears waited for the bishop's response.

"I have come to a conclusion, my lady," Bishop Kingston said, "but I'm afraid you may not be pleased with the results."

Charlotte and I looked to one other, excitedly.

The bishop went on, "My investigation has shown that not only is Mr. Collins a fine minister of upright moral standing, but he is the very model of an excellent clergyman, demonstrating mercy, compassion, and true Christianity for his congregation. Mrs. Collins, also, is everything a parson's wife ought to be: loving, kind, dedicated to helping others, and concerned for the work of the Lord. I am especially pleased to see the work they are doing to rescue ladies of the night, an area of ministry that is sorely lacking or absent in most parishes. If you had not interfered," the bishop directed at Lady Catherine, "their ministry might have made even more headway. Why is it that you are in such opposition again?" Bishop Kingston asked.

"I-I... that is..." Lady Catherine, for once, was speechless.

"Dear Lady," the bishop inquired with a pitying look, "Do you wish to become a better follower of the Lord?"

"Why..." she seemed dazed as she concluded, "of course, my dear bishop."

"Consider looking to the example of Mr. and Mrs. Collins to learn how to follow in the steps of Christ."

Lady Catherine's expression of mortification was priceless.

The bishop continued, "My recommendation, my lady, is that you cease hostilities and instead embrace the opportunity to be of benefit to your community. Your support could further increase the generous stipend I am issuing from the church headquarters to help spearhead their mission." The bishop nodded at us.

Charlotte and I were both surprised.

"Thank you so much, my lord!" Charlotte expressed.

Lady Catherine was still paralyzed.

"Yes, Lady Catherine," Bishop Kingston confirmed, "the Church of England plans to keep Mr. and Mrs. Collins installed in this parish for as long as they wish. Of course, should you still wish to rescind your generous patronage of Mr. and Mrs. Collins, as you hinted in your letter that you might, you are free to do so. It is your money, after all. Only your tithes are required by the church. But you should know that there are many in town who feel you have been less than generous towards the church, as of late, and others who supported you only because you assured them that you were acting according to Christian principles. Once I told them that the church did not agree with some of your principles, they were reluctant to go against the church. It would be in your best interest I think, to regain some of your popularity by supporting the ministries and ministers that your church has sanctioned."

Lady Catherine thought for a few moments, eyes downcast. "Yes, my lord," she answered softly. "You may consider the charges I brought forward to be dropped, and my patronage maintained. I will also do as you request and supply additional funds for the new project, of an amount the church deems worthy," Lady Catherine concluded, defeated. The great lady pulled herself together. Standing straight and proud once again, she turned to Charlotte and me.

"Enjoy your tenure, Mr. Collins. Dinner will be at five o'clock sharp, in the dining room." Lady Catherine announced. "Bishop Kingston, you are to join us also, if you are able. My cook will be serving roast lamb."

"One of my favorites." The bishop smiled, accepting her invitation.

Lady Catherine nodded to us all, before walking up the path towards Rosings.

"Congratulations, Mr. and Mrs. Collins!" Bishop Kingston shook my hand and tipped his hat to Charlotte.

As the bishop left to go back to the inn in town where he was staying, I gave Charlotte a great big embrace. "Praise the Lord, we are saved!" I cried. I planted a large kiss on Charlotte's lips.

"I knew it would all turn out all right," Charlotte said as our lips parted. Then she closed the gap again with another kiss.

Epilogue

Charlotte

The wheels of the carriage clattered as we rode towards Hertfordshire. After the bishop rendered his verdict, things with Lady Catherine went back to normal...more or less. It turned out, she soon forgot about her dispute with us, for her anger was incensed by the prospect that her nephew might break off his supposed betrothal to Anne and unite with Miss Elizabeth Bennet. When we did receive a letter stating that Lizzy and Mr. Darcy had in fact gotten engaged, I was thrilled! William and I knew, though, that Lady Catherine would be most unpleasant company for a time, and so we made our escape to stay with my parents until she calmed down and accepted the matter.

Meanwhile, Anne was working hard to get Magdalena House ready to open. The repairs and alterations were nearly finished, and Vanessa, Lily, Selina, and Isabel were already living in their old apartments, though they planned to give them up for new quarters once the renovation of the adjacent buildings was complete. Anne had offered the tenants a generous package if they would relinquish their lease and vacate, giving her the space she needed to create classrooms and additional housing, and to convert the old apartments into a dormitory for the new residents they all hoped would arrive.

"What are you thinking about?" William broke my long reverie. I turned my gaze away from the coach window and back towards him.

"Just about everything that's happened recently," I told him.

"Yes, it's been quite an eventful year, hasn't it?" he mused. "Our whole ordeal with Lady Catherine, Bartleby's attacks, his death— not to mention the wonderful things happening at Magdalena House."

"Yes! After all she put us through, Lady Catherine gave up rather easily once she was scolded by Bishop Kingston. Her sudden one-hundred-eighty-degree turn back to normal was so surprising, it was as if nothing had ever occurred. It made me think perhaps there is hope that someday she will change. Then she found a new target in Darcy and Lizzy," I said.

"Well, Lady Catherine will always be Lady Catherine," William shrugged, "but there is always hope for change, as long as she lives. We all are given many chances to repent of our ways, to grow, to improve, all the way until the end of our lives." William's somber comment reminded me of Bartleby's sad ending.

"Do you think Bartleby could have ever repented?" I wondered strangely.

William pondered my question for a moment. "That's a difficult question. I'm not certain I know the answer to that."

"I know it must seem odd, for me to be sorry for his sake, over how things ended."

"No," William shook his head. "Knowing what a caring person you are, I would be more surprised if you did not have even a hint of regret over it. As for Bartleby, we will never know whether he believed in the Lord at some point in his life or not; only God could know his heart. He certainly wasn't following the Lord at the end of his life. One thing I do believe is that our merciful God must have already given him many, many chances to turn from his wicked ways. Because he did not repent, God eventually removed him from this world to prevent him from causing further harm to those around him. Only the Lord can see the future and know for certain if Bartleby would have ever changed, but I believe that he would not have, and that's why God allowed his death," William concluded.

I nodded and leaned against William's shoulder for the remainder of the journey.

We stopped at Lucas Lodge just long enough to deposit our trunks, for I was eager to pay Lizzy a visit. My mother was a little miffed that we would not be staying even for tea, but I knew she would forgive me, and we promised to return for supper that evening.

Lizzy was so happy to see us that she ran to the gate as soon as we approached.

"Charlotte!" she cried, hurrying to embrace me. I picked up the pace ahead of my husband in order to meet my friend.

"Congratulations, dear Lizzy! I'm so pleased to hear you've

accepted Darcy's offer. I always thought he was perfect for you."

"Yes, I finally came to my senses and realized I was in love with him, and that only my own stubbornness was holding me back," Lizzy admitted. "But I hear congratulations are in order for you, as well." She patted my stomach gently, causing me to blush.

"William was not supposed to mention anything just yet!" I shot a backward glance at him as he caught up to me.

"I beg forgiveness, dear, but nothing gives me greater pleasure than the knowledge that a new olive branch is about to be added to our family tree," William beamed.

"I keep reminding him, it's a baby, not a new plant for his garden," I laughed.

"What can I say? I am a gardener, after all," my amused husband added, taking my teasing in stride. "Now, let's get you inside, dearest, where you can sit down and put your feet up. You must not overdo it, for the baby's sake."

"I've been sitting all day in the carriage!" I complained. "I'm not a china doll."

"But it is getting chilly out," Lizzy agreed with William, leading us inside.

The rest of the Bennet family greeted us warmly. Even Mrs. Bennet seemed to have forgotten for the moment that I would someday displace her as mistress of the house when the time came for Mr. Collins to inherit. Mr. Darcy was there as well, and my husband immediately went to strike up a conversation with him. Lizzy and I escaped upstairs to her room, where there was peace and quiet.

"How are you feeling lately?" Lizzy asked as we sat on her bed.

"I experience some illness, mainly in the mornings, but nothing too severe," I told her. The discovery of my pregnancy was still recent; less than a week after our visit from Bishop Kingston my monthly flow failed to appear, and not long after, the morning ailments began, confirming what I suspected. I had wanted to keep the news a secret until after the first twelve weeks had past, to be certain, but apparently William was unable to keep any good news to himself, for I found out he had mentioned it in his last letter to Mr. Bennet.

"How are the wedding plans coming along?" I changed the subject.

"They are going very well. Mamma is beside herself with joy. Jane and Bingley agreed with Darcy and me that we ought to have a double wedding. The only question is of the date. Mamma thinks we should marry quickly, before Christmas, and of course Darcy is eager to be married as soon as is reasonable. However, Bingley's sister Caroline has taken a trip to the continent for a few months, and he greatly wishes her to be present, so the wedding may be delayed on account of that until after her return."

"In my opinion, you ought to marry when it is convenient for you both, and don't worry about who may or may not be able to attend the wedding," I said.

"Still, we are coming up on winter now. It would be lovely to wait until spring, when the weather is fine for a honeymoon tour," Lizzy commented, closing the topic.

"By the way," Lizzy said, "you must excuse my failure in replying to your most recent letters. You know, of course, about Lydia's unconventional way of getting married to Mr. Wickham," she sighed. Elizabeth had been faithful to keep me apprised of the whole ordeal, up until her sister's disappearance with Wickham. After that, we had no communication from the Bennets until Mr. Bennet announced the marriage of his youngest daughter.

"Well, things had just calmed down after their wedding, when Darcy and Bingley returned to Hertfordshire," Elizabeth continued. "I only just caught up reading the last of your letters and was about to write to you when we got the news of your imminent arrival, and I realized there was no point when my letter would likely miss you in transit," Lizzy finished.

"It's quite all right," I reassured her. "My life has been anything but calm the last several weeks also." I filled her in on all the latest developments.

"I'm pleased that everything turned out all right in the end," Lizzy told me when I completed.

"So am I. Magdalena House will fill such a need for so many women. Miss de Bourgh has already placed advertisements in papers across the country, asking women in need to contact her, and letters are pouring in. The house will likely be open and full of residents by the time we return to Kent."

Lizzy smiled. "I am amazed at you, Charlotte. All this began simply because you listened to the still small voice nudging you to reach out to Vanessa. I'm proud of you." With that, Lizzy happily embraced me.

∞∞∞∞

William

I was happy to let my wife disappear to catch up with Cousin Elizabeth for a spell. Mr. Darcy was already calling upon my cousins when we arrived, and I felt it my utmost duty to congratulate him in person over his happy situation.

"Mr. Darcy, I must tell you how utterly pleased we were to hear the news of your engagement. I congratulate you on the prospect of your marriage, and I am certain, of all the couples in the world, your happiness in matrimonial bliss shall only be surpassed by that which my own wife has brought to me," I grinned.

Mr. Darcy nodded. "Thank you for your heartfelt wishes. Though, I must disagree with you; it is my belief that the happiness Miss Elizabeth brings to me exceeds even yours and Mrs. Collins, although I give you leave to feel otherwise."

"A fair exchange, so long as we each feel ourselves to be the happiest men on earth," I supplied.

Mrs. Bennet happened to be in the room at the time, and hearing all this, said, "I've always thought that Lizzy would make *any* man the happiest in the world." Her remark seemed directed at me, as if she had forgotten that it was Elizabeth, and not I, who rejected the idea of matrimony between us.

Mr. Darcy saved me from replying. "Be that as it may, I shall be eternally grateful that I am that man, and that I shall be the one to, in turn, make her the happiest woman in the world."

"And I shall be the happiest mother, to see my Jane and Lizzy married off so well," Mrs. Bennet commented, dabbing the corner of her eye with her handkerchief. "Has Mr. Bingley arrived yet?" She said, standing to look out the window. "He is to arrive soon and stay for supper. No, no sign of him yet? Well, I'd best check with cook to ensure that our supper will be ready. Will you and Mrs. Collins be staying?" Mrs. Bennet asked me. I replied that we would not, and then she left us to see to the kitchen.

As the others were all absent from the room for the present, Mr. Darcy took the opportunity to speak to me privately.

"Mr. Collins, I understand you have had a great deal of trouble with my aunt, Lady Catherine lately."

I presumed he heard all this from Cousin Elizabeth, to whom Charlotte had been writing. "Yes, we have, though things are now mended, and her attention has been turned towards you," I said.

"Indeed." Darcy replied. "Though fear not for my sake, my aunt will eventually forgive me on account of my being family, and if she does not, I shall not consider it any great loss. But my intention is to reassure you that, should you have any trouble with Lady Catherine in the future, I should be happy to intercede on your behalf. I too have friends in the church, and many connections which can be used to assist you should you ever need it. It is in my power to ensure you are always properly cared for, both materially, and practically."

"Sir, I can never thank you enough for your tremendous generosity and support of us." I began to tear up. "After all my wife and I have gone through this year, to know that we can continue the Lord's work that He began through us, without any fear for our security and happiness, is a most wondrous blessing. Your magnanimous demonstration is more than I could have hoped for. Truly, you were meant to be a Duke or an Earl or some other station befitting your excellence, your kind-heartedness, your—"

"A simple 'thanks' is all I require." Darcy cut me off, embarrassed by my lavish praise.

I nodded, still feeling a little overwhelmed.

"It was my cousin Anne who related your troubles to me," Mr. Darcy revealed. "I am pleased to see her finally standing on her own two feet and making a life for herself apart from her mother's shadow. She will make a fine mistress of Rosings one day."

"I couldn't agree with you more, sir." I restrained myself from launching into a lengthy veneration of Miss de Bourgh's fine qualities, as well as comparing them to Lady Catherine, in whom I found much fault these days, and who would need time to regain the amount of respect I once held for her.

It was not long before Mr. Bingley arrived. The household returned from their various activities to greet him, and as his friendly and amiable manner pleased everybody, Darcy and I were not alone again, for all members were eager to converse with him in the sitting room where we had kept ourselves. Supper would be served soon. Thus, Charlotte and I finally excused ourselves to walk back to Lucas

Lodge, knowing Lady Lucas would be expecting us, and we had delayed her spending time with her daughter long enough. Noticing where we were, I stopped suddenly.

"What is it?" Charlotte asked me.

"Do you know where we are?"

She laughed. "Certainly. We are on the lane leading to Lucas Lodge."

I shook my head. "No, I mean this exact spot. This is where I proposed to you, last November. That tree right there is how I know." I pointed to an elm beside the lane.

Charlotte looked at the tree I mentioned. "I hadn't realized this was the particular spot. Funny, to think it has not even been one year yet since then. So much has happened. So many trials and tears."

"But plenty of good things too, would you not agree?" I reached out to pat the slight bump on Charlotte's belly, still unnoticeable to most people.

"Yes," she agreed with a smile. "Some *very* good things. Besides becoming a mother soon, I found my purpose, helping lost women find their way to new life. I certainly never expected my life would turn out this way when I agreed to marry you."

"Are you happy you did?" I asked.

"Happy I married you?" Charlotte returned. "Yes. I can say that I am." She pulled me close, taking my hands in hers.

"What about you? Are you pleased that you married me?" Charlotte asked.

"Well, that I'll have to think about…" I teased. Then grinning, I said, "Yes, I am undeniably glad that you are my wife! My dear, amiable, sweet Charlotte! My morning star, my ray of sunshine!" I grabbed her by the waist and twirled her around.

Charlotte laughed, then cried out, "think of the baby! Put me down!" I instantly set her down.

"Oh dear, I haven't hurt him, have I?"

"Him?" Charlotte asked.

"Just hoping!" I smiled.

"I'm sure he— or she!— is fine," Charlotte answered. "It's still early days, after all."

"Nevertheless, I must not be so careless," I reminded myself aloud.

As we reached Lucas Lodge, Charlotte commented, "You know, I think I will enjoy balancing motherhood and ministry."

"It will be quite a challenge. Are sure you're up to it?" I asked.

"With the Lord's help, I think so. After all, I am the parson's wife." Charlotte smiled.

The End.

Acknowledgements

This book has been on a three-year journey to reach this point; a journey for which I am incredibly grateful. From my weekly editions of the early draft, posted on Fanfiction.net, to this refined and finished product, there have been so many people who have encouraged me and helped me to develop Charlotte and William's story into the best possible version.

In particular, I would like to thank my beta readers: Nancy, Jennifer, Bonnie, Charisse, and Lori, and my editor, Pam Crouch. Your constructive criticism, suggestions, and detailed corrections were absolutely indispensable in pushing my manuscript to its fullest for grammatical exactness, historical authenticity, and story and character development.

I would also like to express my gratitude to Mary Batchelor, for her beautiful cover design that perfectly captured my vision of what Charlotte might look like.

Taylor Hohulin, thank you for sharing your "industry intel" with me to help me get started as a self-published author.

Last, but certainly not least, I thank my family for their continual love and support, especially my husband, Moses. Besides providing your feedback as my sixth beta reader, you were the one who encouraged me to pursue my writing as more than just a hobby. You saw my potential and urged me to develop my God-given talents. Without you, I might not have had the courage to move beyond being a casual writer and become a fully-fledged published author. I will always love you, and I thank you from the bottom of my heart.

Free Books!

Thank you for reading my book! I hope you enjoyed it. I invite you to submit your honest review on **Goodreads**, **BookBub** or **Amazon**. Your assessment will help other people like you to find my book and know whether they might like to read it.

Can't get enough of Charlotte and William's love story?

Read more in "Christmas at Hunsford Parsonage", a short story sequel to this book!

Get this story, plus <u>exclusive</u> deleted scenes and extras from "Marriage and Ministry" when you sign up for my newsletter with this link.

You'll also get a link to download a FREE copy of my complete story, Elizabeth's Secret Admirer, a Pride and Prejudice Novella in your welcome email!

Coming Soon by Amanda Kai

Not In Want of a Wife— A Pride and Prejudice Variation

Mr. Darcy is *not* in want of a wife. At least, not one that only loves him for his money. Ever since he came of age, Darcy's been an object of prey to fortune hunters– greedy ladies and their scheming mamas who would do anything to get their hands on his ten-thousand a year and his luxurious estate. Tired of being the most eligible man in any room he walks into, Darcy decides the only way to stave off the fortune hunters is to make himself unavailable to them.

Elizabeth Bennet is convinced that only the deepest love could persuade her into matrimony, and since that has yet to appear, she would do anything rather than marry without affection. Unfortunately, all her mother's thoughts are bent on finding rich husbands for her and her sisters. With the arrival of Mr. Bingley and Mr. Darcy causing a stir among all the mothers of Meryton, Elizabeth knows it is only a matter of time before her own mother pushes her to try to capture one of these rich gentlemen for herself at all costs.

Seeing themselves in virtually the same predicament, Mr. Darcy and Elizabeth come up with a convenient arrangement: they will pretend to court while Mr. Darcy is staying at Netherfield. Mr. Darcy will get a reprieve from the relentless husband hunters, and Elizabeth can satisfy her mother with the notion that she has landed a suitor.

But when the time comes for their partnership to end, the feelings that were merely an act have started to become a reality. Will Darcy and Elizabeth find a way to express the feelings that are in their hearts, or will they part ways for good?

Scan here to order your copy today!

More Books by Amanda Kai

Marriage and Ministry, a Pride and Prejudice Novel
Unconventional: an Austentatious comedy that defies expectations!
Love at the Library
Keys: A Marie Antoinette story

Scan here to get your next Amanda Kai book!

About the Author

Amanda Kai's love of period dramas and classic literature inspires her historical romances and other romances. She is the author of several stories inspired by Jane Austen, including *Not In Want of a Wife*, *Elizabeth's Secret Admirer*, and *Marriage and Ministry*. Prior to becoming an author, Amanda enjoyed a successful career as a professional harpist, and danced ballet for twenty years. When she's not diving into the realm of her imagination, Amanda lives out her own happily ever after in Texas with her husband and three children.

www.ingramcontent.com/pod-product-compliance
Lightning Source LLC
Chambersburg PA
CBHW060143130626
46556CB00006B/2477